TWO OF A KIND

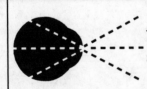

This Large Print Book carries the
Seal of Approval of N.A.V.H.

TWO OF A KIND

SUSAN MALLERY

WHEELER PUBLISHING
A part of Gale, Cengage Learning

GALE
CENGAGE Learning®

Detroit • New York • San Francisco • New Haven, Conn • Waterville, Maine • London

LIBRARY OF CONGRESS CATALOGING-IN-PUBLICATION DATA

Mallery, Susan.
   Two of a kind / by Susan Mallery. — Large Print edition.
     pages cm. — (A Fool's Gold Romance Series) (Wheeler Publishing Large Print Hardcover)
   ISBN-13: 978-1-4104-5878-0 (hardcover)
   ISBN-10: 1-4104-5878-4 (hardcover)
   1. Large type books. I. Title.
PS3613.A453T86 2013
813'.6—dc23   2013015567

Published in 2013 by arrangement with Harlequin Books S.A.

To 2012 Fool's Gold Co-Head
Cheerleader Judie Bouldry and her girls'
great Nana Ellen, who shares her love of
reading. Judie, you're clever and
enthusiastic, and Fool's Gold is
lucky to have you!

CHAPTER ONE

Rational thought and a working knowledge of hand-to-hand combat were useless when faced with the villainous power of the American house spider.

Felicia Swift stood immobilized in the corner of the warehouse, aware of the web, of the arachnid watching her, no doubt plotting her downfall. Where there was one female American house spider, there were others, and she knew they were all after her.

The logical part of her brain nearly laughed out loud at her fears. In her head, Felicia understood that spiders did not, in fact, travel in packs or scheme to attack her. But intelligence and logic were no match for a true arachnophobe. She could write papers, prepare flow charts and even do experiments from now until the next appearance of Halley's Comet. She was terrified of spiders and they knew it.

"I'm going to back away slowly," she said

in a soft, soothing voice.

Technically, spiders didn't have ears. They could sense vibration, but with her speaking quietly, there wouldn't be much of that. Still, she felt better talking, so she kept up the words as she inched toward the exit, always keeping her gaze locked firmly on the enemy.

Light spilled from the open door. Light meant freedom and spider-free breathing. Light meant —

The light suddenly blacked out. Felicia jumped and turned, prepared to do battle with the giant mother-of-all-spiders. Instead she faced a tall man with shaggy hair and a scar by his eyebrow.

"I heard a scream," he said. "I came to see if there was a problem." He frowned. "Felicia?"

Because the spiders weren't enough, she thought frantically. How was that possible?

Fortes fortuna adiuvat.

She tried to rein in her unwieldy brain. Fortune favors the brave? That was helpful how? She had spiders behind her, the man who took her virginity in front of her, and she was thinking in Latin?

Felicia sucked in a breath and steadied herself. She was a logistics expert. She'd never met a crisis she couldn't organize her

8

way out of, and today would be no exception. She would work from big to small and reward herself by doing the Sunday *New York Times* crossword in less than four minutes.

"Hello, Gideon," she said, bracing herself for her hormonal reaction to this man.

He moved closer, his dark eyes filling with emotion. She had never been all that good at reading other people's feelings, but even she recognized confusion.

As he approached, she was aware of the size of him — the sheer broadness of his shoulders. His T-shirt seemed stretched to the point of ripping across his chest and biceps. He looked lethal but still graceful. The kind of man who was at home in any dangerous part of the world.

"What are you doing here?" he asked.

By *here,* she assumed he meant in Fool's Gold and not in the warehouse itself.

She squared her shoulders — a feeble attempt to look larger and more in control. Similar to a cat arching its back and raising its fur. But she doubted Gideon was going to be any more intimidated by her than he would be by a hissing tabby.

"I live in town now."

"I knew that. I meant what are you doing in this warehouse?"

9

"Oh."

An unexpected response, she thought, suddenly less sure of herself. A result of the spider encounter. Their powers were far-reaching. She'd planned to avoid any contact with Gideon for several months. Here it was less than five weeks into her plan and they'd run into each other.

"I'm working," she said, returning her attention to his question. "How did you know I was in town?"

"Justice told me."

"He did?" Something her business associate hadn't mentioned to her. "When?"

"A few weeks ago." Gideon's mouth curved into a smile. "He told me to stay away from you."

His voice, she thought, trying not to get lost in the memories of what the sound meant to her. While olfactory recollections were thought to be the strongest, a sound or a phrase could also shift a person back to another time. Felicia had no doubt she could easily be transported by Gideon's scent; right now she was most concerned about his voice.

He had one of those low, sexy voices. As ridiculous as it sounded, the combination of tone and cadence reminded her of chocolate. Now his voice was a vibration she was sure the spiders could get behind. She should —

Her chin came up as her brain replayed his statement.

"Justice told you to stay away from me?"

Gideon raised one powerful shoulder. "He suggested it was a good idea. After what happened."

Outraged, she planted her hands on her hips, then thought hitting Justice was a far better idea. Only, he wasn't there.

"What happened between you and me isn't his business," she said firmly.

"You're his family."

"That doesn't give him the right to get in the middle of my personal life."

"I didn't see you trying to find me," Gideon pointed out. "I figured you were comfortable with his . . . intervention."

"Of course not," she began, only to realize she *had* been avoiding Gideon, but not for the reasons he thought. "It's complicated."

"I'm seeing that," he told her. "So you're okay?"

"Of course. Our sexual encounter was over four years ago." She had no idea if he'd guessed she'd been a virgin or not and didn't see any reason to mention it now. "Our night together was . . . satisfying." An understatement, she thought, remembering

11

how Gideon had made her feel. "I'm sorry Justice and Ford broke down the hotel room door the following morning."

Gideon's expression changed to one of amusement. It was a look Felicia was used to seeing, and she knew it meant she'd somehow missed an obvious social cue or taken a joking comment literally.

She held in a sigh. She was smart. Scary smart, as she'd often been told. She'd grown up around scientists and graduate students. Ask her about the origins of the universe and she could give a fact-based lecture on the subject without having to prepare. But interpersonal interactions were harder. She was so damned awkward, she thought glumly. She said the wrong thing or sounded like a space alien with bad programming, when all she wanted was to be just like everyone else.

"I meant are you okay *now*," he said. "You screamed. That's why I came in."

She pressed her lips together. For possibly the thousandth time in her life she thought how she would gladly exchange thirty IQ points for just a small increase in social awareness.

"I'm fine," she said, offering what she hoped was a reassuring smile. "Couldn't be better. Thank you for coming to my rescue

— however unnecessary that was."

He took a step toward her. "I'm always happy to help out a beautiful woman."

Flirting, she thought, automatically monitoring his pupil dilation to see if it was real or simply politeness. When a man was sexually interested, his pupils dilated. But it was too dark in the warehouse for her to be sure.

"What made you scream?" he asked.

She drew in a breath. "I saw a spider."

One eyebrow rose.

"It was large and aggressive," she added.

"A spider?"

"Yes. I have issues with them."

"Apparently."

"I'm not stupid. I know it's not rational."

Gideon chuckled. "You're many things, Felicia, but we're all aware that stupid isn't one of them."

Before she could figure out what to say to that, Gideon turned and walked away. She was so caught up in the way his jeans fit his butt that she couldn't think of anything to say, and then he was gone and she was alone with little more than her mouth hanging open, a herd of American house spiders and their plans for her.

Gideon Boylan knew the danger of flashbacks. They could come on suddenly and disoriented him. They were vivid, engaging all his senses, and when they were gone, a man had no way of knowing what was real and what was imagined. After being held captive for two years, he'd been ready to give in to madness. At least it would have been an escape.

His rescue had come just in time, although too late for the men who had been with him. But even being out of the hands of tormentors hadn't given him any sense of freedom. The memories were just as painful as the imprisonment had been.

Focus, he told himself as he loaded the CD and checked his playlist for the next three hours. He had put his past behind him. Some days he even believed it. Seeing Felicia earlier had been a kick in the gut, but he would take a flashback of a beautiful woman in his bed every time. Still, he'd had to take a five-mile run and then meditate for nearly an hour before he'd felt calm enough to head to the radio station.

"We're doing it the old-fashioned way tonight," he said into the microphone. "Just like we always do."

Beyond the control room, the station was dark, the way he liked it. He didn't mind the dark. If it was dark, he was safe. They'd never come for him in the dark. They'd

14

always turned the lights on first.

"It's eleven o'clock in Fool's Gold and this is Gideon. I'm going to dedicate tonight's first song to a lovely lady I ran into today. You know who you are."

He pushed the button and "Wild Thing" by the Troggs started.

Gideon smiled to himself. He had no way of knowing if Felicia was listening or not, but he liked the idea of playing a song for her.

A red light flashed on the wall. He glanced at it, aware someone was ringing the front bell. After hours, the signal flashed back in the control room. An interesting time for visitors. He walked to the front of the radio station and unlocked the door. Ford Hendrix stood in front of the door, a beer in each hand.

Gideon grinned and waved his friend in. "I heard you were in town."

"Yeah, back two days and I'm already regretting the decision."

Gideon took the offered beer. "Welcome home the conquering hero?"

"Something like that."

Gideon had known Ford for years. Although Ford was a SEAL, they'd served together on a joint task force, and later, when Gideon had been left in his Taliban

15

prison to rot, Ford had been one of those who had risked his life to get him out.

"Come on back. I have to put on the next song."

They walked down the long corridor. "I can't believe you own this place," Ford said, following him into the control room. "It's a radio station."

"Huh. That explains all the music."

Ford took the seat opposite Gideon's. Gideon put on his headphones and flipped a switch.

"This is my night for dedications," he said. "I apologize for going digital for a second, but it's the only way to cue up quickly. Here we go. Welcome home, Ford."

The opening of "Born to be Wild" began.

"You really are a bastard," Ford said conversationally.

"I find myself an amusing companion."

Ford was about Gideon's size. Strong and, on the surface, easygoing. But Gideon knew that anyone who had been to the places they'd been and done what they'd done traveled with ghosts.

"What brings you out so late at night?" he asked.

Ford grimaced. "I woke up and found my mom hovering over me in my room. Fortunately I recognized her before I reacted. I

16

need to get out of there."

"So find an apartment."

"Believe me, I'm looking first thing in the morning. She begged me to wait, and I figured moving back home couldn't be too hard. You know, connect with family."

Gideon had made the attempt once. It hadn't gone well.

"My brothers are okay," Ford continued. "But my mom and my sisters are staying way too close."

"They're glad you're home. You were gone a long time."

Gideon didn't know all the details, but he'd heard Ford had left Fool's Gold when he was twenty and hadn't been back much in the past fourteen years.

Ford took a long swallow of his beer. "My mom's already asking if I've thought of settling down." He shuddered.

"Not ready for a wife and the pitter-patter of little feet?"

"No, although I wouldn't mind getting laid." Ford glanced at him. "You're in trouble, by the way."

"I always am."

His friend laughed. "Felicia went after Justice this afternoon. She said he had no right to tell you to stay away from her. When she gets mad, it's quite the show. Talk about

17

a woman who can handle the big words."

"You know her?"

"Not well. The first time I met her was in Thailand."

When both Justice and Ford had interrupted Gideon's night with Felicia. Or rather the following morning. A polite way of saying they'd busted down the door and Justice had insisted on taking Felicia with him. Gideon had tried to go after her, but Ford had held him back.

Gideon hadn't seen her again until today. When she'd been fighting marauding spiders.

"She was pissed at Justice?" he asked.

Ford shook his head. "Leave me out of this. We're not in high school, and I'm not passing notes in study hall or asking her if she likes you. You'll have to do it yourself."

Gideon was tempted. That night had been memorable. She was an intriguing combination of determined, sexy and geeky. But he knew he wasn't her type — he wasn't anyone's. To the untrained eye he looked as if he'd healed, but he knew what was underneath. He wasn't a good relationship risk. Of course, if Felicia was looking for something less serious and more naked, he was all in.

Ford finished his beer. "Mind if I bunk in

18

an empty office?"

"There's a futon in the break room."

"Thanks."

Gideon didn't bother mentioning it wasn't that comfortable. For a guy like Ford, a ratty futon was just as good as a four-star hotel bed. In their line of work, you learned to make do.

Ford dropped the bottle into the blue recycling bin, then headed down the hall. Gideon put in a CD, then searched until he found the right track.

"You Keep Me Hanging On" began to play.

Felicia hurried toward Brew-haha. She was late, which never happened. She liked her life to be organized and calm. Structured. Which meant she always knew where she was going to be and what she was going to be doing. Being late was not part of her plan.

But ever since she'd seen Gideon the day before, she'd been out of sorts. The man confused her. No, she thought as she walked by the park, her *reaction* to him confused her.

She was used to being around physically powerful men. She'd worked with soldiers for years. But Gideon was different. The result of their sexual history, she thought. Percentage-wise, a single night was such a small part of a person's life, yet it could have lasting impact. A trauma of any kind could stay with a person forever. But her time with Gideon had been wonderful, not traumatic. The memories of that night along with their meeting yesterday kept swirling in her head. As a woman who liked her brain as tidy as she liked her life, she was unprepared for being so unsettled.

She paused to wait for the light so she could cross the street. As she stood, she saw a young mother with two small boys. They were maybe two and four, the youngest still a little unsteady as he ran across the grass. He came to a stop, turned and saw his mother and brother, then smiled broadly.

Felicia stared greedily, absorbing the pure joy of the moment, the unselfconsciousness of the happy toddler. This was why she'd come to Fool's Gold, she reminded herself. To be somewhere normal. To try to be like everyone else. To maybe even fall in love and have a family. To belong.

For someone who had grown up as a whiz kid on a university college campus, normal sounded like heaven. She wanted what other people took for granted.

The light changed, and she crossed

quickly, aware of her lateness. Mayor Marsha hadn't said why she wanted to meet and Felicia hadn't asked. She'd assumed her skills were needed on a project of some kind. Maybe setting up an inventory system for the city.

She walked through the open door into the coffeehouse. Brew-haha had opened a couple of months before. Hardwood floors gleamed as sunlight spilled through the big windows. There were plenty of tables, a nice selection of pastries and delicious caffeine in all forms.

Patience, the owner and one of Felicia's friends, smiled. "You're late," she said cheerfully. "I'm excited to know you have flaws. There's hope for the rest of us."

Felicia groaned as her friend pointed to a table toward the back. Sure enough, Mayor Marsha Tilson and Pia Moreno were already seated there.

"I'll bring you a latte," Patience added, already reaching for a large mug.

"Thanks."

Felicia made her way through the tables toward the other women. Mayor Marsha, California's longest-serving mayor, was a well-dressed woman in her early seventies. She favored suits and, during business hours, wore her white hair up in a classic

21

bun. She was, Felicia thought wistfully, the perfect combination of competent and motherly.

Pia, a willowy brunette with curly hair and a ready smile, jumped to her feet as Felicia approached. "You made it. Thanks for coming. It's summer with what feels like a festival every fifteen minutes. I'm happy to be out of my office, even for a business meeting."

She gave Felicia a quick hug. Felicia responded in kind, despite her surprise. She'd only met Pia a couple of times and didn't think they were all that close. Still, the physical contact was pleasant and implied a connection.

Patience brought over the latte and a plate of cookies. "We're sampling today," she said with a grin. "From the bakery. They're too fabulous." She pushed the plate into the center of the table with her left hand. Her diamond ring flashed.

Mayor Marsha touched Patience's ring finger. "What a beautiful setting," she said. "Justice did a very nice job choosing the ring."

Patience sighed and studied her engagement ring. "I know. I keep staring at it when I should be working. But I can't help myself."

She returned to the front of the store. Pia watched her go.

"Young love," she said with a sigh.

"You're still young and very much in love," the mayor reminded her.

"I am still in love," Pia said and laughed. "Most days I don't feel so young. But I'll agree with you on the ring. It's impressive."

Mayor Marsha turned to Felicia and raised her eyebrows. "Not a big diamond fan?"

"I don't get the appeal," she admitted. "They sparkle, but they're simply pressurized rocks."

"Expensive rocks," Pia teased.

"Because we assign them significance. They have little intrinsic value, except for their hardness. In some industrial settings . . ." She paused, aware she was not only talking too much, she was heading into a subject everyone else would find boring. "Fossils are interesting," she murmured. "Their formation seems more serendipitous."

The other two women glanced at each other, then back at her. Their expressions were polite, but Felicia recognized the signs. They were both thinking she was a freak. Sadly, they were right about that.

Moments like this one were the main

reasons she worried about having the family she wanted so desperately. What if she couldn't have children? Not biologically. There was no reason to assume she couldn't procreate as well as the next woman. But was she emotionally sound enough? Could she learn what she didn't know? She trusted her brain implicitly but was less sure about her instincts, and maybe her heart.

She'd grown up never fitting in — a reality she would never want to foist on any child she might have.

"Amber is tree sap, isn't it?" Pia asked. "Wasn't that the basis of that movie? The dinosaur one?"

"Jurassic Park," the mayor said.

"Right. Raoul loves that movie. He and Peter watch it together. I won't let the twins anywhere near the room, though. They wouldn't be able to sleep for weeks after seeing T.rex eating that man."

Felicia started to point out all the scientific inconsistencies in the movie, then pressed her lips together. She believed that many life lessons could be found in clichés, and right now the phrase "less is more" came to mind.

Mayor Marsha took a sip of her coffee. "Felicia, I'm sure you're wondering why we wanted to meet with you today."

24

Pia shook her head. "Right. The meeting." She smiled. "I'm pregnant."

"Congratulations."

The expected response, Felicia thought, not sure why the other woman was sharing the information. But then they'd hugged, so perhaps Pia thought they were closer than Felicia did. She wasn't always good at judging things like that.

Pia laughed. "Thanks. I couldn't figure out what was wrong. Ask poor Patience. I had a complete breakdown in front of her not that long ago. I've been forgetful and disorganized. Then I found out I'm pregnant. It was good to have a physical cause for my craziness and not have to worry about going insane."

She cupped her hands around her mug of tea. "I already have three kids. Peter and the twins. I love my work, but with a fourth baby on the way, I can't possibly stay on top of everything that's happening. I've been wrestling with the fact that I can't be in charge of the festivals anymore."

Felicia nodded politely. She doubted they were going to ask for her recommendation on who should take Pia's place. They would know that better than she would. Unless they wanted her to help with the search. She could easily come up with a list of criteria and —

Mayor Marsha smiled at her over her mug. "We were thinking of you."

Felicia opened her mouth, then closed it. Words genuinely failed her — a very uncommon experience. "For the job?"

"Yes. You have an unusual skill set. Your time with the military has given you experience at dealing with a bureaucracy. While I like to think we're more nimble than most city governments, the truth is we still move very slowly and there's a form for everything. Logistics are your gift, and the festivals are all about logistics. You'll bring a fresh set of eyes to what we've been doing."

Mayor Marsha paused to smile at Pia. "Not that you haven't been brilliant."

Pia laughed. "Don't worry about hurting my feelings. Felicia can be better than me. If she is, I won't have to feel guilty."

"I don't understand," Felicia whispered. "You want me to be in charge of the festivals?"

"Yes," the mayor said firmly.

"But they're important to the town. I know you have other industries, but I would guess that tourism is your main source of income. The university and the hospital would be the largest employers, but the visitors are the real money."

"You're right," Pia said. "Don't get me started on how much per person, because I can tell you within a couple of dollars."

Felicia thought about mentioning she was the sort of person who enjoyed math, then told herself it wasn't pertinent to the subject at hand.

"Why would you trust me with the festivals?" she asked, knowing it was the only question that mattered.

"Because you'll make sure they're done right," Mayor Marsha told her. "You'll stand up for what you believe in. But mostly because you'll care as much as we do."

"You can't know that," Felicia told her.

The mayor smiled. "Of course I can, dear."

Chapter Two

Felicia drove up the mountain. She'd left town a couple miles back and was now on a two-lane road with a gentle grade and wide shoulders. She took the curves slowly, not wanting to find herself grill-to-nose with any wildlife out foraging in the warm summer night. Overhead the sky was a mass of stars with the moon only partially visible through a canopy of leaves.

It was after two in the morning. She'd gone to bed at her usual time, but had been unable to sleep. She'd been restless much of the day. Actually since her meeting, she thought. She still couldn't wrap her mind around what the mayor and Pia had suggested. That *she* run the festivals.

Her usual response to a difficult problem was to brainstorm solutions. Only this wasn't that kind of problem. This was about people and tradition and an intangible she couldn't identify. She was both excited by the opportunity and frightened. She had never shied away from responsibility before, but this was different, and she didn't know what to do.

The result of which was her drive up the mountain.

She turned down a small, paved road that was marked as private. A quarter mile later, she saw the house set back in the trees. Gideon's house.

She hadn't known who else to talk to. She had started to make friends in town, women who tried to understand her and appreciate the effort she made to bond. Funny, charming women who all had a connection with the town. And that was the problem. The town. She needed an outside opinion.

Normally she would have gone to Justice, but he had recently gotten engaged to Patience. Felicia wasn't clear on all the dynamics that went into falling in love, but she was pretty sure keeping secrets broke a major rule. Which meant Justice would tell Patience what Felicia said, bringing her back to needing an outside opinion.

She parked in the wide, circular driveway and got out of her car. There was a long front porch and big windows that would allow in plenty of light. She would guess that light and sky would be important to a man like Gideon.

She walked to the porch and sat on the steps to wait. His shift ended at two, so she would expect him to arrive shortly. He didn't strike her as the type to stop in a bar on the way home. Not that she could say how she knew that about him.

The little information she had on Gideon was sketchy at best. Their time together four years ago had been more physical than conversational. She knew that he was former military, that he'd been assigned to covert ops and that his work had taken him places no man should have to go. She knew that he and his team had been taken prisoner for nearly two years. That had happened before they'd met.

She'd never discovered any details on his captivity, mostly because the information had been classified beyond her pay grade. Technically she could have gotten into the file, but Felicia was less concerned about if she could do something than if she should. What she did know was that Gideon had been involved in the kind of missions that were so exciting in movies but deadly in real life. The kind that if the operative got caught — no one was coming after him. Because of that, Gideon had spent twenty-two months in the hands of the Taliban. She assumed he'd been tortured and abused until death had seemed like the best possible outcome. Then he'd been rescued. The other men with him hadn't made it out.

Headlights appeared through the bushes. She watched Gideon's truck pull up behind her car. He turned off the engine, then got out and walked toward her.

He was tall, with broad shoulders. In the starlight there were no details — just the silhouette of the man. A shiver raced through her. Not apprehension, she thought. Anticipation. Her body remembered what Gideon had done, how he'd touched her with a combination of tenderness and desperation. His hunger had chased away any nerves.

While she'd studied the subject of sexual intimacy, knowing in her head and experiencing in person were two different things. Reading about the states of arousal had been nothing like experiencing them. Intellectual knowledge of why a tongue stroke on a nipple might feel good hadn't prepared her for the wet heat of his mouth on her breast. And knowing the progression of an orgasm hadn't come close to actually feeling the shuddering release that had claimed her.

"You're unexpected," he said, pausing at

31

the foot of the stairs.

In the starlight, she couldn't read his expression. She couldn't see if he was remembering, too. "I need to talk to someone," she admitted. "You came to mind."

His eyebrows rose. "Okay. That's a new one. I haven't seen you in four years and you thought of me?"

"Technically you saw me in the warehouse."

One corner of his mouth twitched. "Yes, and it was meaningful for me, too." The almost-smile faded. "What do you want to talk about?"

"It's work related, but if you don't want to have a conversation, I can leave."

He studied her for a few seconds. "Come on in. I'm too wired to sleep after I work. I usually do Tai Chi to relax, but having a conversation works, too."

He walked past her. She rose and followed him inside.

The house was big and open, with plenty of wood and high ceilings. Gideon flipped on lights as he moved through a great room with a fireplace at one end. There were floor-to-ceiling windows that looked out onto the darkness. While she couldn't make out details of the view, she had a sense of vastness beyond.

"Is the house on the edge of a canyon?" she asked.

"Side of a mountain."

He went into the kitchen. There were plenty of cabinets, lots of granite countertops and stainless appliances. He pulled two beers out of the refrigerator and handed her one.

"I thought you were avoiding me," he said.

"I was, but now that we've spoken there didn't seem to be any need to continue."

"Huh."

His dark gaze was steady but unreadable. She had no idea what he was thinking. His voice was appealing, but that was more about physiology than any interest in her. Gideon had one of those low, rumbly voices that sounded so good on the radio. He could make a detergent sound sexy if he put any effort into it.

He flipped off the kitchen lights. She blinked in the sudden darkness, then heard more than saw him walk across the room and open a sliding glass door. Moonlight illuminated the shadow of him disappearing onto what would be the back deck of the house. She followed.

There were a few lounge chairs and a couple of small tables. Forest stretched out beyond the railing. The trees angled down

— Gideon hadn't been kidding about the house being on the side of a mountain.

She settled in a chair close to his, with one of the tables between them. She rested her head against the cushions and stared up at the star-filled sky. The half-moon had nearly cleared the mountain, illuminating the quiet forest and still mountain.

The air was cool, but not cold. In the distance she heard the faint hoot of an owl. An occasional leaf rustled.

"I can see why you like it here," she said, reaching for her beer. "It's restful. You're close enough to town to get to the station but far enough away to not have to deal with too many unexpected visitors." She smiled. "Excluding me, of course."

"I like it."

"Do you get snowed in during the winter?"

"I didn't last year. We hardly had any snow. But it's going to happen." He shrugged. "I'm prepared."

He would be, she thought, because of his military training. She'd noticed that she and Justice often came at a problem from different angles but with the same objective. And speaking of her friend . . .

"I couldn't talk to Justice about this," she said.

Gideon raised his eyebrows. "All right."

"I thought you'd want to know why. Because he and I are like family." She turned on the lounge chair, angling herself toward him.

He was in silhouette again. A powerful man momentarily tamed. Her gaze drifted to his hands. She was tall, but with Gideon she'd felt delicate. For a few hours in his bed, she hadn't been frighteningly brilliant or freakishly organized. She'd been a woman — just like everyone else.

"So what's the problem?"

For a second she thought he was referring to her study of his hands, and the resulting memories. "It's the town."

"You don't like it here?"

"I like it very much." She drew in a breath. "The mayor has asked me to take over running the festivals. Pia Moreno had been doing it for several years, but she already has three kids and is pregnant with a fourth. It's too much for her."

Gideon shrugged. "You'd be perfect for the job."

"On the surface. The logistics would be easy enough, but that's not the point. It's the significance."

"Of the festivals?"

She nodded. "They are the heartbeat of

35

the town. Time is measured by the festivals. When I go out with my friends, they often talk about festivals from the past, or what's coming up. Why is Mayor Marsha willing to trust them to me?"

"Because she thinks you'll do a good job."

"Of course I'll do the work. It's more than that."

"You're scared."

Felicia drew in a breath. "I wouldn't say scared."

He took a drink of his beer. "You can pick some big word if you want, but you mean scared. You don't want to let them down and you're afraid you're going to."

"I thought *I* was the most direct person in any conversation," she murmured.

Gideon leaned back in his chair and closed his eyes. It was safer than looking at Felicia, especially in moonlight. With her big green eyes and flame-red hair, she was a classic beauty. How would she describe herself? Ethereal, maybe. He smiled.

"This isn't funny," she told him.

"It kind of is." But not for the reason she thought. His situation was more ironic.

He'd built his house and designed his life so that he chose if and when he interacted with anyone. Last night Ford had been his surprise guest. Tonight it was Felicia. The difference was he'd been comfortable around his friend. Not so much with the woman sitting only a few feet away.

It wasn't that he was *uncomfortable,* it was that he was aware. Of the soft sound of her breathing. Of the way her hair tumbled over her shoulders. Of how she occasionally looked at him like she was remembering them naked together.

Wanting stirred. It had been dormant so long that the physical act of blood rushing to his groin was painful. Thinking pure thoughts didn't help, mostly because he didn't have any where she was concerned. Of course now he was left with a hard-on and nowhere to put it, so to speak.

He glanced at Felicia and wondered what she would say if he told her he wanted her. Any other woman would be flustered or embarrassed. A few might start taking off their clothes as a way to say yes. But what about Felicia?

He figured there was a fifty-fifty chance she would discuss the biological process of arousal and an erection in such scientific terms that the blood would retreat in self-defense, thereby solving the problem. On the other hand, she could do what she'd done when they'd met in Thailand — look him directly in the eye and ask if he wanted to have sex with her.

"You were the most beautiful woman in that bar," he told her. "I was surprised when you came over to talk to me."

"You seemed nice."

"No one's said that about me in a long time."

She smiled. "I was still in the military at the time and working with guys in Special Forces. I was comfortable being around dangerous men. I can't explain why I picked you, though. I found you appealing, of course. I suppose I also had a chemical reaction. Perhaps to your pheromones. Attraction isn't an exact science."

She ducked her head, then looked back on him. "It was my first time."

"Picking up a guy? You did good. I was immediately intrigued."

"I was wearing a very low-cut sundress. Most men are attracted to breasts. Plus I'd run in place for a few minutes before going into the bar. The scent of female sweat is also sexually attractive to men."

"I feel used."

She laughed. "No, you don't."

"You're right." They'd had a great night. "I wanted to see you again, but I couldn't find you."

She wrinkled her nose. "I got sent back to the States. I'm sure Justice had something to do with it." She paused. "I didn't mean I'd never picked up a man in a bar before, Gideon. I meant you were my first time. I was a virgin."

Gideon stared at her, his beer halfway to his mouth. He returned it to the table. Memories of that night flashed through his head. Of Felicia exploring his body as if she couldn't get enough. Her eager cries of "more" and "harder." She'd been so clear on what she wanted that he'd assumed . . . No guy could have ever guessed . . .

"Shit."

"Don't be upset," she told him. "Please. I didn't say anything that night because I was afraid you'd turn me down. Or that it would make things difficult. That you'd be too careful or tentative."

"How old were you?" he asked.

"Twenty-four." She sighed. "Which was part of the problem. No one would sleep with me. I was tired of not knowing. Of being different. I'm not saying there's anything wrong with being a virgin. I suppose in a perfect world I would have waited until I fell in love. Only, how was that supposed to happen?"

She sat up and faced him. "I grew up on

a university campus. They had very polite words to describe my situation, but at the heart of it, I was a lab experiment. I joined the Army and was quickly moved into logistics for Special Forces. Guys everywhere, right? Except I was so socially awkward, I think I scared them. Or they saw me as a sister, like Justice. I kept waiting to meet someone. For that first kiss, that first time. But it wasn't happening."

She twisted her fingers together. "I went to the bar for three nights before I saw you. Once I did, I decided you were the one."

He didn't know what he was supposed to do with all that information.

"Are you angry?" she asked.

"Confused. You had me fooled. You seemed to know what you were doing."

She smiled. "I'm very good at research."

"Still, I should have noticed."

"You had an incredibly beautiful woman in your bed. You were distracted."

She was laughing as she spoke, as if making a joke, yet the words were completely true.

"It had been a while for me," he admitted. "You were my first after I was held captive."

Her humor faded. "I didn't know that."

"You and I didn't talk much. Once I realized what you wanted, I wasn't about to say no. I'd spent two years in that hole in the ground, then another year and a half in Bali."

"There are very lovely women in Bali."

"That may be true, but my teacher insisted celibacy was the road to healing."

"Hence the trip to Thailand?"

"I wouldn't have said 'hence,' but it was part of the reason I wanted to take a break." He managed to take a drink of his beer. "I wasn't expecting to find you."

"You didn't. I found you."

A point he would happily concede. "Things didn't end the way I wanted."

"For me, either."

He and Felicia had been lounging in bed when two guys had literally broken down the door. Gideon hadn't known Justice at the time, but he'd recognized Ford. His buddy had shrugged in apology but hadn't stayed to talk.

"I should have reacted faster," Gideon said.

"It's good that you didn't. Then you and Justice would have gotten into a fight and someone would have gotten hurt."

He liked to think it would have been the other guy but figured he would have taken the brunt of the attack. At that point he'd

41

been out of the game for several years. He'd been in good shape but not honed like Justice. He doubted Ford would have taken sides, although he probably would have prevented them from killing each other. A cold comfort, he thought.

"Now you and I are here," he said.

"Not a coincidence. You and Justice both know Ford. Justice met him when he was a teenager and lived here for a while."

Gideon had heard the story. Justice had been in the witness protection program, which had relocated him to Fool's Gold. A perfect place to hide, Gideon thought. No one would think to look for him in such an idyllic town.

All these years later, Justice had returned, fallen in love with Patience, a girl he'd cared about in high school. Talk about a sappy story. Yet it was a situation that Gideon found himself envying. Justice had found peace — something Gideon knew would always elude him. On the surface he looked like everyone else, but he knew what was inside. He knew that he couldn't risk caring. Love made a man weak and ultimately killed him. Gideon couldn't afford to take the risk.

She tucked her hair behind her ears. "Ford talked to you about Fool's Gold and you came to check it out."

He had, and he'd liked what he'd seen. The touristy town was big enough to have what he needed and small enough that he could exist on the fringes of belonging. He could be a part of things and yet separate.

"Are you going to take the job?" he asked.

"I want to." Her voice had a quality of longing.

"You should. You'll do well. It's mostly logistics and you excel at getting things done."

"You can't know that," she said.

He shrugged. "I asked Ford about you. That's pretty much all he would tell me."

"Oh. That makes sense." She twisted a strand of hair around her finger. "I'm not worried about the operation part of the job. It's everything else. I'm not good with emotions. I'm too in my head." She ducked her head. "I wish I was more like you. In the moment. You don't seem like you need to think everything through. That's nice."

He wasn't allowing himself to be in the moment right now, he thought grimly. If he did, he would already have her naked and moaning. He would have explored every inch of her body before settling with his mouth between her legs.

Blood surged at the image. He wanted to

hear her breathing hitch as she got closer. He wanted to feel her tensing before she shattered, her mind nothing more than a hazy mess of pleasure.

"Gideon?"

He forced himself back to the present. "I could teach you some breathing techniques that might help."

She laughed.

The sweet, happy sound filled the silence of the night. It was the kind of sound that could save a man, he realized. Or bring him to his knees.

The need grew and, with it, the understanding that he couldn't take the risk.

"It's late," he told her.

"I'm aware of the time. The movement of the stars and the moon are a clear . . ." Her humor faded. "Oh, you're asking me to leave."

"You have a long drive back."

She stood. "It's three-point-seven miles, but that's not the point. I'm sorry. I didn't mean to keep you so long. Thanks for talking to me. It helped."

He felt as if he'd kicked a kitten. "Felicia, don't read too much into this." He rose. "Look. Like you said, it's complicated."

She looked into his eyes. "People say that when they don't want to tell the truth."

The truth? Tension had returned and, with it, his arousal. Restlessness made him want to move, but he knew the value of staying still.

She put her hand on his shoulder, then moved her fingers to his biceps. "You're very powerful. More muscled than Justice. His body type is leaner, and he has to work harder to bulk up. Your physiology allows you to add muscle more quickly. It's . . . interesting."

As was the warmth of her skin, he thought, watching her green eyes darken slightly as her features sharpened and her gaze intensified. The air seemed charged as energy flowed between them. He didn't know exactly what she was thinking, but he was starting to have a good idea.

"Don't look at me like that," he commanded.

The corners of her mouth turned up. "I'm trying to flirt. Sorry. It's harder than it looks. I guess it's all the nuances."

She swayed toward him. "Our previous encounter was very satisfying. There have been two other men, and it wasn't the same. I suppose it's one of those intangibles that can't be measured. With you, I felt more comfortable. We laughed and talked in addition to making love. I remember that we

45

ordered champagne and you —"

He knew exactly what he'd done with a mouthful of champagne. He remembered everything about their night together.

Unable to stop himself, he put his hands on her waist and drew her to him. She went willingly, her head already slightly raised so he barely had to bend to kiss her.

Yes, Felicia thought, as Gideon's mouth pressed against hers. She let her eyes sink closed as she lost herself in the feel of his lips against hers.

The kiss was gentler than she remembered. As if he were retracing steps. She let herself feel the heat radiating out from a central point low in her belly and get lost in the image of fire dancing across her skin.

She put her hands on his shoulders and leaned against him. He moved his hands from her waist to her back, then slid them up and down. She wanted to stretch and purr, she thought, her brain cataloging the various sensations of his kiss, his fingers, the heat where they touched, chest to chest. She wrapped her arms around his neck and parted her lips. He stiffened and drew back a little.

While she wasn't usually one for insights, she was acutely aware that he had yet to decide. That the kiss had been more reaction than plan and he was still in a place where he could say no. She didn't know *why* he would refuse, but understood he still could.

She opened her eyes to look at him. His jaw was tight, his gaze filled with indecision.

"You don't know what you're asking," he said, his voice nearly a growl.

She smiled. "I know exactly what I'm asking."

Four years ago she had pursued Gideon, she thought. Had picked him from all the other men in the bar that night. As she had said, there was something about him. His strength, of course. Nearly any female would respond well to a powerful man. That was merely biology. But there had been something else. An elusive sense of rightness, although if she did some research, she could probably figure out what it was.

Now the need to be with him was as strong, and for a similar reason, she realized. She was unsettled. Confused. There had been so many changes in her life, and the job offer had provided a tipping point of sorts. She needed to feel anchored and safe. How strange she would seek that in Gideon's arms.

She didn't have many gut instincts —

another hazard of living in her head. But she had learned to trust them when they occurred, and right now her gut was telling her that she wanted to have sex with this man. Hot, hungry sex.

"I want this," she murmured, still working through the questions.

She studied him, his broad shoulders, the slight tremor in his hands. Her gaze drifted down and she saw his erection straining against his jeans.

Anticipation joined satisfaction. There was no time to get her sweat glands working to tip the scales, so to speak. She would have to be more direct.

She quickly pulled off her T-shirt and dropped it onto the lounge chair beside her. Then she undid her bra and let it fall on top of her shirt.

Gideon's jaw tightened, but otherwise, he didn't move. She reached for his hands, took them in hers and placed them on her bare breasts.

Perhaps from instinct or perhaps because he couldn't resist, he cupped her breasts and rubbed his thumbs against her nipples. She hadn't felt them tighten, but when she glanced down she saw the tips were puckered.

He moved his thumbs again, and the

gentle pressure sent pleasure moving all through her. His skin was more tanned against her paleness. His hands large. He moved back and forth against her until she felt her eyelids start to sink closed so she could get lost in how he made her feel.

She drew in a breath. "I'm enjoying everything you're doing and —"

"Shut up."

Her eyes popped open, and she saw him smiling.

"Too much conversation?"

"Yes. This is when it's best to be quiet."

Relief made her nearly as weak as his hands on her breasts.

"So we're going to have sex?"

His answer was to haul her against him and thrust his tongue in her mouth. She met him stroke for stroke, wanting every sensation possible, wanting, no, needing, to be intimate with this man. Vulnerable.

As soon as the thought occurred, she felt herself starting to analyze what it meant. She did her best to turn off her analytical brain and focus instead on the feel of his soft T-shirt under her fingers, of his broad shoulders.

He deepened the kiss, then broke free and stepped back. In a matter of seconds, he'd pulled off his shirt and flung it away. His boots and socks followed. As he reached for the belt on his jeans, she undid her own and pushed them, along with her bikini panties, to the deck.

Before she could even admire his nakedness, he was moving past her to one of the lounge chairs. He raised a bar in back, then released it. The chair collapsed into a flat position.

"How clever," she began, only to find herself being half guided, half carried to the chair. She was placed on the end, in a seated position, then Gideon dropped to his knees.

He buried his hands in her hair and kissed her. His tongue stroked against her lips before dipping inside. She kissed him back, even as she moved her fingers up and down his arms and his back.

He dropped his hands to her breasts. As he began to trail kisses down her neck, he urged her to lie back.

She did as he requested, her body on the cushion, her knees bent, her feet on the wood floor of the deck. As his fingers teased her sensitive nipples, his mouth moved lower and lower, the ultimate destination quite obvious.

He'd done that to her before, she remembered. The other two men hadn't, but Gideon had given her her first orgasm with his tongue. She shivered slightly as he kissed his way down her belly, pausing to lightly circle the inside of her belly button.

She moved her arms so she could use her fingers to part herself for him. He'd taught her that, as well, she thought, her breathing already increasing.

Her insides clenched as he got closer and closer. She was so swollen. Her clitoris would be completely engorged with blood and extremely sensitive.

He shifted his hands so his palms were flat on her breasts. He massaged her, distracting her for a second. She felt the warmth of his breath, then he flicked the tip of his tongue against her. Just once. She gasped as a jolt of involuntary movement caused her to jump. He chuckled, then did it again.

This time she was prepared and felt herself sinking into sensation. He explored all of her, easing his tongue all the way inside her before returning it to her clit. Once there, he settled into a steady, slow rhythm of back and forth and around, his hands keeping pace on her breasts.

The predictable movements allowed her to focus on what she was feeling instead of anticipating what should happen next. As more and more muscles tensed, as her nerve endings fired more quickly, she felt her brain starting to shut down. There was only the sensation. She, who lived in a world of thoughts and ideas, was reduced to simply feeling. It was glorious.

Back and forth, around and around, with each stroke of his tongue, her body began the steady climb to release. She pulsed her hips, an unconscious signal that she wanted more. She was aware of her breathing getting faster and faster. Of small moans.

He moved one of his hands, sliding it down her body before inserting a finger deep inside her and curving up. Scientists argued about the reality of the G-spot, she thought hazily, trying to part her legs more, to press down. Right now she was convinced it existed, and when he rubbed it like that she was —

Her orgasm caught her unawares. One second she was tense and ready and the next she was flying. She rode the waves of pleasure, calling out, gasping and begging, screaming maybe. She wasn't sure. She shook and shuddered. One finger became two, and she pushed down, wanting him to fill her.

His tongue stayed steady, allowing her release to go on and on until there was nothing left. This was what it felt like to be boneless, she thought, barely able to open her eyes.

He straightened.

She half raised herself on her elbows and glanced at his large erection. She smiled as she reached for him, guiding him inside her.

He was large enough to stretch her as he pushed in. She wrapped her legs around his hips, reached her hands to his. He grabbed hers. Their fingers laced together. She tried to keep her eyes open, to watch him as he pumped in faster and faster, but she was unable to stay focused. Not with the need growing inside her. Not when she was drawing closer to the edge once again, straining and straining until they came together.

CHAPTER THREE

Felicia arrived for her morning meeting right on time. As she parked by the warehouse that was the new offices for CDS, she found herself unable to stop smiling.

She'd spent the night with Gideon. They'd slept in a tangle of arms and legs in his big bed, then awakened before dawn to make love again. She'd left around five and had driven back to her place to shower and prepare for her day.

Although it was simple biology, what she'd done sounded so illicit. She liked that. Usually she was the boring one. The predictable friend who was always around and rarely had plans. She didn't have sex with men she hadn't seen in years — certainly not outside. At night.

She had a job offer and the aftereffects of the hormone bath that went with a satisfying sexual experience. Right now life was very, very good. Still grinning foolishly, she collected her backpack and walked into the building.

What had once been one big open space had been partitioned into offices, classrooms, locker rooms and a large workout facility. The plumbing was taking the longest. In addition to the usual toilets and sinks, there were also showers, lockers and a dressing area. Segregated by gender. Angel had foolishly suggested they make the women's locker room smaller, but Felicia had stared him down. Justice and Ford hadn't bothered coming to his defense. Probably because they knew better.

Justice was already there, his large presence seeming to fill the room. He sat at a battered desk he'd picked up at a garage sale a few weeks ago. Their "real" office furniture was on order.

"Hey," he said as she entered, not bothering to look up from his laptop. "Did you file the permits for the shooting range?"

"Yes." Her tone indicated she really meant "Of course," but why state the obvious? "I took them directly to the city officials myself. They'll be processed by the fifteenth."

There was a professional mission statement in the articles of incorporation, but at its heart, CDS was a bodyguard school. It would provide advanced training for those in the industry as well as refresher courses. Ford would be working with corporations who wanted a unique team-building facility, while Angel would be in charge of the actual training. Justice was going to run the place.

In addition, CDS would provide classes for the community. Self-defense mainly with a few gun safety lectures and some hands-on training.

Felicia had been offered any job she wanted with the company, but knew she needed something different. She was ready to be as close to normal as she could get. She wanted to be part of a community, to fall in love, get married and have kids. A common dream, she thought, but one that seemed especially difficult for her to accomplish.

The job Mayor Marsha had offered was a big step in that direction. If only Felicia was brave enough to accept it.

She pulled her own laptop from her backpack and walked over to the desk. She pulled up a second chair and sat opposite Justice. Once the machine booted, she logged on to the internet and began typing.

"The equipment Ford and Angel ordered for the obstacle course will be delivered by the end of the week. The cherry picker is coming next Monday to help with installation of the suspension bridge."

Justice glanced at her, his eyes bright with excitement. "Can't wait to try it."

"It's high, it's a bridge, what's the big deal?"

He grinned.

She knew he was really looking forward to having one of his friends on the bridge and trying to shake the other guy off. The three business partners looked all tough and burly but in their hearts, they were still boys who liked to play practical jokes.

At least they were smart about them, she thought. They were all keenly aware that each of them was trained to be a deadly killer. It would be easy for any situation to get out of hand and they made sure that didn't happen.

The main door opened, and Angel and Ford walked in together. Wearing jeans and T-shirts, they should have looked like a couple of regular Joes. But they didn't. After her years in the military, Felicia was an expert at spotting men with special training, and these two had all the characteristics.

There was a confidence in the way they walked. Anyone looking at them would know they could handle themselves, regardless of the situation. Ford was a couple of inches taller and maybe twenty pounds heavier. He had dark hair and dark eyes, and an easy laugh. On the surface, he was the most fun-loving of the group. But Felicia knew that was a facade. Underneath, he was as emotionally distant as any man who'd spent his career viewing life through a sniper rifle.

Angel might have gotten out of the military sooner than any of them, but he'd moved into the type of private security that was just as dangerous as black ops. He had pale gray eyes that had seen too much and an intriguing scar across his neck, as if someone had tried to cut his throat.

Felicia had started to ask him about it once, and he'd stared her down. As she wasn't usually intimidated by the men she worked with, she considered that a testament to his mental powers. She knew Angel had been married before, and that his wife and son had been killed in a car accident. How sad to have everything and then lose it, she thought.

Justice, Ford and Angel would be the partners in the company. There would be several permanent employees, including her friend Consuelo, who was due to arrive shortly. Felicia knew the team wondered if they could fit into life in a small town, and they worried about blending in. She had only been in Fool's Gold a couple of months, but she was pretty sure that in a test of wills, the town would win. Justice had already changed; it was just a matter of time until the others found themselves behaving in ways they would have sworn wasn't possible.

There was little scientific data to back up her assertion, but she was willing to stake her reputation on her supposition all the same.

"Is my gym ready?" Angel asked. "I've been using the one in town, and there are too many people there."

Felicia smiled. "You mean women, don't you?"

Angel turned to her. "Look, dollface, you don't know what it's like."

"It's Eddie," Ford said, snickering. "She came up to him yesterday and asked about his scar. Then she wanted to touch his biceps."

Angel's face took on a pained expression. "The woman is what? A hundred? What the hell was she doing in a gym?"

"Mostly checking out cute guys," Felicia said cheerfully. "From what I hear, she and her friend Gladys do it all the time. I don't think she's much past her seventies, by the

way. In case, you know, that makes a difference."

Angel glared at her. Justice and Ford
laughed.

Felicia grinned in return, pleased to have
made a joke. "The gym equipment is coming this week," she told him by way of a
peace offering. "It will be installed and
ready to go before the weekend."

Ford pulled up a chair and sat by the desk.
"Didn't we say we were going to let people
in town work out here if they wanted?
Should we send Angel's new friend an in-
vite?"

Cool, gray eyes turned glacier. "You really
want to take me on?" Angel asked.

"Any day, old man."

Felicia glanced at Justice, who shook his
head. This was familiar territory with Angel
and Ford. They exchanged banter and
insults, staged ridiculous competitions and
generally drove each other crazy.

As Angel was probably forty or forty-one,
the "old man" comment was simply part of
their fun.

"Can we get on with the meeting?" Justice
asked. "If you two can hold off on your play-
time for a few minutes. Felicia, bring them
up to date."

They spent the next two hours talking

about the business. Ford had a few leads on potential corporate clients, and Angel had some interesting ideas for team-building exercises. When the meeting finished, Ford and Angel went off to wrestle or race or something that required one to win and the other to lose. Felicia shut down her computer, then looked at Justice.

"I've seen Gideon."

Justice studied her. "Okay."

She thought about mentioning they'd had sex but didn't think her friend wanted that level of detail. "I might continue to see him." Hopefully with and without clothes, she thought. She wanted to get to know him better. Perhaps not the traditional sequence for a relationship, but she hadn't found any traditional path that worked for her.

"I know you want to protect me," she continued, "but you can't. It's important that I learn in my own way. Make my own mistakes and suffer the consequences."

"As long as you're admitting Gideon is a mistake."

She sighed. "You know what I mean."

"I do. Look. I'll admit I don't like the guy very much."

"You don't know him."

"I know what he did to you."

She rolled her eyes. "I picked him up in a

61

bar. I practically begged him to have sex with me, and he complied. He did nothing wrong."

Justice winced. "Could we not talk about that part of it?"

"Why not? It's the reason you're upset. Justice, I was twenty-four. It's not unexpected I would have sexual relations with someone by that age. I wasn't irresponsible. You had no right to barge in back then, and you're not invited to do the same now. I love you. You're my family. But I'm twenty-eight years old and you don't get to tell me what to do with my personal life."

Justice opened his mouth, then closed it. "Fine."

She waited.

"I mean it," he grumbled. "I won't say anything about Gideon. You can see him if you want."

She resisted pointing out she'd just told him she didn't want his opinion or involvement. "Thank you."

"Just wait to have sex with him this time, okay? Get to know him a little."

She did her best not to smile. "You're probably right."

"I am."

Like many things in Fool's Gold, Jo's Bar

defied expectation. Instead of catering to men and their love of sports, Jo's served mostly women. The lighting was flattering, the decor feminine and the large screens were tuned to shopping shows and reality TV. Men were welcome, as long as they retreated to the back room where there was a pool table and plenty of TVs showing sports. If they insisted on staying in the front of the house, they were expected to keep quiet about the signs counting down the days until the new season of *Dallas Cowboy Cheerleaders — Making the Team.*

Felicia liked the bar. When she came here, it was to meet her friends. Because in the few months she'd been in town, she'd made friends. Women who didn't seem to mind that she was socially awkward and often said the wrong thing.

She sat at a table with Isabel, Patience and Noelle. They'd already put in their orders and each had a soda or iced tea.

"I'm thinking Labor Day," Noelle said, stirring her diet soda with her straw. She laughed. "A traditional Christmas holiday."

Noelle planned to open a new store in town. The Christmas Attic would celebrate the season. Like Felicia, Noelle was new to Fool's Gold. The tall, willowy blonde was friendly and funny, but there was something about her eyes. Felicia would guess secrets but had no idea what they were.

Isabel, also a blonde but a little curvier, had grown up in the area. She was back in town for a few months helping her family with Paper Moon — a wedding gown boutique. Isabel was irreverent and self-deprecating. She was the one who teased first and laughed the longest. Felicia secretly admired Isabel's sense of style and easy grace.

Patience had made Felicia the most nervous at first. The pretty brunette was the single mother of a ten-year-old girl and engaged to Justice. When Felicia had first arrived, Patience thought there was more to her and Justice's relationship than friendship, but their siblinglike connection had become apparent. Since then, Patience had welcomed Felicia to her world and had made her feel welcome.

"There will be lots of tourists," Isabel was saying. "We fill up for all the major holidays, and Labor Day is when people want that last rush of summer. Which is why it's called the End of Summer Festival. I think you'd get a big crowd in the store."

Noelle sighed. "I hope you're right. Maybe it's too early for people to be thinking about Christmas."

"I know what you mean," Patience said. "I'm going to have to figure out when to start decorating for the various holidays. It's not anything I had to worry about before."

Felicia often helped Patience out at Brewhaha, picking up a shift a few times a week. The work wasn't very challenging, but she enjoyed the chance to work on her people skills in a low-key setting. She was also able to eavesdrop on people's conversations and try to learn from them.

"I think the abundance of tourists would outweigh any concern that you're asking them to think about Christmas too early," Felicia told Noelle.

"She has a point," Isabel said. "The day after Labor Day is the traditional start of the fall season. And then comes Santa."

"You're right." Noelle nodded slowly. "If I can pull it all together by then, I'll open over Labor Day."

Patience leaned toward Isabel. "Justice and I are talking dates. How long do I need to order a wedding dress?"

Isabel grinned. "I can't wait for you to come in and try on dresses. As for timing, it depends on the manufacturer."

"I want something simple. It's a second marriage for me."

Felicia didn't know the details of Patience's past, but she'd heard that her ex had disappeared shortly after Lillie had been born and he'd never come back.

"It's a first marriage for Justice," Isabel reminded her. "He'll want you to be a princess. You are perfect princess material. There are some great dresses you'll love."

Patience blushed. "Maybe. We'll see. I'll come in and try a few things on this week." She waved her hand. "Okay, enough about me. Someone else talk, please. One of you must have news."

Felicia thought about her job offer, then hesitated. She wanted to accept, but still wasn't sure she was the right person.

"Wow, I saw that," Isabel said, staring at her. "Okay, you have to tell us."

"I'm not sure I . . ." Felicia hesitated, then decided to plunge ahead. "Pia Moreno is going to step down from her position running the festivals. Mayor Marsha asked me to take her place."

All three women stared at her.

"That's great," Patience said. "You'll be perfect for the job. It's all about staying organized, and you're really good at that."

Isabel nodded. "I don't know how Pia managed with three kids, and now she's pregnant with her fourth. The town is lucky she lasted as long as she did."

Noelle patted Felicia's arm. "I know nothing about the festivals, but I can't imagine you not being brilliant at anything, so well done you."

"Thanks." Felicia hated the insecurity welling up inside her. "I wasn't sure what people would think. I'm new in town. Maybe someone who has been here longer would understand the nuances of what goes on better."

Patience shook her head. "No, no and no. Noelle's right. You'll be great. As for being new, I'm sorry, but you're already one of us." She sighed heavily. "I suppose this means you won't be filling in at Brew-haha anymore."

"I don't think I'll have the time."

"Don't worry. I need to hire more full-time people. I'm blessed with many customers." She raised her glass. "To festivals and whipping them into shape."

Everyone drank.

Isabel leaned toward her. "Okay, so what's the scoop on some fighter chick coming to town? I've been hearing rumors that we're getting our own girl soldier. Is that true?"

"Yes," Felicia said. "Consuelo Ly should be arriving in the next couple of weeks. I haven't heard from her recently, so I don't have an exact date. She'll be teaching classes at CDS. Self-defense, hand-to-hand, some advanced weapons training."

"Seriously?" Noelle asked. "I can't decide if I'm excited to meet her or terrified."

"I'm excited," Isabel said. "Have you seen how Ford and Angel walk around town like they're so hot and we should all be falling all over them?"

"They haven't been like that," Patience said.

"Ford struts. I've seen him strut."

Patience's expression turned knowing. "Someone is worried about her past."

"I'm not," Isabel said firmly. "I refuse to be. I was a child and he can't hold that against me."

From what Felicia had heard, years ago Isabel had had a crush on Ford and been devastated by his departure. There were also rumors that Isabel had written to him regularly, but Felicia wasn't sure about that.

"I don't think Consuelo is interested in Ford," Felicia said. "Or Angel. She's known both of them for years. She says they're not her type."

"Too bad," Patience said. "I'm so into this being in love thing. I need one of you to join me. I want to be able to talk about how wonderful Justice is and how my heart beats faster when he walks in the room."

"You can talk about it all you want," No-elle told her.

"It's not the same." Patience glanced at each of them. "I want one of you to fall in love. I mean it."

"I'm leaving town in March," Isabel said. "This is a bad time for a relationship. I refuse to fall for some guy and then have to decide between him and my career. It's not going to happen."

Noelle shrugged. "Sorry, but I'm getting over a bad breakup."

Patience pressed her lips together. "You're sure you don't find Ford or Angel attrac-tive?"

"They're very sexy, but not my type."

Patience turned to Felicia. "What about you? You like both Ford and Angel."

"Kind of how I like Justice," she said. "Biologically speaking, humans aren't gen-erally attracted to family members. It keeps the gene pool healthier if we're not."

"I'm very disappointed," Patience told them. "You're all letting me down."

Felicia knew her friend was just kidding, but she still felt guilty. An odd phenomenon and not one she was comfortable with.

"I slept with Gideon," she blurted, unable to stop the words.

All three of them turned to stare at her.

Isabel raised her eyebrows. "It's always the quiet types. Have you noticed that?"

"Gideon?" Noelle asked. "Radio Gideon of the dreamy voice? OMG, I love listening to him."

Patience stared at Noelle. "You didn't just say OMG."

Noelle laughed. "Sorry. I love to read teen fiction. It's a flaw, but one I can live with."

Isabel leaned toward the center of the table. "Patience, honey? You're missing the point. Felicia had sex with the mysterious Gideon."

Patience turned to Felicia. "How did that happen?"

"In the usual way. We were outside on his deck and . . ." Felicia stopped and cleared her throat. The three of them were staring at her with identical expressions of confusion.

"You mean you're curious about the order of events that led up to our encounter. Not where and in what position."

Isabel leaned back in her chair. "You know, I'm going to have to think about that. No one has ever given me a choice like that before."

Noelle patted Felicia's arm. "You're one of my favorite people, you know that?"

"Because I'm a freak?"

"You're not a freak. You're honest. There aren't enough honest people in the world. How do you know Gideon? You must know him because I can't see you jumping into bed with a perfect stranger."

A lovely assessment of her character, Felicia thought, however false. Because that's exactly what she'd done. Twice.

"We met four years ago, in Thailand. It was a brief, um, encounter. When I got here, I heard him on the radio and realized it was the same man. I didn't know what to think or do, so I've been avoiding him for the past couple of months."

A plan that had been going really well, until spiders had worked their arachnid mojo and changed everything. Although she couldn't really say she objected to the ultimate outcome.

"I wanted to talk to someone about the job offer," she continued. "So last night I drove to his house to speak with him."

"You drove to his house?" Patience repeated. "Just like that? You're so brave. I wish I was like that. Direct and fearless. I overthink everything."

Felicia thought about explaining why she'd picked Gideon, then stopped herself. It was possible her friends wouldn't understand her reticence in speaking with them

71

about the job.

"What's his house like?" Noelle asked. "Is it fabulous? I bet it's fabulous."

"The part I saw was nice."

"They did it on the deck," Isabel said, reaching for her drink. "I'm guessing there wasn't a tour."

"Oh, right. The deck. That's pretty hot." Noelle smiled. "You two make a cute couple. Ooh, I wonder if he's going to dedicate a song to you tonight. I'll have to listen."

"I'm sure he won't," Felicia said, knowing now she, too, would have to listen. Just in case.

Is that something a man would do after a night with a woman? She wasn't clear on what normal people did in relationships. She might have slept with Gideon, but he was still a mystery to her. She'd had sex, but never love. A physical encounter but not a boyfriend. She hadn't ever even been on a traditional date.

How was she supposed to find a man and fall in love when she couldn't even get asked out on a date?

"Good evening, Fool's Gold," Gideon said into the microphone. "I'd like to start tonight with a favorite, for a friend of mine."

72

He pushed the button, and the Beatles' "I Saw Her Standing There" began to play. He thought about mentioning the spiders but knew that would lead to questions, and he enjoyed his nights without the phone ringing to interrupt.

The red light on the wall flashed.

So much for a quiet night. Gideon walked to the front door. For a second he wondered if Felicia had come by, then decided if she wanted to see him again, she would be waiting at his house, not interrupting his work.

He opened the back door and found Angel standing on the steps, a six-pack in his hands.

"Hey," he said, motioning for his friend to follow him back to his desk. "Tell me you're not looking for a place to crash. Ford already claimed the back room here."

They walked into the control room. "I'm good," Angel said. "And you'll be free of Ford soon, too. We're renting a house with Consuelo. It's furnished. We'll have the keys in a couple of days."

He passed over a beer.

Gideon took it and popped the top. "You're going to live with Ford?"

"You sound surprised."

"You'll kill each other."

Ford and Angel had always been competitive. They would bet on anything and liked to create elaborate challenges with ridiculous payoffs.

"We'll be fine," Angel said. "Consuelo will keep us in line."

"Or smother you with a pillow if you get to be too much trouble."

He'd only met the feisty brunette a few times. She was small but muscular, and she fought dirty. He'd watched her take down a trained fighter twice her size and not break a sweat.

He pushed another button to start the next CD.

"Besides," Angel said, waving his can. "I always win."

"You don't always win. You win more than half the time, which is the problem. Ford gets defensive, you get cocky. It's not a good scenario. It's like when the two Terminators fight. They both walk away and the town is left in ruins."

Angel grinned. "I like the Terminator movies. I see myself as a T-1000."

Gideon rolled his eyes. "I see you as the old beat-up Schwarzenegger."

"Hey."

"I'm just saying. You're over forty, my friend."

"It beats being dead."

Gideon raised his can. "I will drink to that. How's the business coming?"

"Good." Angel looked around the studio. "You should join us. Get out of here."

"I like it here."

"You have to miss the work."

Gideon knew what he meant. That it was difficult for some guys to walk away. They craved the excitement or the constant travel. Without danger, they couldn't relax. One of those counterintuitive truths he was sure Felicia could explain.

"I'm happy being like everyone else," he said.

He couldn't go back. Couldn't pick up a gun and kill again. There wasn't enough left inside. The damage was permanent and his pretense at normal tissue-thin. He wanted a sameness to his days. He wanted ordinary.

"We've got plenty of work," Angel said. "Ford's been selling the hell out of the company, and we're getting corporations signing up. I've been talking to the big security companies, and they want us to do their training. Easier and cheaper for them. We could use the help."

"No, thanks."

"You'll change your mind," Angel insisted.

"I won't. Just like you won't go back into the field."

Angel's mouth twisted. "I've seen enough death to last me a lifetime."

And he'd come close to losing it all, Gideon thought, his gaze drifting to his buddy's scar. The one on his neck. He only knew pieces of that story, but he was sure Angel's life had been spared by mere seconds.

Gideon's decision to walk away had come over time. He'd had nearly two years of being held captive and tortured to think about what he would do if he ever got out. The problem was being physically released hadn't changed the fact that his head was still in their control. He'd felt trapped. Recovering from that was harder. He doubted the nightmares would ever disappear.

"I heard a rumor that you'd bought two stations," Angel said.

"The rumors are true. AM and FM. Plenty of talk and local news on the AM station and music on FM. At night, it's all oldies, all the time."

Angel raised his head, listening to the music. "What is this stuff? It's what? A hundred years old."

"Very funny. My show is all '60s. 1960s for those of you who have trouble with math."

"Try something from this century."

shelves or moving furniture.

Her new job would demand more of her time, and she was looking forward to that. She'd spoken with the mayor the day before, officially accepting the position with the city. She'd filled out piles of paperwork and had thought about explaining how they could streamline the hiring process. In the end, she'd decided not to frighten anyone too soon. She could talk to the human resources department in a few weeks. When she wasn't the new girl.

The store was quiet, with only a few customers sitting at tables. Felicia took advantage of the lull and washed out the milk carafes and spoons. The front door opened, and she turned to see Charlie Dixon walking in.

Charlie was one of the town's firefighters. She was tall and physically strong, with a practical and pragmatic approach to life. Felicia enjoyed her company and always looked forward to their visits.

"Your usual?" Felicia asked.

Charlie nodded. She drank a large latte, to go. No fat-free milk for her, no flavors. Nothing with frills, Felicia thought, smiling as she pressed the button to grind the right amount of beans.

"I wanted to let you know I got a note

from Helen," Charlie said. "The woman whose husband was abusing her."

"Right." The couple had come into Brew-haha shortly after Felicia had arrived in town. The man had been horrible, and Felicia had reacted. She'd physically restrained him and then had dislocated his shoulder.

She'd put it back in place, but the pain had distracted him long enough for Charlie and the mayor to get Helen away.

"How is she?" Felicia asked, almost afraid to hear the answer. So many women were unable to break the cycle and truly end the relationship with their abuser.

"She did what she said. She left the bastard and is starting over in another state under a new name. She's already registered for classes at her local community college."

"I'm glad."

"Me, too. She wanted you to know that you inspired her."

Felicia poured the steamed milk into the to-go cup and passed it over. "That's nice. Thank you. I don't usually inspire anyone."

Charlie passed over a brightly colored card. "Here. It's an invitation to a party." The firefighter shrugged. "We're having a luau at the new hotel."

The Lady Luck Casino and Hotel being built on the edge of town was due to open next week. That morning the mayor had mentioned how the business was working to support town events, and the hotel-casino would be mentioned in advertising around the state.

"Thank you," Felicia said, glancing at the information printed over the picture of a beach with a palm tree. "Should I dress in costume?"

"Not necessary. It will be casual." She sighed. "Clay and I still can't agree on the wedding. I want to elope, he wants the big church wedding. Crazy man. We're getting a lot of pressure from people in town who want us to decide. We're thinking a big party will calm everyone down."

"It's very generous of you to have a large event," Felicia said, "but I don't think it will solve the problem. It's not the party your friends want, but the ritual. A wedding is a statement to your social group that you've moved into another stage of your lives. Years ago, changing from single to married often meant different responsibilities in the —"

Felicia stopped talking. "Sorry. You probably weren't looking for a dissertation on marriage."

"It was interesting," Charlie told her.

Felicia wished that were true. "I'm sure the party will be a lot of fun."

"I hope so. Oh, you can bring a date." Charlie grinned. "That was an offer, not an instruction. You don't have to if you'd rather not. There will be plenty of food and good company either way. Just show up and I'll be happy."

"Thank you. I will."

Another woman walked into Brew-haha and hurried over to Charlie. "Stop hiding from me!" she said loudly. "I swear, Charlie, you're making this we—" She came to a stop and smiled at Felicia. "Hi. I'm Dellina, Charlie's party planner."

Felicia smiled back at the pretty blonde. "She just mentioned the luau. It sounds like it's going to be a lot of fun."

"It is," Dellina said, glaring at Charlie. "If certain people will ever make decisions."

Charlie grumbled something under her breath. "Fine. I'll decide on the stupid flowers." She glanced at Felicia. "Ignore my complaints. The party will be great."

"I'm looking forward to it."

Charlie grabbed her latte and left with Dellina.

Felicia fingered the invitation. She wanted to go to the luau, but wasn't sure what to do about the date issue. The only man she would ask was Gideon, but she wasn't sure how he would feel about both the asking and the event itself. They'd had sex, but she knew that was different than a relationship. Women might bond during intercourse, but often a man was simply getting laid. Unless he was in a relationship, then the experience might be emotionally significant for him, too.

It was all so confusing, she thought, as an older couple walked into the store.

"Hello," she said with a practiced smile. "How can I help you?"

They placed their order and she went to work.

Considering all the variables, it was somewhat surprising that men and women ever got together in the first place. A testament to tenacity, or a higher power with a wicked sense of humor? To be honest, she wasn't sure which.

Gideon walked down the sidewalk, aware he was going to have to make a decision. Go get a cup of coffee or not.

On the surface, the choice wasn't life-changing. Or even notable. But he knew that his interest in entering Brew-haha had a whole lot more to do with the woman behind the counter than any beverage offered on the marquee.

He'd had sex with Felicia. More startling,

when they'd finished, he hadn't asked her to leave. They'd dressed, started talking, and then before he had known what he was doing, he was asking her to stay.

In his *house.*

He rarely had anyone over, didn't like visitors or surprises or change. Sure, the sex had been great, but why hadn't he encouraged her to leave? And what was he doing walking into Brew-haha today?

He held the door open for a couple of older tourists, then stepped inside. Felicia was behind the counter, her long red hair pulled back in a ponytail, her curvy body covered with a cheerful apron sporting the coffee shop's logo.

She didn't notice him right away, giving him a chance to study her. Her green eyes were wide and filled with amusement. She was smiling. Sunlight filtered in through the sparkling windows, illuminating her face.

She was beautiful — the result of a horrible car accident in her late teens and subsequent plastic surgery. After their night together in Thailand, he'd made it his business to find out who she was. It had taken two months, but he'd finally tracked her down. He'd seen the picture of her before the surgery, and while she was more conventionally attractive now, she'd been just as appealing back then. He'd thought about going to see her. Only, he'd known better.

Despite his studies, despite the meditation and Tai Chi, the long runs and the superficial calm, he wasn't like everyone else. He was broken in so many places, he would never be whole. That which wasn't broken was missing. He'd known better than to inflict himself on her.

Now he'd found her again, and for the life of him, he couldn't figure out what to do about her.

He walked to the counter and stood in line. He wasn't looking directly at her, but he was aware of the exact moment she noticed him. Her body stiffened in surprise, then relaxed.

He placed his order with the teenager manning the cash register, then walked over to where Felicia was handing a latte to another customer.

"Gideon." She reached for a to-go cup and smiled at him. "A latte? Really?"

He shrugged. "See me as more of a drip guy?"

"Yes."

"I like to change things up every now and then."

"I get that."

She worked efficiently, pouring the shots

of espresso into the cup, then starting to steam the milk.

"Did you make your decision?" he asked.

She nodded. "I took the job."

"Good. You'll like it."

"I hope I meet expectations. This town values tradition and connection."

Two things she wouldn't have a lot of experience with, he thought. But she was trying. He admired that about her. Most people ran from what was difficult. Not Felicia. She threw herself in, headfirst.

"You'll handle the logistics easily and figure out the rest of it as you go." He smiled. "Just like everyone else."

Instead of smiling back, she bit her lower lip. "I do want to be considered normal." She glanced around, as if checking to see who was close to them, then lowered her voice. "I should probably warn you, I mentioned our encounter to a few friends. I didn't mean to — it just sort of happened."

He leaned against the counter. "One of them was Patience."

She nodded. "There's an excellent chance she'll tell Justice."

"You worried about me? I think I can take him."

She handed him the latte. "You're bigger and stronger, but he's still in the protection

86

business, which means his training is more recent. I would prefer if the two of you didn't fight."

She was so damned earnest, he thought. "I'll do my best to honor your request."

"Thank you."

"You're welcome. Why did you tell your friends about us?"

She bit her lower lip. "I'm not sure. We were talking, and it just came out. For what it's worth, they were very impressed. The women in town enjoy the sound of your voice. You've also cultivated an air of mystery that's appealing. It probably goes back to the time of marauders, when women were physically kidnapped by neighboring tribes. Being taken by a handsome stranger is a primal female fantasy."

He sipped his latte. "Is it?"

She nodded. "Culturally, we tell stories to bond or learn lessons. In this case the handsome stranger is kind, thereby ensuring our safety and the future of our unborn children." She paused. "Not that you have to worry about an unexpected pregnancy. I'm on birth control."

He nearly choked. "Thanks for telling me that." Because he hadn't been thinking about protection or anything but the feel of her body and how much he wanted to be inside her.

He swore silently. He knew better. Had known since he was a teenager and his father had given him "the talk." How had she rattled him so much he'd forgotten?

"I wonder if Patience and Justice will have children." Her voice was wistful. "That would be nice."

He fought the need to back away. "You looking for a white picket fence?"

"If you mean I want what it represents, then, yes. In reality, I've never found that kind of fencing to be efficient. The upkeep alone would be daunting."

Okay — he didn't know how she did it. One second he wanted to run, and the next he wanted to pull her close and kiss her senseless. She could look him in the eye and tell him the specifics of her sexual interest and yet be nervous about taking a job because of her emotional connection to the town.

"You didn't come here for coffee," she said.

"I didn't?"

She shook her head. "You're checking on me. You want to know if I'm okay, which is very sweet considering I'm the one who initiated our sexual encounter."

"Are you?"

"I'm fine. The physical intimacy was better than I remembered, which is extraordinary. I have an excellent memory. I don't want you to worry. I don't feel that I've bonded with you as a result of my orgasms, but if it starts to happen, I'll handle it myself."

Which should have made her the perfect woman, he thought. But all he could think was that she'd spent so much of her life by herself. Separate from everyone else — never quite fitting in. She must have been lonely.

Emotion stirred inside him. The need to protect. He knew the danger of getting involved and vowed that he wouldn't, but damn, she was something.

She smiled. "It seems unfair to only discuss my emotions. Are you okay with what happened between us?"

"I'm feeling a little used, but I'll deal." He cocked his head. "You show up at my place in the middle of the night and demand sex. What's a guy to think?"

She laughed. "I think you can handle the pressure."

He was about to ask when she wanted to pressure him again, but stopped himself. He wasn't the picket fence kind of guy. Maybe he had been once, but that part of his soul had long since turned to dust.

She reached for something on the counter and picked up a small brightly colored card. "Do you want to —"

The smile faded, and uncertainty filled her big, green eyes.

The battle was clearly visible. Her shoulders drew back as she steeled herself to continue what she'd been about to say.

"My friend Charlie and her fiancé are having a party in a couple of weeks. At the new casino and hotel. It'll be open by then. She said I could bring a date." Felicia paused. "I've never been on a date before. I'd like to know what it's like, if you'd like to go with me."

He would rather she'd shot him. Or immobilized him with a Taser. Or cut out his heart.

No. His answer was no. He didn't date, didn't get involved, didn't . . .

The card shook slightly in her pale fingers. The woman who had calmly removed her shirt and bra and put his hands on her breasts only a few days ago had never been asked out by a guy? How was he supposed to ignore that? Ignore her? How was he supposed to squash her hopes and dreams?

"I'm not that guy," he told her. "The forever guy."

"I assume you're referring to marriage and not immortality."

"I am."

One corner of her mouth twitched in amusement. "It's a party, Gideon, not an eternal commitment."

"Yeah, I know. Sure. I'll go."

Relief joined amusement. "Thank you. I look forward to it."

"Me, too." Which was actually kind of true. He started for the door, then turned back. "Felicia?"

"Yes?"

"Just so you're clear, it's a date."

"The new office space is available," Pia said. "It has been for a while now. I feel kind of guilty for not taking advantage of it, but there was no way I could take on the task of moving, along with everything else." She motioned to the tiny office, overflowing with filing cabinets and boxes of promotional material. "It's a mess."

Felicia glanced around. "You've clearly outgrown your space."

Pia sighed. "Clearly. I feel like such a slacker. I used to be able to stay on top of things."

"Before you had a husband and three kids?"

Pia nodded. "But other women work with families."

Felicia had never understood why women took on guilt when they were overwhelmed, but she recognized the symptoms. "Pia, from what I've heard, you went from being a single working woman to married with three kids in less than a year. Two of the children were twins."

And not even biologically hers. When a close friend of Pia's had died, leaving her custody of embryos, Pia had had the tiny babies implanted. Then she'd fallen in love with Raoul Moreno. Before the twins had even been born, they'd adopted ten-year-old Peter.

"Your expectations are unrealistic," Felicia continued. "In less than two years, everything about your life changed completely. Yet you've carried on with the festivals and created a successful family unit. You should be proud of yourself."

Tears filled Pia's eyes. "That's so nice," she said, sniffing. "Thank you." She waved her hands in front of her eyes. "Sorry for the breakdown. I'm hormonal."

Felicia would guess she was also physically and mentally exhausted. "I hope I can do as good a job as you," she said, wondering if it was possible.

"You'll do better," Pia told her. "I suppose the good news is you can set up the next office however you like it." She reached into her desk drawer and pulled out an envelope. "The address and the key. Seriously, it's just sitting there. The landlord said to let him know when I was ready and he'd paint the place. I guess I should call."

"I'll do it," Felicia told her. "From now on, you tell me what needs to be done and I'll take care of it."

Pia sighed. "Can you do that for me at home, too? It sounds wonderful."

"I think you'd find me too detail-oriented."

Pia grinned. "Is that possible? I'm not sure it is." She glanced at her desk. "Okay, let's do this. Brace yourself and I'll begin the info dump."

She turned and pointed to the dry erase board dominating the largest wall. "That is the master calendar. It's in computer form, too, but I find this is easier to work with. I can physically see everything happening."

She went over to the file cabinets. "Starting at this end we have information on previous festivals. Next is vendor info. There's a whole section on vendor disasters. You'll want to cross-check that info whenever we have a new application. Permits are

93

in the third cabinet."

Felicia had been taking notes on her laptop. She glanced up. "Permits are done on paper? By hand?"

Pia winced. "We have a process for filing online, but I never really got into it. We tend to have the same people coming year after year, so I just make a note that the information is the same and let it go. Are you judging me?"

"Of course not," Felicia said automatically, even as she started a "to do" list. Right under notifying the new landlord was starting a vendor database.

"I want to believe you," Pia murmured. "Okay, festivals." She returned to the dry erase board. "We have at least one every month. Most months have two, and December has a million. From mid-November through the Live Nativity, it's crazy. Fortunately, this office isn't responsible for the Dance of the Winter King, which is Christmas Eve, so once the animals are back home after the Live Nativity, you're done for the year."

Pia grinned. "Of course it starts up again in January with Cabin Fever Days."

She stood and walked to the small bookcase by the front door. "Notebooks," she said, pointing at the thick binders. "One for every festival. What it's about, how long it takes, is it the kind of event that generates heads in beds?"

Felicia looked at her. "Heads in beds? Nights in a hotel?"

"Right. The longer tourists stay in town, the more money they spend. In addition to meeting monthly with the city council, you meet quarterly with the hotel, motel and B&B owners. They'll want to know any changes to upcoming festivals. They're also a good source of advertising. The festivals are mentioned in their printed materials and on their websites."

Pia returned to her seat and began to explain the logistics involved. There were more notebooks and a very large, slightly tattered Rolodex filled with names and phone numbers.

She flipped through it. "You'll probably want this in a database, huh?"

"It will be easier," Felicia said.

"We have one. A database. It's supposed to be great. I never actually learned how to use it." She sighed. "There are also check-lists of what needs to be ordered and how far in advance. Porta-Potties are now on a yearly contract, which is much easier, let me tell you. But there are things like decorating and —" Pia shook her head. "You have to get on the city schedule for things like decorating and the move. Which is another problem. They're really busy in the summer. I know there's not that much to move, but still, it could be a while. I'm sorry. I should have thought of that."

Felicia glanced at the file cabinets and the small desk. "Do I have to use city maintenance? Can I bring in my own moving crew?"

"Do you have one?"

Felicia grinned. "I know a couple of guys capable of heavy lifting."

"Right. The bodyguards. Sure, use them if they'll do it. Just don't tell the city. They'll be worried about injuries and insurance."

"The guys will be happy to do it," she said confidently. Justice and Ford both owed her, and she had a feeling Angel could be easily manipulated into helping. She would only have to suggest that Ford could lift more than him and he would be all in. While men were traditionally viewed as the stronger of the two sexes, they were often emotionally delicate.

Gideon recognized the cell immediately. It was maybe ten by twenty. Stone, with a barred window up high and a big wooden door too thick to break down. Not that he could. He was kept chained.

The floor was dirt. The only bathroom was a bucket that was emptied every few days. Gideon sat with his back against the wall, dripping sweat as the temperature climbed to what had to be a hundred and twenty degrees.

"Gideon, please."

He ignored the words, the plea. Dan had been asking for days. No. Not asking. Begging.

"I can't hold on," his friend said, his voice nearly a sob. "They're threatening my family. I can't stand it. The torture. All of it. I'm going to break."

Dan, once a tall, proud soldier, lay curled up against the wall. He was bloodied and nursing a broken arm. Gideon had tried to set it but didn't think he'd done a good enough job.

After sixteen months and twenty-two days of captivity, Dan was the last one left. The others had either died of their wounds or provoked their captors enough to be killed.

"Maddie," Dan moaned. "Maddie."

Maddie was his wife. There weren't any kids. Dan had said they were going to start trying when they got home. He talked about her all the time, claimed her love sustained him, but Gideon knew he was wrong. Dan's love kept him anchored in this place. His love made it impossible for him to go so deep in his head that they couldn't hurt him anymore.

Gideon glanced toward the window and saw the sun was near its zenith. That meant they'd come for him soon.

Later, he felt the blows as he was hit over and over again, felt himself vomit, although there was nothing in his stomach. Gideon wrestled with his captors, but it only made it worse. When they were finally done, they started to drag him down the hall back to his cell. He felt the dirt in his wounds, the dry dust in his mouth mingling with the copper taste of his blood.

Then the door swung open, and he couldn't look away. Not from the sight of Dan slumped over, the chain restraining him wrapped around his neck.

The guards tossed Gideon aside and raced to Dan, but it was too late. Gideon had refused to kill him, so he'd killed himself. Gideon lay on the dirt, wondering if his friend had been desperately weak or incredibly strong.

And then, as quietly as it had appeared, the cell was gone and he was awake. Awake and drenched in sweat.

He knew the folly of trying to sleep again,

so he rose and ripped off his T-shirt, then walked out onto the deck. The night air chilled him, but he didn't care. Then he sat cross-legged on the deck, closed his eyes and began to breathe.

CHAPTER FIVE

Consuelo Ly stared at the single-story ranch-style house, half expecting to blink and find it gone. Or maybe see unicorns grazing on the lawn. Because as far as she was concerned, the suburbs and unicorns were equally unrealistic.

She'd heard about both, of course. TV sitcoms enjoyed mocking the suburbs, and she loved *Modern Family* as much as the next person. But living in them? Not her. She had always assumed she would end her days in a hail of bullets. Or, in her less dramatic, more realistic moments, with her neck broken, her body dumped on the side of some road. But here she was, staring at a ranch-style house. Updated, she thought, taking in the new roof and big windows, but still originally constructed in the 1960s.

She parked in the driveway next to Ford's god-awful Jeep. It wasn't the vehicle she objected to as much as the aftermarket two-tone black-and-gold paint job. Jeeps were hardworking machines and deserved more respect. Next to the Jeep was a Harley, which meant Angel was also here.

Sure enough, she'd barely gotten out of her car when the front door opened and the two men stepped out. They were big and tall, both towering over her five feet two inches. Not that they intimidated her in the least. She could take either one in a fair fight, and if they wanted to play dirty, she could geld them in ten seconds. Fortunately for her, they both knew and respected her skill set.

"Ladies," she said as they approached.

Ford got to her first. "Consuelo!"

He wrapped both arms around her and pulled her against him. It was like hugging a warm, muscled wall. Before she could catch her breath, he passed her over to Angel who did exactly the same thing.

"Chica," he murmured in her ear. "Still looking good."

She pushed away from him and rolled her eyes. "You're both flabby," she complained. "We're going to have to start real workouts in the morning."

Ford's expression turned wounded. "I'm not," he said, pulling up his T-shirt to expose a perfect six-pack. "Go on. Hit me."

"You wish."

She walked to her trunk and opened it, then pulled out two duffels. The guys hovered, obviously unsure if they should help or not. She liked the slight edge of fear in their eyes. She preferred any situation where she was in charge.

"Here," she said, handing over her duffels. "How long have you been in the house?"

"Got the keys this morning," Ford said. "We were thinking of going to the store. For beer and maybe food. We were talking about ordering a pizza for tonight."

"One of you should start cooking," she said, leading the way into the house. She held in a snicker, knowing neither of them would have the balls to suggest she should be preparing meals. She might be female, but no one would accuse her of being domesticated.

She walked through the open front door and found herself in a large living room. The furniture was oversize but looked comfortable. Black leather sofa with a couple of chairs and a low coffee table. She could see the dining room beyond and a doorway leading to what she assumed was the kitchen.

She turned the other way, heading down the hallway toward the bedrooms. There was a hall bath, two average-size bedrooms. At the far end, one of a set of double doors stood open.

"The master?" she asked, even as she headed toward it.

"We, ah, weren't sure who would, ah . . ." Ford verbally stumbled to a stop.

Consuelo stepped inside. There was a king-size bed, a long dresser and a desk. The attached bath was small but had everything she needed. The closet was more than adequate.

She saw the duffels by the bed and raised her eyebrows.

Ford and Angel exchanged a look and quickly put her luggage on the bed, then carried theirs out. Low conversation carried back to her. She only caught an occasional word — something like "No, *you* tell her," and she smiled. It was good to be the meanest, baddest bitch in the house.

Thirty minutes later Consuelo had showered and dressed in jeans and a tank top. She brushed out her thick brown hair, thinking she should never have allowed herself to be talked into a layered cut. Her hair had a natural wave that took over if she didn't keep her hair well past her shoulders. Now she wrestled the unruly strands into a ponytail. She slipped her feet into sandals and tucked her wallet and cell phone into her jeans pockets. She left the master and headed to the front of the house.

Ford and Angel were in the kitchen. A table stood by a window, and there were bar stools pulled up to the granite counter. Stainless steel appliances gleamed against dark cabinets. The guys each had a beer.

For a second, she felt the separation between them and her. Not just because she was female, but because at the end of the day they were warriors and no matter how hard she tried, she couldn't see herself as more than a street kid who'd stumbled into a circumstance where she could excel.

"Want one?" Ford asked, pointing to the refrigerator.

"No, thanks. I'm meeting Felicia soon."

She pulled a hundred dollars out of her wallet and put it on the counter. "Each of you put in the same, and we'll get the place stocked with basics. Breakfast and snacks only. We each provide our own lunch and dinner." She cocked her head. "Unless you two want to have one of your bets. Loser cooks for a week and the other two pay for the food. Fair enough?"

The men nodded.

"I'll take care of the initial shopping," she continued. "After that, we'll take turns doing it. Make sure you pay attention to brands and sizes." She narrowed her gaze. "You will do your own laundry, and you will not leave clothes in either the washer or dryer. In this house, I don't work for either of you. Is that clear?"

More nods.

They would have to get a cleaning service in, but they had time on that. She'd roomed with men before and knew everything went more smoothly when she took care of the details up front. Otherwise, she was going to have to knock a few heads together, and that always meant someone getting hurt. Not her, of course, but someone.

She studied the two men watching her warily. "I know both of you. Everything's a competition. I have no problem with that, but leave it outside."

With that, she turned and walked out of the house.

Felicia waited outside Brew-haha. Consuelo had sent a text saying she was on her way. She watched anxiously, excited to see her friend.

During her military career and later with the security company, Felicia had mostly worked with men. Women had not been allowed in combat. *Ipso facto,* she hadn't had much of a chance to make female friends. Consuelo had been one of the few on the team. She was beautiful but deadly and had often been sent on assignments that required covert contact and distraction.

There had been times when Consuelo had seduced the enemy, gained the information she needed, then killed him before disappearing into the night. A different kind of assassin, Felicia thought. Snipers took lives, but what Consuelo had done was more personal and more dangerous.

Felicia turned and caught sight of her friend crossing the street. Although Consuelo was only five foot two, she was strong. A sexually appealing combination of curves and muscle. Men couldn't help turning to gape at her. But when they looked into her dark eyes, they usually backed off. Consuelo had perfected what she jokingly called the "don't eff with me" stare.

Felicia had worked to copy her friend's deadly glare, but when she tried it people tended to ask if she wasn't feeling well. It must have been an innate gift.

Now she watched the petite fighter walk along the sidewalk. She wore jeans, a lime-green tank top and sandals. She should have looked like any other tourist, yet she didn't. From the tip of her long, shiny ponytail to her controlled stride, she radiated confidence and danger.

Consuelo saw her and smiled. They hurried toward each other and embraced.

"Finally," Felicia said with a smile. "I've been waiting what feels like forever for you to get here. Of course it's only been three months, but missing you makes time seem to move more slowly in the context of our friendship."

Consuelo laughed. "You are such a freak."

"I know."

"It makes you special and me love you more." Her friend smiled at her. "How are you? I've missed you, too."

They hugged again, then headed into the store and ordered iced coffees. After collecting their drinks, Felicia led the way outside, and they sat down at one of the tables shaded by an umbrella.

"So, tell me everything," Consuelo said before taking a sip of her drink. "What is this place?"

"Fool's Gold? It's such an interesting town. Large enough to have an assortment of amenities, but still small enough for the residents to connect with each other."

Consuelo wrinkled her nose. "It's not natural. Have you seen the house Angel and Ford picked? It was built in the '60s or something."

"A ranch style. They used space efficiently, separating the living area of the house from the bedrooms. Very traditional."

"It's weird and I don't like it."

Felicia knew her resistance came from her unfamiliarity with the situation. Consuelo was used to being in the field or living in a city. Small-town America was bound to be unsettling.

Her friend looked at her. "My complaints aside, you look happy."

"I am," Felicia said, and realized it was true. "I've wanted to find a home, and I believe I have. I have a new job."

She explained about the festivals and how she would be in charge. "I'm a little concerned about meeting everyone's expectations."

"You'll do great."

"I'm less worried about the logistics than the undefinable 'people' factor."

"You do better with people than you give yourself credit for," Consuelo told her. "Everyone has a different style. You have yours. It works. Go with it."

"I wish . . ." Felicia shook her head. "I understand the futility of wishing."

"That doesn't make the need to do it go away. Look at the bright side. At the end of the day the worst anyone is going to find out about you is that you're even smarter than they first thought. After that, it's all easy."

Felicia understood the unspoken part of her friend's statement. The worst someone could learn about Consuelo was what she'd done in her past. Those who didn't live in the gray area of black ops and covert missions might judge her or be afraid. They might not see that behind the attitude and killer reflexes was a lonely woman who simply wanted to belong.

Early in their friendship, Consuelo had told Felicia a little about her past. At first Felicia had thought they were practicing traditional female bonding, but over time she'd realized Consuelo was testing her. Trying to see if she was a real friend or someone who couldn't take the truth. Eventually Felicia had convinced her she was unshockable. She frequently participated in mission debriefings. The soldiers she knew were killers. Consuelo was no different and had her own ghosts to deal with.

"You need a man," Felicia said.

Consuelo stared at her. "Whatever you're thinking, stop. If I want to get laid, I'll find somebody."

"I wasn't thinking about sexual release,

although that's very pleasurable. You need a relationship, a place where you can allow a man to really know you and believe he cares about you."

Dark eyes turned dangerous. "We are not having this conversation."

"All evidence to the contrary?"

Consuelo made a sound that was suspiciously like a growl. "Don't make me hurt you."

"I'm unmoved by your threats. They're meaningless. You'd never resort to physical force, and you're only mentioning them because they work on the guys." She allowed herself a small smile. "I'm smarter than them."

"You're also a pain in my ass."

"Both cheeks?"

Consuelo laughed. "Yes, both cheeks. Fine, I can't threaten you into silence. I don't want a man."

"I think you want what I want. A place to belong."

"It's sure not here."

"Why not? You're taking a job here. Logistically it makes sense to find a relationship close to your employment."

"It doesn't work like that."

"I acknowledge the element of chance in pair bonding. I'm just saying while you're here, it wouldn't hurt to look."

"I'm not the PTA type."

"You don't have children. Why would you join the PTA?"

Consuelo raised her eyebrows.

"Oh," Felicia said slowly, once again slightly out of step with the conversation. The difference was with Consuelo, she didn't have to feel self-conscious about it. "It's like a picket fence. I get that. You're not traditional. Neither am I, although I'm trying to move in that direction." She thought about the women she saw around town. Young mothers with children. Teenagers talking together and laughing.

"Anyone you're interested in?" Consuelo asked.

"Gideon."

Her friend's dark eyes widened. "Gideon from Thailand? That Gideon?"

Felicia nodded.

"He's here?"

"He owns two radio stations. We've had sex."

That statement earned her a momentary jaw drop, which was very satisfying.

"I didn't mean for that to happen. I went to talk to him, but as I spent more time with him, I found myself attracted to him." She smiled. "It was late at night, and we did it on his deck. It was very primal."

"You go, girl. And after?"

"He came to check on me. It was sweet. He seemed torn between worry and wanting to run."

"That's pretty typical for a guy. What did you do?"

"I asked him out. To a party. He said yes." She could feel herself smiling. "It's a date."

"My little girl is all grown up."

"Gideon explained he wasn't a forever guy. It means —" She paused, remembering that she was the only one who had trouble with casual idioms. "You know what it means."

"He's not into commitment. Look, Felicia, when a guy tells you something like that, he's not lying. When a man says he's never been faithful or doesn't want anything long-term, you should believe him."

"I do. He has no reason to lie to me."

"My point is, don't fall for him."

"If I spend time with him, I'm not sure I can control my emotions. I like being around him. I like anticipating seeing him, and I'm hoping we'll have sex again. Doesn't that, by definition, put me at risk of falling in love?"

Felicia knew her friend well enough to read the emotions moving across her face.

Indecision joined worry, and she understood the cause for both.

"I want this," Felicia admitted. "I want to know what it's like to have butterflies in my stomach. I want to feel rather than think all the time. I've never been on a date, let alone fallen in love. If he hurts me, I'll heal. People do."

"It always sounds so easy," Consuelo murmured. "Right before you get your heart ripped out. Fine. Go fall in love with Gideon and have great sex. Maybe it will all work out."

Felicia grinned. "Maybe I won't fall for him, although I do look forward to more sex."

"It's good to have a plan." Consuelo slipped on her sunglasses and stood. "Come on, you. Show me this weird little town of yours. Tell me there are more than two stoplights."

"There are. We also have California's longest-serving mayor and festivals every month. At Christmas, there's a Live Nativity. I heard last year there was an elephant."

"At the nativity?"

Felicia nodded. "Her name's Priscilla. She lives on a ranch with several goats and a pony. Want me to tell you about the Dog Days of Summer Fair?"

"Only if you promise to shoot me first."

Gideon arrived for the meeting a few minutes early. As a business owner in town, there were events he was expected to attend. He did so just often enough that no one came calling to ask why he wasn't involved. Easier to participate on his own terms, he thought, finding a seat in the back of the room.

After a couple of bad nights, he'd finally managed to get some sleep. He was always grateful when the dreams didn't attack him.

He glanced around the room and nodded at a few people he knew. The mayor walked in with Charity Golden, the city planner. They moved to the front of the room. Mayor Marsha saw him and pointed to a seat up by the podium. He shook his head, and the older woman chuckled.

He watched the door, not sure if Felicia would be attending. While he wanted to see her, he wasn't sure it was a good idea. He still couldn't believe he'd let her spend the night. The sex he understood. Four years ago Felicia had been exactly what he'd been looking for — a wild, uncomplicated ride. She'd rocked his world, and he'd been disappointed to have things end so quickly. Discovering her a second time had been an added bonus.

When a woman like her expressed sexual interest, it would take more self-control than he had to say no. Sex was relatively easy — but spending the night? He didn't do that. Didn't like it. Yet he'd slept with her as easily as he'd made love with her. An uncomfortable truth he'd yet to reconcile.

She walked into the conference room with several other women. He recognized the chick who wanted to open a Christmas store, and he was pretty sure the tall blonde was named Isabel. She owned the shoe store or the dress shop.

For this meeting there wasn't a conference table. Rather, chairs had been set up in rows. Felicia glanced toward him and smiled. He felt the kick in his gut, along with a jolt of heat that moved lower. Damn, she was beautiful, he thought.

She spoke to her friends, then moved to join the mayor and Charity at the front of the room. Isabel and the Christmas store woman walked back several rows and settled a few seats in front of him.

"Do you think he'll be here?" Isabel asked, her voice carrying just enough for him to hear.

Her friend sighed. "You're going to have

to pick. Either you want to see Ford or you don't."

"Why do I have to decide, Noelle? Why can't my decision change with my mood? I don't always wear the same shoes."

"Because you spend half your time trying to figure out where he's going to be in town and the rest of the time avoiding that exact spot. It's exhausting. Also, you have a thousand pairs of shoes. I'm surprised you wear any of them more than two days in a row."

Isabel glanced at the door. "Oh, God. It's Justice. Ford might be with him. I have to hide."

Gideon followed her gaze and saw Justice walking in with Patience. The two of them took seats together in the second row. Isabel writhed in her seat.

"Looks like he's not coming," Noelle said. "Good news or bad news?"

Isabel slumped back in her seat. "I can't decide."

Several more people walked into the conference room. Gideon recognized the Stryker contingent. Rafe and his business partner, Dante, who owned a large real estate development company. Shane Stryker had a horse ranch. His brother Clay had started a Haycation business on the Castle

Ranch. Rafe's wife, Heidi, sat with them. She sold goat cheese and soap.

"Is anyone sitting here?"

He looked to his right and saw a petite blonde standing there. She had big hazel eyes and looked like she was maybe twelve.

"This is a meeting for adults," he said. "Did you mean to be somewhere else?"

She laughed and settled next to him. "I'm twenty-four. Want to see my ID?"

He was sure the chagrin showed on his face. "Sorry, no."

Her grin stayed in place. "Don't worry. I'm used to it. It's a size thing. I'm small and cute so people assume I'm still a child. The occasional tantrum doesn't help the maturity meter, that's for sure."

He glanced to his left and thought about sliding a few seats over.

"The thing is," she said in a conspiratorial whisper, "I'm not supposed to be here. Technically I haven't started a new business."

"You find city meetings compelling?"

"I'm *thinking* of opening a business. A street food cart. What you would call a trailer. I'm still renovating." She paused, as if waiting for a reaction.

"Like a taco truck?"

She winced. "Okay, sort of. Slightly more

gourmet than that, although I do love a good taco. Street food is very big these days. There are fairs in L.A. and San Francisco celebrating street food."

"Good to know."

"I'm Ana Raquel Hopkins, by the way."

"Gideon."

She tilted her head. "You're the radio guy. You play that old '60s music, right? My best friend's grandmother loves you."

Good to know he was popular with the seniors, he thought grimly.

"She says that bedroom eyes are what everybody talks about, but a bedroom voice is much better." Ana Raquel grinned. "She's going to be so excited I met you. I'm going to tell her you're really hot. You know, for an older guy."

He was thirty-six. Not exactly ready for his AARP card. But to a twenty-four year old, he was on the far side of interesting.

He looked toward the front where Mayor Marsha had stepped up to the podium.

"Thank you all for coming," she began. "I thought it would be a good idea for those of you starting a new business in town to get to know each other. This isn't going to be a formal presentation. I wanted a chance to welcome all of you to our community and answer any questions you might have. Also,

I'll be bringing in members of the city government you're most likely to have contact with. I'm going to start with Felicia Swift. She recently took over our festivals, and we're delighted to have her expertise and energy."

There was more talking, but Gideon didn't bother to listen. Instead he studied the leggy redhead and let his mind drift back to the feel of her mouth on his. She made love without inhibition. There was only the moment and the pleasure.

He liked that she didn't play games. She was brutally honest. A man would always know where he stood with her. Not that he was looking to get involved, but she was a temptation.

"Wow!"

He turned to Ana Raquel and saw her staring at him.

She swung to face Felicia. "So you two are together."

He stiffened. "Why do you say that?"

"Because of how you were looking at her. Jeez, if a guy ever looked at me with that combination of passion and need, I'd probably go up in flames." She flopped back in her seat. "Is it hot in here, or is it me?"

He shifted uncomfortably. "I have no idea what you're talking about."

She grinned. "Right. I get it. You don't want everyone to know. I can be discreet. Trust me, I know how sensitive guys can be."

"I'm not sensitive. Don't you have a trailer to remodel?"

"Yes, but that can wait. This is way more interesting."

He crossed his arms over his chest. "Felicia and I are dating."

"For how long?"

"Our first date is in a couple of weeks. A party."

"Seriously? You're going to wait that long for your first date? I don't think you'll last. Besides, look at her. You think someone else isn't going to make a move?"

"It's not like that."

Ana Raquel patted his shoulder. "Sorry to tell you, but when a man looks at a woman the way you looked at her, it's *always* like that."

Gideon shifted his attention back to the presentation. Felicia was done speaking, and someone else from the mayor's office had taken her place. He found himself glancing toward the woman in question, studying the curve of her cheek and how she was listening attentively, no doubt committing every word to memory.

She looked at him and smiled. Beside him, Ana Raquel muttered what sounded like a very smug "See?"

He ignored her.

But after the meeting, he found himself walking to the front of the room. He paused by Felicia, clueless as to what to say or do.

"Hi," she said. "Wasn't this great? I think Mayor Marsha is wise to help the new business owners create a social bond. We do better as a society when we have an emotional connection with each other. There's strength in community."

If he asked, she could probably write down the mathematical formula for the origin of the universe. He would guess she knew more than most engineers about flight and strength tolerances and everything else learnable. She spoke close to a dozen languages. But, as she'd admitted very recently, she'd never been on a date.

They were going to that party, he thought. It should be enough. But it wasn't. He'd been her first lover — a fact that still made him break out in a cold sweat. Still, he couldn't help thinking that he didn't want some asshole taking advantage of her.

"Would you have dinner with me?" he asked. "Tonight? At my place?"

She pressed her lips together. "You're asking me to dinner?"

"Yes."

"Like a . . ."

"Date."

"We already have a date. For the party."

"Did you want to wait until then to have dinner with me?"

"No. I enjoy spending time with you. Thank you. Dinner would be nice."

"I'll see you at seven."

She nodded.

He turned and saw Ana Raquel by the door. She grinned and gave him a thumbs-up. He held in a groan.

CHAPTER SIX

Felicia knew wine was a traditional gift when invited to dinner. She'd gone online and read about several other interesting options, including bringing a dish for the meal, or dessert, along with flowers or other hostess gifts. However, she was fairly certain Gideon wasn't the pretty-silver-frame or napkins-in-a-matching-holder type.

She arrived on time, wine in hand, and knocked on the front door.

In the few seconds it took him to answer, she worked on her breathing to slow her heart rate and reduce her anxiety to something closer to anticipation. Nervousness wasn't pleasant, and considering she hadn't eaten much all day, the sudden need to throw up surprised her.

Perhaps she'd taken too long worrying about her appearance. She'd tried on several outfits, and although none of them had been inappropriate, she hadn't been satisfied with any of them. Jeans had been too casual and a dress had seemed too formal. She'd finally decided on white crop pants and a dark green silk T-shirt. The V-neck dipped low enough to show the shadow of her cleavage, which men seemed to like. She wasn't sure the choice was flattering but realized she didn't know enough about fashion to be sure. It wasn't an area she'd ever had reason to study.

The door opened, and Gideon stood in front of her.

"Hey," he said, his voice low and sexy.

She felt her stomach muscles clench. "Hi." She held out the bottle of wine. "I went online and found several options for dinner. Not knowing what we were having made the choice more difficult, but statistically at a barbecue one is more likely to eat red meat, so I went with a full-bodied red wine."

He smiled at her. "We're having steaks. Come on in."

She followed him into the house.

Days were still long this time of year, and sunlight poured into the house. She could see through the great room to the deck beyond and the view that seemed to stretch for miles. The last time she'd been here, she'd only sensed the vastness beyond. Now it was clearly visible.

Trees carpeted the side of the mountains. Beyond them was another set of mountains and between them a distant valley.

Gideon led the way into the kitchen. It was large, with dark cabinets and stainless appliances. Overhead lights reflected off the granite countertops.

He opened the bottle of wine, collected two glasses then poured. Felicia took one, he grabbed the other and they went out onto the deck.

Close up, the view was even more impressive. She walked to the railing and pointed halfway down the mountain.

"You can see where an avalanche tore up trees," she said. "That group in the middle is significantly shorter. Based on how quickly these trees grow each year, I would say it happened sometime in the past forty years." She looked to the left side of the house. "With this area leveled off, it's unlikely to happen again, but it must have been a powerful event to observe."

Gideon smiled. "Assuming you weren't watching it from below."

She laughed. "Yes. One would want to be above or to the side of an avalanche."

She was aware of the furniture on the deck. They weren't exactly where they had been last time, but if she turned slightly, she could see the lounge chair where they'd had sex.

Wanting surprised her with an intense surge. She found herself thinking about stepping closer to Gideon so she could lean against him and have him hold her. She wanted to kiss him and touch him.

"Are you working tonight?" she asked.

"My shift starts at eleven."

She did the calculations in her head. "So a sexual encounter is unlikely."

He'd been swallowing and now started to choke. She monitored his coughing to see if she should offer assistance, but decided he would recover. A few seconds later, he caught his breath.

"It's not a time issue," he told her, his voice raspy.

"I suppose that's true. We *could* not have dinner."

He shook his head. "I was thinking more along the lines of this being a first date. I'm not the most traditional guy around, but I'm pretty sure we're supposed to wait. Maybe get to know each other."

"Oh." She considered that. "Establish an emotional bond before having physical intimacy. You're right. That's how it usually happens."

Although she'd very much enjoyed making love with Gideon, she could see the appeal of waiting. From what she'd been told, sex was even better with someone who mattered. She couldn't imagine making love with Gideon being more pleasurable than before, but finding out would make for an excellent experiment. Plus, if she wanted a normal kind of life, she needed to act in a normal way.

"You're right," she told him. "This is a first date. We should get to know each other." She turned to face the house. "How long have you lived here?"

"Just over a year. Some guy from L.A. had bought the land and started construction only to realize he didn't like being this far from the big city. I bought it from him and had it finished. Made a few modifications."

She would guess he'd put in more windows, maybe the skylights.

"What happens when you get stuck up here because of weather?"

"I'm prepared. There's a generator, and I keep plenty of food on hand."

"Occupational hazard," she said.

He shrugged and picked up his wine. "Being prepared isn't a bad thing. What about you? Where did you grow up?"

She drew in a breath. Right — he wouldn't know about her past. That night together four years ago hadn't had much in the way of conversation.

"Outside Chicago." She paused, cautious about the details of her past. People reacted in unexpected ways when she told them how she'd grown up. "I wasn't the easiest of children," she began. "I was reading by the time I was two, doing complex math equations at three. When I was four, I used items I found under the kitchen sink to make a bomb."

Gideon raised one eyebrow. "On purpose?"

"I knew there would be an explosion, and I thought it would be funny. I wasn't trying to destroy anything. My parents didn't see it that way."

"Got in trouble, huh?"

"They felt I needed a more structured environment. Somewhere I could be mentally challenged. I was more than they could handle."

She knew she was making excuses, saying what she'd always said. While it was true, it also avoided any emotional reaction to the stark reality. Her parents had been afraid of her. They hadn't wanted her around.

She sipped her wine. "They were approached by several professors at the university. I was to study with them, learn as much as I wanted, and in return they would try to understand what made me different."

Her parents had signed her over to be a lab experiment, she thought, telling herself it was fine. *She* was fine.

"I had access to every class on campus, to the finest professors. I studied with Nobel prize winners and scientists. It was an amazing opportunity."

He looked at her. "You were by yourself."

"There was always adult supervision. The staff made sure of that."

"But no family. No friends."

There wasn't any pity in his voice, but she braced herself for it. "I wasn't in a position to have friends," she admitted. "I was too young for the other students to relate to and the adults saw me as someone to learn from, not an equal. Some of them were afraid of my intelligence. I became an emancipated minor when I was fourteen. I published papers and wrote a few books to pay the bills. When I was sixteen, I decided I wanted something else."

"I knew you'd gone to college when you were young, but I didn't know . . ." He trailed off with a sympathetic look on his face.

"You don't have to feel sorry for me," she told him. "I was happy. Yes, I lived a more solitary existence than most, but I'm not sure I would have done any better with a normal upbringing. I've had the most extraordinary education."

"There's more to life than what you learn in school."

"I agree. Some of the students made an effort. One of them had been a soldier. He was wounded, lost his legs. Getting around was difficult for him, but he never complained. He was nice and funny and treated me like a kid sister." Her mouth twisted. "He died of complications from his injuries. I was sixteen. The following week I faked my ID and joined the army. I never told them about my various degrees. To them, I was just someone who had enlisted."

"How long did that last?"

She grinned. "Long enough. I was able to fit in. There are rules and I do well with rules. My interest in logistics led to me being assigned to a Special Forces team, and you know the rest."

She glanced toward the trees. "I'm sure there are owls in the forest. I wonder if we'll see any at dusk."

"Felicia."

She turned to Gideon. His gaze was intense, but she had no idea what he was thinking.

"I'm fine," she told him. "You don't have to worry about me."

"Then I won't."

But she wasn't sure he was telling the truth. More confusing, the idea of him being concerned actually made her happy. Shouldn't she want a man to believe she was completely self-sufficient? She sighed. Mating rituals were complicated in every species, but with humans, the rules were always changing.

Gideon slid the steaks onto plates, and Felicia carried them over to the table. They'd prepared a salad together, and then she'd made a dressing while he'd put the meat on the grill. They sat across from each other as the setting sun cast shadows on the deck.

She cut into her steak. "Perfect," she said. "I understand the conditions required to cook food, but I can't always make the transition from theory to practice. Baking continues to elude me. Consuelo says my flaws keep me likable, but I'm less sure that's true. Even if nobody likes a know-it-all."

He shook his head. "You're not a know-it-all. It's an attitude thing." She was painfully brilliant, but in a way that made sense. With her, it was like being tall, or having perfect

131

pitch. It simply was.

"I hope you're right. I want people to like me. That's one of the appeals of this town. I have friends." She sighed. "Girlfriends. We have lunch and get drinks together after work."

Normal, he thought. What she would have missed while growing up. The army should have offered her the opportunity, but in Special Forces, there weren't many women. Between her long hours and constant traveling, she wouldn't have had the chance to find other women to hang with.

She smiled at him, her green eyes bright with amusement. "You're a frequent topic of conversation," she told him. "Women find your voice sexually appealing. Plus they admire your physique when you walk around town."

He managed to swallow his bit of steak without choking. "Don't tell me that."

"Why not? It's true and you should be flattered."

"I don't think so."

She glanced at his left arm and lightly touched the tattoo visible below his shirtsleeve. "This also intrigues them. The older women equate tattoos and your former profession with danger. The younger ones simply find you sexy. Yet both can listen to your voice every night, which makes you more approachable. It's a tempting combination." She paused for a second, then laughed. "Like catnip to a cat."

"Look at you, all one with the clichés."

"I find them helpful in social situations. The structure of my speech is on the formal side."

"It might just be your word choices."

She nodded. "I agree. I know too many words, and I enjoy precision in my speech. But others find it off-putting."

"They need to develop a sense of humor."

"I wish I had one. I don't always get the joke. I have trouble with cultural references. I've caught up on the television I missed while I was growing up, and I've read the significant books." She flashed a smile. "I understand the worlds of Harry Potter and *Twilight.*"

"Magic and vampires? Not my thing."

"Yes, but you've proven my point. You know what they are, even without having read the books or seen the movies. From the time I was small until I was sixteen, I missed out. I could tell you about the progress made in work on the origin of the universe, but I completely missed the rise in popularity of the American Girl doll."

She started to say something else, then

stopped. Her gaze sharpened. "You know exactly what I'm talking about," she said quietly. "While you were held by the Taliban, you experienced the same phenomenon. Existing out of time."

She touched his arm again, her fingers warm against his skin. "Not that I'm equating what I went through with what you did."

"I wasn't getting *USA TODAY* delivered, if that's what you're asking."

He kept his tone light and was prepared to deflect any questions. He didn't talk about his past — not with anyone. It was done, he'd moved on. He wanted to say he'd healed, but he knew that would never happen. The nightmares were proof. Some wounds stayed open forever. But he got by and, for the most part, managed to fool everyone into thinking he was just like them.

"I would have kept looking," she said, returning her attention to her dinner. "If you'd been one of my team. They were wrong not to keep looking."

He noticed that while she seemed fascinated by her steak, she wasn't eating.

"No one knew," he told her. "That was the point of my assignment."

"Someone always knows. Someone has to get you in and have a plan to get you out. Equipment is supplied. They shouldn't have

134

left you."

She didn't know the details, but she could guess. And she was right — someone *had* known. His team had been dropped off and told they were on their own. But someone had known where they were.

"Politics," he murmured and reached for his wine.

"How many others?" she asked.

"Three."

Three men he'd watched die. Slowly, painfully. One by one, they'd given in to the torture, to the madness.

He set down his glass. "They had families. Some had kids. They talked about them, how they missed them, how they wanted to see them again. They had hope. They believed. They told me it made them strong, but they were wrong. Having something to live for meant they had something to lose. Those bastards hurt them more because of it. I walked away because living and dying were the same to me."

He'd learned his lesson then. It was safer to just be his own man. To not care. Having nothing left to lose had saved his life.

"Love is death?" she asked.

"Something like that."

"I want to explain that you're wrong, but you have no reason to believe me. The mental and emotional scars of your imprisonment would be significant. Lessons learned in traumatic situations stay with us always." She gave him a shaky smile. "I was trapped in a closet with a spider when I was five. It was only for a few minutes, but I still remember screaming."

She angled her chair to him. "Am I correct in assuming that you're not interested in any kind of emotional commitment? That even though you enjoy my company and find the sex very pleasurable, you don't want to form an attachment?"

Not exactly how he would have phrased it, but, "Yes."

"I want to belong," she told him. "I want to fall in love. I understand much of the feeling is chemical, but I still want to know what it's like. Eventually I want to get married and have children. I want to be part of a family. I want roots. Nothing you're interested in."

"No."

"Then spending time with you doesn't help me achieve my goal."

Stark words, he thought, surprised at the kick in the gut he felt. But she knew what she wanted, and he had no right to keep her from it.

"I told you before, I'm not the forever guy."

She nodded. "Even so, I find myself reluctant to stop seeing you. I wonder if I'm attracted to the traditional bad-boy elements of your personality. Or it could be our sexual compatibility. I do like thinking about us making love and having orgasms together." She sighed. "I'm not sure what I should do."

His suggestion, mostly screaming from his suddenly hard dick, was that they practice a few of those orgasms right here, right now. Dinner and her life goals be damned. But he liked Felicia nearly as much as he wanted her, and there was no way he was going to screw up everything because he needed to get laid.

"You should walk away," he told her, the words physically painful to speak.

"A sensible solution." She stared at him. "I don't want to be sensible. Why is that?"

"You're a woman?"

She laughed. "I believe my ability to reason is far greater than yours, but the sexist comment is charming." She nodded. "I need to consider this. Do you mind if I think about what I want and then get back to you?"

She was like no one else he'd ever met.

Damned if that didn't make him want her more. "Take your time."

"And it's all right if we finish dinner?"

"Sure."

"Good." She smiled. "Would you like to talk about sports? I have a working knowledge of baseball and can discuss team rankings along with player statistics."

He started to laugh, then leaned close and kissed her. She stared at him.

"Why did you do that?"

"Because I couldn't help myself."

She smiled. "What else can't you help doing?"

"No way, young lady. You have to make your decision first. No-strings sex and practice dating, knowing it will never last, or walking away and waiting for Mr. Right."

She nodded. "Yes, that's the sensible course." Her eyes widened. "This is what women mean when they talk about Mr. Right Now. They're attracted to a man like you."

"Not exactly," he murmured. "But close enough."

CHAPTER SEVEN

"This could be higher," Ford yelled from the top of the rope hanging from the base of a thick tree branch a good twenty feet off the ground.

"It could," Consuelo shouted back to him. "We could also dig a moat and float a few alligators. How does that sound?"

"Sweet!"

Gideon shook his head. One day Ford and Angel were going to kill each other with their brainless competition. But as they'd been trying to best each other for years, he knew he wasn't going to change anybody's mind. As it was, he'd been brought in to offer suggestions for ways to make the obstacle course more challenging for the professionals while keeping it doable for "normal people." He wasn't sure why anyone thought he would know more than either Ford, Angel or Consuelo, but, if nothing else, he would enjoy spending a morning in the forest.

Angel patted one of the larger trees. "The trunks tend to have a flat side. We could set up targets."

"No shooting in the forest," Consuelo snapped. "Do you want to get someone killed? We'll have a special shooting range on one side or the other of the warehouse. What the hell is wrong with you?"

Angel stared at her. "What?"

"Tell him," Consuelo demanded, pointing at Angel. "Tell him he's an idiot."

"You're an idiot," Gideon obliged.

Angel glared at him. "Hey, what's with taking her side? We're friends. You just met her."

"I like her better."

Consuelo grinned. "Likewise," she told him.

Angel snorted in disgust and stalked away.

Gideon chuckled, remembering that this was what it was like in the field. Sure there was danger and stress, but in the downtimes there was fun. Life had to be lived all the more because it could end at any second.

Consuelo was short, but she was strong and moved as if she knew what she was doing. Ford had introduced him, saying she would be teaching hand-to-hand and street fighting, along with a few tactical classes. Gideon would guess she knew ways to kill a man that would make the hardiest of souls shudder.

More important to him, he knew Consuelo was one of the few people Felicia considered a friend. As he had suddenly found himself wanting to look out for the beautiful redhead, he was inclined to side with Consuelo.

Ford slid to the ground and stepped away from the rope. "What's the course?" he asked.

Gideon pointed to the west. "Easy two-mile jog to the edge of the vineyard, head north for another mile. Targets are set up. Shoot at a hundred feet. Center target and bottom left." He looked to his left and right. "Do you two want to try? I dropped something along the way. One of you could bring it back." Angel and Ford nodded with gleams in their eyes. Gideon paused. "Okay, go."

Angel and Ford took off at a run.

"What happened to the easy jog?" Consuelo asked.

"You ever see them do something the easy way?"

"Good point." She sighed. "I hope Ford wins. The loser will cook for a week, and Angel's better in the kitchen." She glanced at him. "I'm Felicia's friend."

He met her dark gaze. "I heard."

"What are the odds of her getting out of this with her heart in one piece?"

"She hasn't decided if we're dating yet."

Which didn't answer the question, but he should get points for trying.

Consuelo raised her eyebrows. "What does that have to do with anything?"

"I don't want to hurt her," he said. "I want her to be happy."

"With you?"

"No," he admitted. "Not with me." At one time, maybe. But not for a while now. Ignoring the fact that he didn't have the skill set, he wasn't interested in belonging. In caring. He liked living on the edges, pretending he fit in when he knew better. It was easier. Safer. Comforting.

"You tell her?"

"In many ways."

"Is she going to listen?"

"Do women ever?"

He half expected that to earn him a quick flip over her shoulder with a hard landing, followed by her boot on his throat. Or at least the attempt. He knew the counter moves, but it had been a while. He might work out regularly, but he didn't spar with anyone.

"Women usually hear what they want to

hear," Consuelo said grudgingly. "Felicia might be smarter than most, but she's no different when it comes to reading men."

Part of that was a lack of experience, Gideon thought. Felicia had missed out on what most women her age took for granted. She'd never dated. He might not be able to give her a picket fence — despite her claim it made for lousy containment — but he could let her practice on him. Let her figure it out with a guy who only wanted the best for her. As long as they both remembered his limitations.

In the distance they heard two quick gunshots. Nearly fifteen seconds later, another set echoed off the mountains.

"What did you leave for them to find?" Consuelo asked.

Gideon grinned. "A thumb drive."

"Damn," she muttered. "I really hope Ford wins."

Felicia couldn't get comfortable in Pia's office. This was her third day and she still felt like an interloper. In her head she understood that the space didn't belong to anyone. Technically someone could own a building or a house, but this was different. She'd been given the keys to the office. The issue wasn't her right to turn the lock — it was what happened when she stepped inside.

The office itself was small. Not much more than a desk, a few chairs and a lot of filing cabinets. The large dry erase board listed all the festivals, and under each festival was a to-do list. The remaining free wall space was taken up by posters of various events.

No matter that she knew where everything was or understood in her head that she was now in charge of the festivals — she couldn't shake the feeling that she didn't belong.

She felt dominated by the monster Rolodex and all the stacks of paper. Pia's system was well organized but still relied on actual paper. There was a scent to the small office. Nothing unpleasant. Instead, it seemed as if she'd entered an ancient and sacred place where change was forbidden and those who tried were punished.

Felicia was itching to start a searchable database and put everything on the computer. Then she could relegate the old filing cabinets to storage and have some room. But not here, she thought, chiding herself for feeling superstitious yet unwilling to challenge the sense of unease.

Just one more week, she told herself. She was already set to move next Monday.

Justice, Angel and Ford would be helping her. She would pack up herself and have everything ready to go. Once she was settled in her new place, she would feel more connected to her new job. At least she hoped so.

She was still worried about doing everything right. Not the logistical parts of the job — that was easy. But the rest of it. The connecting with people, the making memories. What if she got it wrong? What if she was a square peg in a round hole?

The use of the cliché made her smile. She liked clichés and common phrases. Not only did they fit easily into many situations, they implied universal understanding. Clichés provided a commonality with those around her.

Someone knocked on her half-open door. A blonde woman in her mid-fifties smiled as she walked in. She was of average height, with pretty features and a welcoming air about her.

"Hi. I'm Denise Hendrix. Do you have a second?"

Felicia knew about the Hendrix family. Ford was the youngest of the three boys. He had three younger sisters who were triplets. This must be his mother, although Denise looked much younger than she was.

"Of course," Felicia said, coming to her feet. "I know Ford."

Denise moved toward her, hand out-stretched. "The young woman who is so good with logistics. Yes, Ford has mentioned you. From what he says, you're going to whip our festivals into shape."

"I'm hoping to keep them going," she said. "I want to respect the history of the town and its celebrations. I'm not sure I'll need a whip."

She paused, hoping the joke made sense. Denise laughed and took a seat. Felicia settled behind the desk, relieved she'd managed to be a little funny. Humor was so complicated, she thought. Nuanced and subjective. She preferred situations where she could predict the outcome.

Denise leaned forward. "I want to rent a booth in the Fourth of July festival. Is it rent or lease? I don't know the exact termi-nology. But I want a booth."

"The city requires an application," Felicia told her. "It's a fairly straightforward pro-cess. Will you be cooking and serving food? That makes it more complicated. There are sanitation laws and the like."

"No food," Denise assured her. "I want to set up a booth so I can find a wife for Ford."

Felicia stared at her. She must have misheard the other woman's statement. Or not understood precisely what she meant because . . .

Denise sighed. "You think I'm crazy."

"No, ma'am."

"All right. Not crazy, but misguided." Denise shrugged. "I can accept that. I refuse to get desperate, so I'm taking matters into my own hands."

Another cliché, Felicia thought still stunned. "It helps to be in control," she said, not knowing what else to say.

"Exactly." Denise nodded. "Ford was gone for so long. I missed him every day. I know why he left and I can't really blame him, but now that he's home I want to keep him around. So I thought if he fell in love and got married to a local girl, he'd want to stay. From what I can tell, he's not dating, which means this is going to take a while. That's when I realized I don't technically need him to find the right girl. I can find her for him."

Felicia honestly didn't know how to respond. This time it wasn't her lack of social conditioning that had her silent, but the fact that her brain had suddenly, unexpectedly, gone completely blank.

"Does Ford know that you —"

"Plan to marry him off?" Denise shook her head. "No. He'll find out soon enough, but by then it will be too late. Oh, and I'm going to find someone for Kent, too. He has finally given up on that ex-wife of his. Thank goodness. Lorraine turned out to be a total bitch. I could forgive her walking out on her marriage. It's wrong, but, okay, relationships fail. But she walked out on her son, on my grandson, and that crosses a line in my book."

Felicia felt as if she'd lost the ability to reason. There was too much going on and she didn't know which thought to address first.

"I, ah . . ."

Denise smiled. "I thought I'd decorate the booth simply. Maybe with an eye-catching sign. 'Do you want to marry this man?' or something like that. I'll have baby pictures of my two boys to show the women. That way they'd have an idea of what their children will look like." She leaned forward and lowered her voice conspiratorially. "It's all about the grandchildren. Kent has Reese and Ethan has Tyler and Melissa and Abby. My girls are all married with children. Ford owes me. I want him married, and if he won't take care of that on his own, I'll do it for him."

She reached down and pulled a folder from her purse. "I have a list of traits I'm looking for. I was thinking I'd have the young women fill out an application and then I'd sort through them myself." She handed over a piece of paper.

Felicia glanced at it. Sure enough, it was an application for a wife. The three-page document was surprisingly thorough. There was a medical history, a place to explain about previous relationships, along with a few lines about future goals.

"Intelligence passes through the mother," Felicia murmured. "You might want to confirm their educational history."

"Thanks. I will." Denise looked at her. "So, can I have a booth?"

"Sure."

Felicia stood and collected the papers necessary for the permit. "There's still time for you to have space in the Fourth of July festival," she said.

"Good. I want to be in a heavy traffic area. I know the right girl is out there for each of my boys, and I'm going to find her."

Felicia couldn't decide if she wanted to be around when Ford found out what his mother was doing, or somewhere far away. She knew Consuelo would laugh herself sick when she learned what was happening.

Denise took the sheets of paper. "Thank you for all your help."

"You're welcome."

The other woman left.

Felicia turned back to her computer only to realize that Denise had never once considered her for either of her "boys." She was single, intelligent and reasonably attractive. Yet Denise hadn't said a word or even hinted she would be welcome into the Hendrix family.

Why was that? Could the other woman tell by looking at Felicia that she didn't fit in? Was it a Mom thing? It wasn't that she wanted to date Ford and she'd never met Kent, but still. Shouldn't she be able to make the short list?

Apparently not, she thought sadly. Which meant if she wanted to fall in love and have a family, she was going to have to figure out how to be more normal. She was going to have to fit in better. And she only knew one way to make that happen.

"Be faithful, gentlemen," Gideon said into the microphone. "Or you know what will happen." He pushed a button and Elvis's "Suspicious Minds" began to play. He chuckled to himself as he stretched in his chair.

The world righted itself when he was here. It was just him and the night and the music.

He'd been around people too much lately, and that always wore him down. He needed his solitude, his routine.

When he'd first found his way to Fool's Gold, he hadn't known what to expect beyond what Ford had told him. That the town was small but lively and that he might be able to settle here. Gideon had wanted to disappear and had assumed a big city was the best place to do that. Still, he'd visited and had been unexpectedly taken in by the pretty streets and friendly locals.

The first person he'd met had been Mayor Marsha. She'd stopped him outside the Fox and Hound, stared at him for several seconds and asked, "Gideon or Gabriel?" He'd been so rattled that she'd not only known his name but the name of his twin, that he'd taken off without saying a word.

He'd gotten in his car and driven mindlessly, wondering who she was and how she'd guessed his identity. Twenty minutes later he'd found himself outside the radio station. The big For Sale sign had made him laugh. It was a radio station, for God's sake. Not a garage sale. But he'd walked inside and asked for a tour.

Less than a month later, he owned both the AM and FM stations.

The purchase had about cleaned out his

savings. He'd had enough left to finish the house he'd bought and little else, but he was fine with that. The stations did well, and he was able to put most of his salary away. He didn't need a whole lot. While he would never be anyone's idea of a business mogul, he was unexpectedly successful, and when the nights got bad, he remembered that.

Mayor Marsha had visited him on his first shift. She'd apologized for telling people he was Gabriel rather than Gideon and had explained she was so sure his brother would be the one coming to town. A statement that hadn't made sense. His brother was a doctor working with the most gravely wounded soldiers. Saint Gabriel, Gideon thought grimly. Or was it Angel Gabriel? He hadn't spoken to his brother in years. Not because of any particular disagreement but because there wasn't much to say.

The song ended. Gideon moved on to the next one on his playlist, but thoughts of his brother led to thoughts of his family. He should probably call his mother in the next week or so. She worried if she didn't hear from him every now and then. But first he needed to spend some time alone. He would go running in the morning. Let the miles work their magic and heal him.

The light on the wall flashed, indicating someone was at the door. He glanced at the clock. It was nearly midnight — late for visitors. He stood and walked down the hall.

While he knew he would most likely find Ford or maybe Angel waiting, his gut tightened slightly at the thought of other possibilities. Or just one. And if his need to see a leggy redhead who spoke her mind and looked at him as if she wanted him tied up and naked was dangerous, it was a flaw he was willing to live with.

He walked to the door and pulled it open. Felicia stood there, her mouth twisted and her expression troubled. Need flared, both to have her back in his bed and to offer comfort. He wanted to hold her and tell her whatever was bothering her could be fixed. The latter pissed the hell out of him.

"What?" he barked, more sternly than he intended.

She raised her chin and glared at him. "I need to speak with you."

He held the door open wider and motioned for her to enter, then led the way back to the studio. At least if he walked in front, he didn't have to look at the way her hips swayed with each step.

When he was safely behind his equipment and she was seated across from him, he risked looking at her again.

"What's wrong?" he asked, his voice less hostile.

She drew in a breath. "Denise Hendrix came to see me."

It took him a second to figure out who that was. "Ford's mother?"

She nodded. "She wanted to have a booth at the Fourth of July festival." Felicia went on to explain about the purpose of the booth.

"It's not that I'm interested in Ford. He's like a brother to me, and I've never met Kent, but that's not the point." Felicia pressed her lips together, as if fighting emotion. "Why didn't she consider me? I meet her criteria. I'm single, I live in Fool's Gold, there's no reason to think I can't produce healthy offspring. That's what she said she wanted. Grandchildren. So why am I not good enough?"

He didn't know which was worse — the slight tremor in her voice, the pain in her eyes or the vicious jealousy ripping through him. The thought of her with Ford or someone else made him want to slash and burn.

He was in trouble, and he knew it. Staying centered, keeping calm, were essential to his survival. He'd been to hell, and he didn't want to go back.

"I think she knows the truth about me," Felicia continued. "Somehow she sensed there's something wrong with me."

"There's not," he said, focusing on the words and ignoring his unease. "You're a beautiful, intelligent woman who wants to settle down. What potential mother-in-law wouldn't put you at the top of her list?"

"Denise Hendrix." Felicia stared at him. "I want to be like everyone else."

"A state that's highly overrated."

"Easy for you to say. You fit in wherever you go. You understand how to speak to people. You walk into a room and you know you can figure out what to say."

"I walk into a room and I'm looking for exits."

She nodded slowly. "You're right. I know you are. I didn't mean it like that."

He shook his head. "Don't. I know what you meant, Felicia. I was being a jerk."

Mostly because he was still pissed about her wanting Denise to pick her for Ford. Although if he actually *listened* to what she was saying instead of reacting to her words, he understood her point.

"You fit in," he told her.

"Not like everyone else. I do want to belong. I like it here and I want to stay. I

155

want to get married and be part of a family." She stared at him. "I want us to date."

His head snapped to the right, and he calculated how far it was to the door.

She giggled. "I didn't mean for those two thoughts to sound related. You don't have to panic."

He turned to her. "I didn't panic."

"You went pale and looked like you were going to run from incoming fire." Her humor faded. "You warned me before about what you want and don't want. I had decided that dating you didn't help me achieve my goal, but I'm less sure of that now. You understand how to fit in."

He didn't like where this was going. "Felicia," he began, then stopped, not sure what to say.

"I want to learn from you," she said firmly. "Well, from 'us.' I just want to go out, like a regular couple. Show me what people do on dates, how they act. I want to be like everyone else."

He didn't have the heart to tell her that was never going to happen. She was too special. But she wouldn't understand the compliment, and he didn't want to upset her.

She smiled. "In return, we'll have sex. You have to admit our sexual chemistry together is excellent."

He was willing to put a check mark in the yes column for that one. "Sex is dangerous."

"I don't think so. We'll use protection, and as long as we keep the locations relatively safe then we should be able to . . ." Her brows rose. "Oh, you're talking about the potential for emotional connection. You don't want me to fall in love with you."

"You'd get hurt."

"I appreciate your concern. You have no worries for yourself?"

He hesitated, not wanting to hurt her feelings. "I'm not capable of loving anybody." There wasn't enough of him left inside.

"I think you're very capable," she told him, "but I understand what you're telling me."

"Saying."

"What?"

"I understand what you're saying."

"Why wouldn't you? I'm using very plain language."

He chuckled. "No. Don't use the phrase 'I understand what you're telling me.' It's too formal."

Her eyebrows drew together, then she nodded. "I see your point." She smiled. "Was that your way of agreeing to date me and help me learn to be like everyone else?"

He knew all the reasons he shouldn't. The odds of this ending badly were greater than he liked. But how was he supposed to resist a commitment-free sexual relationship with a beautiful woman? More important, time with Felicia, both in and out of bed. He couldn't be what she wanted or deserved, but that didn't mean he could resist her.

"Yes," he said.

She laughed, then stood. "Did you want to start with us having sex here at the radio station?"

He swore under his breath. In the time it took him to process her statement, he was already hard.

"You don't have to pay in advance," he told her.

Her smile widened. "I don't consider physical intimacy with you payment. I enjoy it very much."

He groaned. "You're killing me, you know that, right?"

She circled the console and walked toward him. When they were close enough, she hugged him, pressing her curvy body against his.

"Thank you," she murmured. "I really appreciate this."

"You're welcome."

He allowed himself to put his hands on her waist, with the idea he and the woman in his arms weren't going to do anything tonight. If they were dating, then he would follow the appropriate rules. No matter how much he wanted her.

She stepped back. "We should plan our first date." She paused. "Although technically we had that already, so this would be our second date."

"I'll take you to dinner," he said quickly, knowing if she showed up at his house, there wouldn't be any eating, or dating. There would just be him and her and how they made each other feel.

She beamed at him. "I'd like that." She kissed him lightly on the mouth, then waved and left.

He stood rooted in place until he heard the front door close. Then he sank onto his chair and sucked in a breath.

This was dangerous — possibly for both of them. But Felicia wanted to learn how to be like everyone else and he . . . Well, he wanted to pretend, even for a couple of weeks, that he was still close to an actual person.

He flipped through his CDs until he found the one he wanted, then put it into the slot. He put on his headphones and cranked up the volume. It was a night for the Rolling Stones. As they reminded him, "You Can't Always Get What You Want," but with Felicia, he could get damn close.

CHAPTER EIGHT

Felicia casually checked the clock behind the bar, then picked up her glass of wine. She had a bit more time before she had to head home and get changed before her dinner with Gideon.

They were going on a date. A real date, she thought happily, somewhat confused by her level of excitement. While dating Gideon would help her understand the rituals that could lead to marriage and children, he wasn't the one she would spend her life with. He was a means to an end — therefore her enthusiasm level should be more contained. But there was a definite tightness in her chest and a fluttering in her stomach.

"What?" Patience demanded. "That's like the fourth time you've looked at the clock in the past fifteen minutes. Are you late for something?"

Isabel, Noelle and Consuelo all turned to her, their expressions equally curious.

"Not late," Felicia murmured. "I have a date."

Four sets of eyebrows rose in unison. If she hadn't been the subject of their speculation, she would have enjoyed analyzing their identical reactions. As it was, she felt a sudden and inexplicable need to squirm in her seat.

"A date," Isabel repeated. "With a man?"

Felicia nodded. "I've never had any sexual feelings toward women."

"Good to know," Consuelo said, reaching for her beer.

"With whom?" Noelle asked.

"Gideon," Patience and Consuelo said together.

Isabel and Noelle looked at each other.

"Obviously, you two knew," Isabel said. "Are you keeping secrets?"

"No one tells us anything," Noelle told her. "It's because we're blondes. They're jealous."

"Maybe." Isabel turned to Felicia. "When did hot monkey sex lead to dating?"

Felicia cleared her throat. "We're not dating in the traditional sense. We're going out so he can help me learn how to be more like everyone else."

"Why is instruction necessary?" Consuelo asked.

"Because I'm a freak," Felicia said, thinking the answer should be obvious.

"You're a lot of things," her friend told her. "Freak isn't one of them."

"I'm not like the rest of you."

"I'm really boring," Isabel said. "You don't want to be like me."

"You've been married. You've fallen in love. I want that."

Isabel touched her hand. "You'll find the right guy. I'm with Consuelo. I'm not sure you need to be practicing."

Felicia sighed. "There's something wrong with me. A couple of days ago Denise Hendrix came to see me. She wants a booth in the Fourth of July festival."

She went on to explain what Denise had been after. When she was done, she leaned back in the booth and waited for their understanding.

Patience's jaw dropped. "No way," she breathed. "Seriously? Denise Hendrix is taking applications to find a wife for Ford and Kent?" She turned to Isabel. "So you should apply."

"No way. I'm not interested in Ford." Isabel clutched her margarita. "Nope, not interested. It's been years." She sighed. "Maybe if *he* was interested." She shook her head. "No. Not interested. I'm determined to pretend he doesn't exist. I'm strong."

"And a little bit crazy." Consuelo rolled her eyes. "That booth is going to be nothing but trouble."

"Denise is the crazy one," Isabel said. "Ford isn't going to be happy. I wouldn't think Kent would be thrilled, either."

"It's nice she cares about her sons," Noelle said. "Even if you have to question the viability of the plan."

Felicia glared at all of them. "Excuse me," she said loudly. "You're missing the point. I was sitting right there. I'm an intelligent, articulate, single woman of breeding age. Why didn't she ask if I was interested in either of her sons?"

"You already know Ford," Consuelo said. "Maybe she was thinking if you two were going to get together, it would have happened already."

"What about Kent?" Felicia asked. "Face it. She never saw me as an option. I don't know why, but there it is. The truth is I'm different, and I don't want to be different anymore. I want to be exactly like everyone else. So I'm going to date Gideon until I can figure out how to make that happen."

Felicia stared at the table, not wanting to see their pitying looks.

"I hope it never happens," Consuelo said flatly. "You being like everyone else. That would be a shame. I think you're great, just the way you are."

Felicia glanced at her friend. "Thank you. I appreciate the support, but I want more than what I have."

"You should be out there dating, looking for the right guy," Consuelo told her. "But you don't need to practice."

"I can be very awkward."

"You should have seen me with Justice," Patience admitted. "I didn't know what to say when he showed up in the salon a few months ago. I'd been so crazy about him when I was a teenager." She sighed. "But it all worked out and now we're getting married."

"Speaking as the recently divorced," Isabel said, raising her margarita, "I'm intensely bitter."

Noelle raised her glass of wine. "Me, too. But in a 'I'm so happy for you' kind of way."

Conversation shifted to potential wedding dates. Patience admitted to wanting a fall ceremony but was concerned about the potential for early snow.

Felicia glanced at the clock and realized it was time to leave. She dropped ten dollars on the table and slid out of the booth. "I have to go," she told her friends.

"We'll want a report," Isabel told her. "With details."

"I should go, too," Patience said, when Felicia had left.

"Handsome man waiting at home," Noelle said with a smile. "I'm envious but understanding." She paused, frowning slightly. "This has been a happy hour with a full range of emotions. I'm exhausted."

Isabel laughed. Consuelo waited for the other two women to say they had to leave, too. Or wait for her to go. She'd only just met them, and that was only because Felicia had invited her.

Consuelo knew she had nothing in common with the other women at the table. They'd grown up in quiet towns and cities, on the right side of the tracks. It wasn't that she would guess no one else at the table had scars from bullets or knives, it was that if they knew what she'd done — at first out of necessity and then because she was good at it — they would never want to have anything to do with her again.

"Have a good time with Justice," Isabel said, then glanced at Consuelo. "Noelle and I were going to stay for dinner. Will you join us?"

"Say yes," Noelle urged. "We can be very fun."

"That would be nice," Consuelo said, before she could think of a reason to leave. In truth, she wanted to fit in, too. She shared Felicia's desire to be normal but for different reasons. Like her friend, she probably wouldn't get there, but she could fake it.

Isabel waved toward the woman behind the bar, who nodded, indicating she'd be over soon. "One of the advantages of living in Fool's Gold. We can walk everywhere, so there's no drinking and driving issue." She crossed her arms on the table and leaned forward. "Okay, I know you're friends with Felicia and that you've been in the military. Were you in logistics, too?"

"Not exactly."

They both stared at her expectantly.

"I was an operative. Some undercover work."

Noelle's blue eyes widened. "You were a spy? Like James Bond? Only, you know, a girl?"

"That's me," Consuelo said lightly, then smiled. "Actually it's not that interesting. I would move to an area, get to know the locals, find out what was going on." Seduce an enemy agent and, if necessary, kill him.

167

But she wasn't going to share that part.

"So you're trained in self-defense and stuff?" Isabel asked.

Consuelo nodded. "I'll be in charge of a lot of the training at CDS."

Noelle looked confused for a second. "You mean the bodyguard school. That's what we town folk call it."

"Town folk?" Consuelo asked.

Noelle grinned. "Uh-huh."

"I'm with her." Isabel wrinkled her nose. "Town folk? What is this, the 1940s?" She looked at Consuelo. "You have the best abs. You probably work out, huh?"

Consuelo thought about the punching bag she'd spent an hour on that morning. "Most days."

Isabel sighed. "I should work out. I think about it. I don't suppose that counts."

"Sincerity totally counts," Noelle told her. "It's all about attitude."

"Sit-ups help, too," Consuelo said drily.

Isabel smiled. "I seriously don't see that happening, but you will be my inspiration."

The woman from behind the bar walked over. She turned to Consuelo. "I'm Jo. We haven't met."

"Consuelo."

"You're with CDS," Jo said, and chuckled. "For what it's worth, both Angel and Ford

168

are scared of you."

"Good. That's how I want things."

"I can respect that." She glanced at the nearly empty glasses. "Another round?" she asked.

"Yes," Isabel said. "And chips and guacamole, and then we'll talk about dinner."

Jo wrote down their order and left.

Noelle picked up her margarita, then put it down. "Are you going to lecture us on not eating right?"

"No," Consuelo said. "I'm going to order an extra bowl of chips."

"We're going to be such good friends." Noelle sat up straighter. "I know. What if you taught an exercise class? Something like 'exercise for the woefully out of shape'? I could do that. You'd make it fun."

Isabel nodded. "I agree, although I'm painfully aware you'd also kick our butts. But I'm going to be thirty in a couple of years."

Consuelo smiled, liking Isabel's breezy personality. "You just said you weren't interested in exercise."

"I'm not, but I can be motivated by fear. Gravity is going to start making things move. At least that's what my mother has always told me."

"Your mom is in town?" Consuelo asked.

"Not at the moment. She and my father are taking a cruise around the world. It's actually a series of cruises with lots of weeks here and there in between. They're going to be gone nearly a year. That's one of the reasons I'm back in Fool's Gold. I'm working in the family business." She paused for effect. "Paper Moon."

"It's a bridal shop," Noelle added. "Very nice. They carry prom dresses and other kinds of gowns, too."

Isabel rolled her eyes. "My sister is too busy popping out kids to deal with the business. My parents want to sell it and I'm recovering from a divorce, so here I am. I'm going to fix it up, find a buyer and when it sells, I get a cut of the proceeds. Then it's *adios* for me."

"You're not staying in town?" Consuelo asked.

Isabel shook her head. "Been there, done that, and I have an entire wardrobe of festival T-shirts."

One of the servers returned with two margaritas, a beer, chips, salsa and guacamole.

Noelle reached for a chip. "I don't get wanting to leave. I love it here."

"You just arrived," Isabel said. "Give it twenty years."

"I'll love it more, I swear. If only I could

170

find the right guy."

"I hear Mrs. Hendrix is taking applications," Consuelo said, thinking she couldn't wait for Ford to find out about his mother's plan. That was going to be quite the show.

"I haven't met Kent," Noelle said, then lowered her voice. "But I couldn't date Ford. Isabel's still in love with him."

Consuelo wondered if Ford knew and, if he did, what he would think about that tidbit of info.

Isabel glared across the table. "I'm not. I haven't spoken to the man in years."

"You *were* in love with him."

"It was a crush." She looked at Consuelo. "I was fourteen and he was engaged to my sister. She cheated on him, he left town and I wrote him. End of story."

"It's not really the end of the story," Noelle said confidentially. "She has feelings."

"I feel like I'm going to have to lock you in a closet or something."

Consuelo sipped her beer. "Don't make me separate you two."

Noelle leaned toward her. "You said that so casually, but it was totally scary. How do you do that? You're petite and yet completely intimidating. I admire that."

"It's a lot of training," Consuelo said, knowing that she'd learned how to take care of herself early on. Growing up on the street meant figuring out how to survive. One of her favorite movies was *The Shawshank Redemption*. Whenever she got into a tough spot, she reminded herself she had to get busy living or get busy dying. She'd always chosen to err on the side of living.

"You could still date Kent," Consuelo said, to distract them.

"I haven't met Kent," Noelle admitted again.

"He's nice enough." Isabel scooped salsa onto a chip. "He's a typical Hendrix. Tall, dark hair and eyes. Good-looking enough, I guess."

"But not Ford?" Noelle teased.

Isabel rolled her eyes. "I'm ignoring you." She turned to Consuelo. "He's a math teacher. Has a son. Reese. He's eleven or twelve. There was a divorce, and I don't know much more."

"Maybe I'll go apply," Noelle said. "Of course then I'll be one of the many. The potential for rejection seems huge." She raised her eyebrows. "What about you, Consuelo? Any interest in either Hendrix son?"

"No, thanks. I've known Ford a long time and he's not my type."

"Why not?"

"The last thing I want in my life is another

swaggering soldier."

Noelle poked Isabel in the arm. "Does Ford swagger? Does it make your heart beat faster when he does?"

"You're really annoying, you know that?" Isabel turned to Consuelo. "Kent isn't a soldier."

"It wouldn't be a good fit," Consuelo said lightly. In truth she knew there was no way a guy smart enough to be a math teacher would be interested in a woman like her. Especially a man with a child. He would take one look at her, see her for what she was and walk away. It had happened before.

Isabel sighed. "I'll bet you walk in the room and all the men turn and stare."

"With their tongues hanging out," Noelle added. "Must be nice."

The sun was still high in the sky, but large trees provided shade. Felicia smoothed her napkin across her lap, trying to convince herself there was no reason to be nervous. She'd had sex with Gideon — this was only dinner. Shouldn't it be easy? After all, they were both wearing clothes.

But from the second he'd picked her up, through the drive to the Hibiscus Winery, to being seated at this lovely outdoor table, she'd found herself unable to think of a single thing to say.

Maybe it was how Gideon looked. He was wearing dark-wash jeans and a long-sleeved pale blue shirt. Not dressy but not completely casual, either. His shaggy hair had been trimmed, and he'd recently shaved.

Because this was a date, she thought. And she didn't know how to be on a date.

"This is nice," he said, glancing around.

Trees shaded the west side of the patio. Beyond them and north of the property were vineyards.

"The trees are mostly indigenous," she said. "Various pine, white fir and California black oak. Black oak is one of the more useful trees in the area. Over fifty species of bird are thought to use the trees, and the acorns provide a substantial part of the winter diet for squirrels and black-tailed deer. The California black oak has adapted to the wildfires that used to be common in this part of the country. Its thick bark provides protection from smaller fires, and it grows back easily after a major fire."

She paused. "Which is probably more than you wanted to know about a local tree."

Gideon gave her a slow smile. "You're not boring. I like that." He glanced at the trees. "I have a lot more respect for the California black oak than I did."

She wasn't sure if he was teasing her in a gentle, "I like you" way or making fun of her. She hoped it was the former.

A young woman in black pants and a white shirt walked toward them. "Good evening. Thanks for joining us for dinner. I'll be your server. Tonight we have several specials along with three different wine flights."

She explained about the wine choices. Felicia and Gideon decided they would each try the red wine flight and ordered a selection of appetizers to start.

"How's the new job going?" he asked.

"I'm still adjusting and learning. I went to the X-treme Waterski festival with Pia. She walked me through what happened before, during and after." She paused, wondering how honest she could be.

"What?" he asked.

"It was disorganized. Some of the booth placements surprised me, and the bathroom situation wasn't efficient."

She smoothed her napkin again. "I liked meeting the competitors. They're remarkably skilled. While I understand the physics of waterskiing, I doubt it's something at which I could succeed." She wrinkled her nose. "In fact, I picture myself falling over and over."

"You'd look good in a bikini, though."

Felicia opened her mouth, then closed it. She felt heat on her cheeks. The involuntary response to unexpected attention, she thought. Or perhaps it was the sexual innuendo in the compliment. The pleasure of knowing he enjoyed her body.

"A one-piece bathing suit is more practical for sports."

He sighed heavily. "Well, if you have to be practical."

She laughed.

The server appeared with five glasses of wine for each of them. There was only a small amount in each. She explained about the various wines and then laid out the appetizers and left.

"Dinner's gotten complicated," Gideon said.

"The different wines and foods allow us to find the most pleasing combinations. Salty with sweet, spicy with acidic and so on." She pressed her lips together. *Not every conversation has to be a lecture,* she reminded herself. "Sorry."

He frowned. "Why are you apologizing?"

"I have too much information in my head. Not everyone wants to know that the phrase 'Get your ducks in a row' in Latin is *Instrue omnes anates tuas in acie.*"

He picked up the first glass. "I'll sleep better with that information."

"You're just being nice."

"Ask around, Felicia. I'm not nice."

"Actually you are. The people in town think well of you."

She watched him as she spoke, noting the moment he stiffened, as if finding himself in a trap.

"That compliment doesn't make you happy?"

"No."

His honesty surprised her. "Because you're not capable of fitting in and if they think you do, they'll expect too much?"

He studied her. "Got it in one. I should remember you're familiar with the warrior psyche."

"As much as I can be. I'm not one of those who believes that men and women have the same neurophysiology. Our brains are wired very differently, and because of that, we process information differently. But I was with the military long enough to have a working knowledge of how soldiers think and react." She paused. "As much as one can generalize from the group to the individual."

She put down her glass of wine and thought briefly about running. Anywhere would work, as long as it wasn't here.

"I'm doing it again," she murmured. "I'm nervous. That seems to make the rambling worse."

"You're being too hard on yourself. I like the facts you share. It makes me think about my world in different ways."

"Thank you." She hoped he was telling the truth, because not everyone felt that way.

She thought about Denise Hendrix and how the other woman hadn't seen her as a potential wife for either of her sons. "I believe I have a clear grasp on my personality flaws," she told him. "Ignoring them won't make me fit in."

"Followed by a husband and children."

"I'd like that, yes." She took a sip of her wine. "Some of the scientists at the lab where I was raised had family. I remember how excited they got when a child was born or a milestone achieved. These were brilliant men who proudly talked about a baby's first step or first word. We're hardwired to want to procreate, to pass on our DNA. More than that, being part of a close group — a family — satisfies us emotionally. I'm sure you've heard about the studies that show people live longer when they have a community around them."

"I'm not arguing your goals," he told her.

"Just how much effort you have to put into it."

"You're a strong, tall, good-looking man. You'd never lack for female companionship, and if you let it be known you wanted to get married, you'd have tons of women volunteering."

He dodged the compliment by pushing the plate of bruschetta toward her. "Try it."

"Why?"

"Because I'm sure it's delicious, and I'm not going to convince you there's absolutely nothing wrong with you."

If only that were true, she thought sadly. "If there's nothing wrong with me, why are you here? You've made it clear you're not interested in having a romantic relationship. Therefore, you're with me to help. If I didn't have a problem, I wouldn't need help."

He groaned. "Remind me not to challenge your brain again."

She nodded. "It's a good rule. For what it's worth, you'd beat me in any physical activity that required upper-body strength. I work out, but I can't achieve the muscle mass you have."

"Small comfort. So I can win in the caveman category."

She smiled. "You also have a very sexy

voice. I enjoy listening to your show."

"You listen?"

"Nearly every night."

"In bed?"

"Sometimes." His show was late at night. Being in bed shouldn't be a surprise.

"Naked?" he asked, his dark gaze settling on her face.

"I usually wear a T-shirt and . . ." Information connected. "Oh." She realized they were flirting. She leaned toward him and lowered her eyes so she had to look at him through her lashes. "Sometimes I'm naked."

His expression tightened and his pupils dilated.

Sexual interest, she thought happily. Which was one of the purposes of flirting. Inciting it as well as indicating one's own.

"Should I mention I touch myself?" she asked. "Don't men find that arousing?"

Gideon had just taken a sip of wine. He started to choke and cough. He was able to inhale, so she didn't offer to pound him on the back. After a few minutes, he cleared his throat.

"Better?" she asked.

He nodded.

"Was that a no on talking about masturbation?"

"It was a no," he said, his voice low and hoarse.

"There are a lot of rules to dating. Someone should write a book."

"I'm sure you can find one on the internet." He waved at her. "We need to talk about something else."

"All right." What would be a suitable topic? "I've been reading some papers on using Lagrangian mechanics in the flow of crowds. I thought it might be useful for the festivals."

He studied her for several seconds, then smiled. "I want to hear all about it."

CHAPTER NINE

"I'm confused," Felicia said.

Consuelo picked up the packing tape and used it to seal the box. "Not about moving, right? Because this office is tiny."

Felicia shook her head. "I'm happy to be moving into the larger office. I'm going to be more comfortable in my own space. It's about my date with Gideon."

Her friend paused. "What happened?"

"We went to the winery and had drinks and appetizers. We talked." She'd told him more about her time growing up at the university and he'd . . . She frowned. Gideon had deflected most of her questions. She didn't know any more about him today than she had this time last week.

"Yes? He what?"

Felicia shook her head. "I don't know why he's helping me. I thought it was for sex, but all he did after our date is kiss me on the cheek. Based on his physical reaction to me, I don't think he's lost interest. So why didn't he want to do more?"

Consuelo shrugged. "Men are strange and fragile creatures. They pretend they're all macho, but it's not true. Did you ask him what was wrong?"

"No. I wanted to, but I didn't know what to say. I felt confused."

"Welcome to the world of dating. But you like him?"

"Yes. I enjoy the sense of anticipation I feel when I'm going to see him. He's easy to be with and I like how being around him sexually arouses me."

Consuelo laughed. "I just love you so much."

Felicia knew her comment didn't warrant her friend's response, so she must have been inadvertently funny. Again.

"Should I not mention being aroused?"

"No, it's not the share, it's the language choice."

Felicia considered that. "I like how he turns me on? I like how he's hot?"

"Better. Do you have another date scheduled?"

"Yes. Gideon's going with me to the Sierra Nevada Balloon Festival. Then he's my date for Charlie and Clay's luau. He doesn't seem to mind spending time with me."

"He obviously enjoys your company. That's a good thing."

"I know, it's just . . . I'd like it better if he couldn't control himself around me."

Consuelo grinned. "What? Just push you to the floor and do it?"

"I'd like a little more finesse than that, but it would be better than a kiss on the cheek."

"See, this is what guys complain about. If they want us, we call them animals and pull back. If they don't attack us, we think they're not interested. Men can't win."

"I'm not being deliberately difficult," Felicia told her. "I just wish there'd been more." She'd wanted to make love with Gideon. She'd wanted him in her bed. Not just for the orgasms, but because she liked touching and being touched by him. "Maybe he's afraid I'll get too emotionally connected, although I have told him that if that happens, I'll deal with it myself. He's explained he's not the type to want a relationship, so if I fall in love with him, isn't that my problem and not his?"

"You'd think so, but it's rarely that simple."

"Maybe I *should* fall in love with him. For practice."

Consuelo winced. "Don't go looking for

heartbreak, kid. It'll find you fast enough on its own."

Maybe, but it would be wonderful to know what love was like — just once.

She glanced at the clock. "The guys are due to arrive shortly. We need to get finished."

The office was nearly packed. There were two more boxes to fill. Felicia had arranged use of the service elevator, which meant the file cabinets could be moved with their contents in place. She'd already emptied the desk and storage cabinets, not to mention the small closet. With Justice, Ford and Angel each wielding hand trucks, she calculated the move would only take three hours. As long as everyone did what she said, things would go smoothly.

She and Consuelo finished packing about three minutes before Justice, Ford and Angel arrived.

"You couldn't hire movers?" Ford asked as he took in the stacked boxes, with neat numbers written on the side.

"The city provides movers," Felicia told him. "However, they have other responsibilities, and I didn't want to wait. So you volunteered."

"I don't remember volunteering," Ford grumbled.

"Me, either," Angel said.

"Your lack of recall isn't my problem," she said firmly. She'd actually told them when and where to report. Which was almost like volunteering.

"Consuelo will supervise this end of things," she continued. "I'll be at the new place. When you take the boxes, please do so in order." She paused for emphasis. "Once you are in my new office, you will stack them in order. Not all the odd numbers in one section and the evens in another. Not by prime numbers or weight, but in numerical order. Is that clear?"

Justice grinned. "I'm not sensing a lot of trust."

"I know you. All of you." She did her best to glare at them, not that she'd ever been especially intimidating. But a girl could dream.

"If you don't listen to her, you answer to me," Consuelo said firmly. "Got that?"

Angel and Ford exchanged a look, then nodded.

"The desk stays," Felicia said, picking up her tablet and tapping on the screen. "So do the bookcases. You have the address. You may begin now."

She started for the door, then turned back. "Thank you very much for your help.

186

I'll have beer and pizza waiting for all of you when we're finished."

Two minutes later she was on the street. As she exited the building, she was surprised to find several women on the sidewalk. They weren't walking, and there wasn't a festival. Instead they seemed to be waiting.

"Is it now?" one of them asked her.

"I wish it was hotter," her friend said. "Then they'd want to take their shirts off."

Felicia looked to the left and saw more women waiting. "I don't understand."

A woman wearing a bright purple track-suit walked over. "We're here for the parade," she said cheerfully. "You're Felicia, right?"

"Yes, ma'am."

"I'm Eddie Carberry. Your bodyguards are moving your office today. We're here to watch the show."

Felicia still didn't understand. "You want to watch men use hand trucks to move boxes and file cabinets?"

Eddie smiled at her. "We want to stare at rippling biceps and great butts. The boxes are just the delivery system."

"Okay," Felicia said slowly, thinking there was so much about small-town life she still found confusing.

She walked along the sidewalk. The gauntlet of women stretched to the corner, and when she made the turn, she saw it went on even longer. Her new office was on the other side of City Hall. As she approached that building, Mayor Marsha came out and started toward her.

"I don't know how word got out," the mayor said with a sigh. "I swear, the women in this town are like children. Promise them a half-naked man and they go wild."

"The men won't be half-naked, so I'm not sure they're going to get what they came for."

Mayor Marsha looked grim. "Honestly, I doubt that will matter."

Felicia looked back at the still-growing crowd of women. Angel had just rounded the corner, and the women cheered. She heard calls of "Work it, baby" and "Take off your shirt!" Instead of appearing insulted, Angel only grinned and moved a little more slowly.

Ford followed, looking just as pleased with the attention. At least until he noticed his mother pointing at him while she spoke to a woman in her twenties. Only Justice seemed the least bit chagrined.

One of the upstairs windows in a building across the street opened and loud music poured out. The throbbing beat set the women to cheering even louder.

"This isn't what I expected," Felicia admitted.

The mayor gave her a weary smile. "You get used to it," she said. "Some days it's even endearing. Of course, the other days, it's just plain embarrassing."

If it wasn't so damned early, Gideon was pretty sure he would be enjoying himself. The morning was clear and crisp, the sky a deep black-turning-blue with only the slightest hint of light at the top of the mountains. He was in the company of a beautiful woman he very much wanted to sleep with. The fact that it was 4:30 and he'd been up since the previous morning was about the only downside. That and the other five thousand or so people, which meant the odds of him having his way with Felicia were slim to none.

Around them, with the mountains to the east and the vineyards to the west, were close to a dozen hot air balloons. Their brilliant colors weren't yet visible. Right now they were more shape than substance.

He stood off to the side of the crowd, where Felicia had left him. She'd gone off with Pia to discuss festival details. Gideon shoved his hands into his jeans pockets and wished he hadn't gulped his coffee so quickly. He could sure use it now.

"Morning."

Gideon turned and saw Justice and Patience approaching. The other man had a sleepy girl in his arms. Patience carried an open bottle of champagne and a stack of glasses.

"Morning," he said. "You're up early."

"This is when the balloons take off," Patience said with a smile. "Isn't it lovely? I felt guilty, taking a morning off work, but I had to see this. Lillie wanted to see it, too, but she seems to be lacking enthusiasm at this point."

Her daughter stirred sleepily but didn't speak.

"She'll wake up when they take off," Justice said, his hands holding the child protectively.

Gideon accepted the glass of champagne Patience offered and wished it were coffee.

More people crowded around them. He heard snatches of conversation, saw couples standing close together. There seemed to be lots of hand-holding and plenty of snuggling. It was the hour, he thought. Or maybe the sight of the huge balloons slowly filling with hot air as the sun began to climb the mountains.

"Is there coffee?"

The question came from behind him. He turned and saw Ford, Angel and Consuelo approaching.

"Champagne," he said, holding up his glass.

Angel grimaced.

"It's a tradition," Ford said, accepting a glass from Patience. "We toast them taking off."

"I'd rather be in bed," Consuelo grumbled, but also took a glass.

"Dollface, just say the word."

Angel had barely finished speaking when Consuelo thrust her glass at Ford, twisted slightly, kicked out her leg and dropped Angel onto his back. The entire move took about three-tenths of a second.

She pressed her booted foot against his neck and smiled.

"Really?" she asked.

He swallowed, then held out both hands, palms up. "Sorry. Reflex. It won't happen again."

"I didn't think so." She removed her foot and retrieved her champagne. "When do the balloons take off?"

"Five minutes before sunrise," Felicia said, walking up to them. She had a tablet in her hands and looked a little frazzled.

"They'll head south, following the mountains. Air flow over the peaks will push them steadily west until they land close to Stockton. There are maps if you want to follow the projected route. I anticipate a seventy-two percent chance of them landing as planned."

She looked at Angel, who was still brushing himself off. "Whatever you said, you know better."

"It was an accident."

Felicia wiped off several leaves. "You know an accident like that can get you killed." She turned to Gideon. "Is this nice? Are you enjoying yourself?"

Hanging out with this many people before seven in the morning was his idea of hell. But her expression was slightly frantic, and he had the feeling she was just as uncomfortable as he was — if for different reasons.

"It's great," he said.

She looked at him. "I want to believe you," she said.

"Then you should."

She nodded. "The event is relatively easy. No booths or parades. Just the balloons launching this morning, followed by balloon rides for the public this weekend. Assuming the weather cooperates. I created my own computer program to collect the most current weather data."

"Because you can't trust one of the online sites?" he asked, trying not to smile.

"I like to confirm the data." She glanced over her shoulder. "I should get back to Pia. She's giving me lots of information about the other festivals. If I don't see you before you leave, I'll see you for the luau?"

"I wouldn't miss it."

She paused, then raised herself up on tiptoe and pressed her lips to his cheek. The soft kiss was over nearly before it began, and then she was gone.

He stared after her, not exactly sure how he'd gotten sucked into her ridiculous plan of learning how to date so she could fall in love with someone else and get married. While the process made sense, he couldn't shake the feeling that he was headed for trouble. Probably because when it came to a happily ever after, he knew he wasn't going to be able to make that happen.

The more he got to know Felicia, he more he was aware that he was going to regret having to let her go when the time came. She wasn't the kind of woman a man forgot easily. But walk away he would — not just because it was the right thing to do for her, but because when it came to himself, he didn't have an option.

■ ■ ■ ■

The Lucky Lady Casino Resort sprawled over nearly a hundred acres north of town. While the facility was modern and large, the construction had made use of the natural forest, framing the parking lot with trees and continuing the natural theme through the main entrance.

Felicia was both excited and nervous as Gideon guided her toward the ballroom. He kept his hand on the small of her back, as if she needed assistance. Or maybe it was a dating thing. She was starting to get confused.

In the past week Gideon had taken her to dinner at the winery, gone to the balloon festival, although they hadn't spent much time together there because she'd been working, and now they were attending Charlie and Clay's luau. Even ignoring their first dinner at his place, this was their third date. Shouldn't something be different between them?

The problem was she was just as nervous and unsure of herself as she had been the first time they'd gone out. She had that fluttery sensation in her stomach, and she questioned everything she wanted to say.

She wanted to feel him touch her, and at the same time, she was unable to ask when they were going to have sex. Being around Gideon made her shy.

"Clay was one of the first people I met when I came to town," Gideon said as they circled a selection of slot machines. "He came to the station to talk about advertising his Haycations."

"I don't know him very well," she admitted. "But I like Charlie. She's direct, which makes her easier for me to deal with. I also enjoy her sense of humor."

"They sound like a fun couple."

Felicia nodded.

They'd reached a wide hallway with signs directing them to the ballroom. Up ahead she could see double doors standing open. Music with a reggae beat spilled out, and she could hear people talking and laughing.

"You'll be fine," Gideon murmured.

"What?"

She glanced around and realized she'd come to a stop — as if afraid to walk into the room. Mostly because she was. Social situations in large crowds made her uncomfortable. The more people she didn't know, the greater the odds of her saying the wrong thing. She was just starting to get comfortable in town. She didn't want to appear any more awkward.

"I understand my fears are irrational," she told him.

He smiled at her. "So says the chick afraid of spiders. Next thing you know you'll be handing me jars to open because you're not strong enough."

"I'm comfortable with my physical strength and my use of leverage. And except for the spiders, I'm not afraid of most living things. People are different."

She glanced down at the yellow floral print dress she'd chosen to wear. It was strapless, but not too fussy. The top was fitted, and the skirt flowed over her hips with a fullness she found appealing. She'd painted her toes a bright coral color and slipped on gold strappy heels.

Gideon had it easy, she thought. He'd chosen a Hawaiian shirt and jeans. What could be simpler?

"I was nervous at the balloon festival," she admitted. "But busy. I felt a part of things because I was helping behind the scenes. This party is different."

The song switched from something fast to something slower. Gideon surprised her by pulling her close and taking her hand in his. He put his other hand on her waist and started to move in time with the song.

"What are you doing?" she asked.

"Dancing. I guess if you have to ask, I'm doing it wrong."

"We're in a hallway."

"Uh-huh."

"People don't dance in hallways."

His dark eyes flashed with amusement. "How about kissing? Do people kiss in hallways?"

Before she could answer the question, he'd drawn her closer still and lowered his mouth to hers.

His lips claimed hers with an intensity that took her breath away. Technically she could still breathe, but the expression was exactly right, she thought, letting herself get lost in all the sensations. Her eyes drifted closed as her hands settled on his shoulders, and she let herself lean into him.

Wanting swept through her. It was fast and intense, making her want to touch him all over — or maybe just rip off her dress so he could touch her. Either would work, but both would be better.

He moved his mouth against hers. She parted for him immediately and was rewarded by the feel of his tongue against hers. Nerves reacted like a waterfall, cascading all the way down her body. Heat settled in her belly and moved lower.

When he drew back, she smiled. "You make me hot."

He grinned. "You don't want to tell me about your chemical reaction?"

"I can, but in this case I think the vernacular works better."

"You make me hot, too," he murmured, wrapping his arms around her and pulling her against him. "And I like it when you talk technical . . . about any of your girl parts."

She rested her cheek on his chest, enjoying the sensation of being safe and the feel of his hard penis against her belly. His heartbeat was steady, the rhythmic sound relaxing her.

He drew back and kissed her forehead. "Better?"

"Than what?"

"I wanted to distract you so you wouldn't be so nervous."

Because of the party, she thought. "Your plan worked," she said with a smile. Like she'd said before — Gideon was very nice to her.

They turned toward the entrance to the ballroom. Gideon took her hand and together they went inside.

The room itself had a stage at one end with what appeared to be a reggae band.

There was a long buffet and three bars, along with a dessert station that featured a chocolate fountain. One side was open to a wide patio with lots of seating and a view of the mountains. Felicia suspected that the glass doors could be left in place or pushed out of the way, depending on the season or the event.

She and Gideon were offered tropical drinks in an assortment of colors. Servers walked by with trays of food. She caught sight of Charlie with Clay. Charlie had on a beautiful white dress in a tank style. While Charlie was more a cargo pants kind of woman, the simple lines of the dress combined with the silky fabric suited her. Dellina walked up to Charlie and whispered something. Charlie nodded. Clay leaned over and kissed Dellina's cheek, which Felicia thought was strange. It was almost as if he was thanking her. Interesting.

Felicia and Gideon walked through the crowded room. They were greeted by several people they knew. Justice and Patience came over and began to chat. She saw Consuelo having what looked like an intense conversation with Mayor Marsha and Isabel ducking behind a large plant. Obviously her friend had decided to continue hiding from Ford.

About an hour later, a very beautiful,

middle-aged woman stepped onto the stage. She was petite and fit, dressed in a red-and-white sarong.

"Thank you all for coming," she said into the microphone the band had set up. "My name is Dominique Dixon, and I want to welcome you. This party is for my wonderful daughter, Charlie, and her fiancé, Clay."

She motioned to the couple, who had moved to the front of the crowd.

Dominique's eyes filled with tears. "I love you so much, Charlie. I hope you'll always be happy."

Just then Mayor Marsha joined Dominique on the stage. The mayor wore one of her suits — this one in a light pink. An odd choice for a luau, Felicia thought. Just one of many.

The mayor hugged Dominique, then took the microphone.

"Welcome," she said with a smile. "I have to say this represents what I love about Fool's Gold. Friends coming together to celebrate. It has been my honor to be a part of nearly every birth and wedding here, for many, many years. Today is no exception. If those of you in the middle of the room could move to the left or the right, please. We need to create a center aisle."

Felicia didn't understand. What were they doing?

Gideon took her hand and drew her back. It was then she was able to see Charlie had moved to the back of the ballroom. She was in the same dress she'd worn before, but now she had a bouquet of white roses and lilies in her hand. Clay had left her side and was standing by the stage. A girl of maybe ten or eleven stepped in front of Charlie. She had obviously been burned at some point, but still smiled happily as she tossed out rose petals.

Felicia found herself oddly teary and excited, without knowing why. A very pregnant Heidi and her husband, Rafe, stepped between Charlie and Clay and the flower girl. Annabelle and Shane joined.

"Oh, there's going to be a wedding!" someone squealed.

The mayor smiled again. "Yes, there is. Apparently Charlie and Clay couldn't decide whether to have a big wedding or a small one, so instead they picked something unconventional. Less hassle, more fun." She paused. "Charlie said to tell you all she and Clay are going to Fiji for three weeks in the morning and they don't want any calls."

Everyone laughed.

The band played a Calypso version of the

Wedding March and Charlie started down her makeshift aisle. Felicia couldn't believe it. A wedding. Just like that.

Everyone turned to the front again, as Charlie and Clay took their places in front of Mayor Marsha. Their family gathered around them. Felicia saw Charlie's mother and Clay's mother linking arms, both smiling and crying.

She looked between the couple and saw the love in their eyes. They belonged together, she thought. They were happy and starting their lives together.

Yearning welled up inside her, but she reminded herself not to worry. She'd started down a path herself. She would learn what she needed to, and then she would find the man she belonged with. One day she would be getting married. Maybe not exactly like Charlie, but however it happened, it would be a memory she would treasure always.

CHAPTER TEN

Felicia had the entire Fourth of July festival reduced to a diagram and a flow chart. She'd organized by time, location and type of booth. She was ready. Or as close to ready as one could be before the actual event took place. It wasn't as if she could cook the food or anything, but if she could, she would have that started, too.

Thirty-seven hours and counting, she thought. Thirty-seven hours until the vendors arrived and started setting up. The deliveries had been confirmed, as had the workers who would help. The decorations were in place. Every light pole on the main streets had either bunting or a flag. She knew the exact time the parade would start and who would be in it.

She'd planned ops before. She'd been responsible for moving millions of dollars' worth of equipment, not to mention soldiers, planes and boats, but nothing had prepared her for what it was like to be facing her first festival in Fool's Gold.

"I can do this," she told herself as she stood in the center of her office. She was strong. She was smart. She was not going to start hyperventilating. If she did, she might pass out, and hitting the floor would likely cause some kind of injury.

Focus on your office, she told herself. She liked her office. It had lots of windows and commercial grade internet connections, and everything was organized the way she liked. She'd put Pia's massive Rolodex into a database and then downloaded it to her tablet. She had access to more information than any president before 1990.

Neutiquam ero. I am not lost.

Right. Because she wasn't lost. She knew exactly where she was and what she was doing. She would keep breathing and everything would be fine. She was sure of it.

"I don't understand."

Felicia smiled politely and pointed to the map. "Your booth is here."

The tall, dark-haired woman in jeans and a T-shirt with a tarot card of the Magician glared at her. "I can see what's printed on the page. I'm saying I don't understand because that's not my spot. I have the same spot every year. It's over there, by the corn dog stand. I get a lot of business from people eating corn dogs. No doubt they've guessed that hideous, processed meat is going to kill them so they want to find out when their life is ending. I can help them with that."

She moved her lips in what Felicia thought might be a smile, but it was hard to tell. It looked a little like a snarl, too.

"I've moved your booth," Felicia told her.

"Move it back. People come looking for me. I need to be where they'll find me."

"They'll find you very easily." Felicia did her best to appear patient, even if she was getting frustrated by the woman's obvious lack of vision. "You're now going to be on the way to the park. People will pass by you as they go listen to the band playing. They'll be able to sit and enjoy your reading without having to juggle their corn dogs. You'll get more business."

The woman put her hands on her hips. "I want to be by the corn dog stand."

"That's not possible. Rather than having the food scattered throughout the festival, I've created a food area. There's no room for your booth there."

"This is stupid. Where's Pia?"

Felicia thought about pointing out that if

205

the woman was as psychic as she claimed, she would have known her booth was moving before she got to Fool's Gold. But she knew saying that wouldn't help. "I'm in charge now."

"She quit?" The tarot reader shook her head. "Figures. You get one person in a job who knows what she's doing and she leaves. Now I'm stuck with you." Her gaze narrowed. "You know I can put a curse on you, right?"

Felicia thought about the fact that she'd been trained to disarm an assailant in less than three seconds, but knew physical violence wasn't an option. Or her style.

"I'm sorry you're disappointed by your new booth location. I hope you'll at least try to make it work. According to my calculations, you should have thirty-two percent more traffic, and that will translate into an increase in revenues."

"Whatever," the woman muttered and stalked off.

Felicia drew in a breath, determined not to let a single difficult incident color her view of her new job. Change was often met with resistance. By the end of the long weekend, the vendors would see what she'd done was a good thing.

"Hey, you that Felicia person?"

She turned and saw a big guy wearing a short-sleeved shirt with the name "Burt" on the pocket.

"Yes."

"I've got the extra Porta-Potties you ordered, but I can't put them where they go. There's some guys building a stage or something."

"Right. The Porta-Potties are going to be in a different location this time. In fact, in several."

The man groaned. "Seriously? You're doing this to me the afternoon before the Fourth of July. Where's Pia?"

"It's eye-catching," Isabel said, sounding doubtful. "The colors are bright, and the pictures turned out really well."

Consuelo stared at the cheerful yellow booth framed with red, white and blue balloons. The sign would draw attention, she thought, staring at the large letters asking: "Do you want to marry one of my sons?" Two twenty-four by thirty-six-inch pictures of each man graced the front of the booth. Denise Hendrix sat at a desk in the shaded space, several photo albums on the surface, along with a stack of applications.

"It would scare the hell out of me if I were Ford or his brother," Consuelo said.

"Kent," Isabel said absently. "The other brother is Kent. He's a math teacher. And he has a kid."

Kent had the same dark hair and eyes as Ford, but his expression was gentler, Consuelo thought. There was something about his easy smile that drew her to his picture.

"Divorced?" Consuelo asked.

"Yes. I don't know the details, though. Her name was Lorraine. When she took off, Kent handled it badly. Pining for her, because men are inherently stupid. Anyway, he moved back here and got a job at the high school. He's smart enough and nice, I guess. A good guy, but you know, not very interesting."

Consuelo turned to her friend. "Not dangerous enough for you?"

Isabel flipped her blond hair over her shoulder. "I'll have you know I was wildly in love with Ford long before he was dangerous. No one truly loves like a fourteen-year-old girl."

"And now?"

"I don't know him." She glanced around and lowered her voice. "Essentially, I'm still avoiding him. It's not that hard. I suppose working in a bridal shop helps."

Denise, an attractive woman in her early fifties, looked up and saw them. "Hello, girls," she said, waving them into the booth. "Come to apply?"

"Not exactly," Isabel said. "But the booth is fabulous."

Denise smiled. "I've been getting a lot of applications." She motioned to a pile of papers in a plastic box in a corner of the booth. "I'm also taking pictures of each of the girls that I'll attach to the applications. I'm going to be checking all the information and their references before telling either of the boys."

"Speaking of the boys," Isabel said. "Do they know?"

Denise's smile turned slightly wicked. "Not yet. I'm sure they'll be upset when they find out, but that will pass. In a few months, when they're happily married, they'll thank me."

"It's good to have a plan," Isabel said, then turned to Consuelo. "I'm sorry. I should have introduced you two. Denise, this is my friend Consuelo Ly. She's new to Fool's Gold. She'll be working at the bodyguard school. Consuelo, Denise Hendrix."

Consuelo shook hands. "Nice to meet you, ma'am."

"Denise, dear. Call me Denise." Her dark gaze swept over Consuelo. "Are you single?"

"Yes."

"Ever married?"

"No."

"How old are you?"

"Thirty."

Denise frowned. "Is there a reason you haven't married?"

"I traveled a lot for work."

"Any children?"

"No, ma'am." Consuelo fought the need to take a step back. She knew she could easily shut down the other woman — physically or verbally — but this was Fool's Gold, and she had a feeling she was supposed to treat her elders with respect.

"Do you like children?"

The question shouldn't have surprised her, but it did. When she'd been a little girl, her mother had always told her to take care of her younger brothers. That she was the oldest and it was up to her. She'd done her best. Had tried to keep them out of trouble, but the neighborhood was tough and the allure of the gangs was irresistible.

Her youngest brother had died before his fourteenth birthday, the victim of a drive-by shooting. The other spent his life in and out of jail. She'd wasted years trying to show him there was another path, but he didn't listen. Now they barely spoke. The only time he called was to ask for money, and she refused to give him any. If her mother were still alive, she would be crushed to know her family had fallen apart.

"I always wanted children," Consuelo admitted. A chance to start over. To live somewhere nice. To belong. Loving a man was a risk she wasn't sure she could take, but a child seemed safer. With a child, she could offer all she had.

Denise reached for an application, then pulled it back. "Are you planning on staying in Fool's Gold?"

Consuelo nodded.

Denise's smile returned. "Excellent." She handed over the application, then turned to Isabel. "Unfortunately, I've heard you're leaving in a few months, so you'll understand why I don't want you to apply."

Isabel took a step back. "Not a problem. Good luck."

"Thank you, dear."

Isabel grabbed Consuelo's hand. "We should go."

Denise moved toward them. "Don't you want to fill out an application?" she asked Consuelo.

"Um, no, thanks. I already know Ford and he's not my type."

"What about Kent? He's very smart. And a good father."

Isabel tugged, and Consuelo followed her out of the booth, while calling out a quick "Sorry."

Isabel kept walking. "If it wasn't ten-thirty in the morning, I'd suggest we go to Jo's and get drunk. Was that as scary as I think it was?"

"It was unusual. You have to give her credit for initiative."

Isabel laughed. "Is that what we're calling it? I swear, if I wasn't avoiding Ford, I would hang around the booth just to watch the explosion when he finds out what his mother is doing."

She kept talking, but Consuelo wasn't listening. Instead she found herself glancing over her shoulder and looking at the picture of the other Hendrix brother. The one with kind eyes.

Felicia understood the various causes of a headache. Ruling out a brain tumor and an aneurysm, she was left with a host of innocuous causes. Most likely the throbbing in her temples came from a lack of sleep and the steady stress of her new job. When she next saw Pia, she would apologize for ever thinking what the other woman did was easy. Because in truth, this was the most difficult challenge she'd ever faced.

It was nearly five on Friday afternoon, which meant they were in day two of the festival. They'd gotten through the fireworks the previous night, along with the first concert. Tonight was concert number two — the main draw being a bluegrass band with the unlikely name of A Blue Grass Band.

"We're in the park," the lead singer was saying for possibly the eighth time in as many minutes. He had moved from the street to the sidewalk, perhaps in an attempt to intimidate her by appearing taller.

"I know," Felicia said, hoping she could maintain her air of patience and under-standing. In truth she wanted to pick up the nearest large object and beat the man with it until he stopped complaining.

"Why are we in the park? We're never in the park."

Felicia drew in a breath. "You'll have more seating there. We've set out chairs on both sides, with a large grassy area in the middle. The sound will travel better without the buildings so close. The food court leads directly to the park, increasing traffic flow. People who didn't plan to come hear the music will be drawn in. Attendance was up last night by twenty percent, as were CD and T-shirt sales. You're going to have to trust me on this."

"I don't think you have the right energy for this job. Where's Pia?"

"Unavailable," Felicia said, doing her best not to grit her teeth. "And if you want to complain, you'll have to get in line. I believe someone is already putting a curse on me."

"This sucks," the twentysomething man told her. "And you bite."

With that eloquent insult, he stalked away, leaving her clutching her tablet.

She had forty-eight more hours, she thought grimly. With luck, she would be in bed by midnight and able to sleep until six. The same on Saturday. Which meant twelve of the forty-eight hours would be spent pleasantly. She couldn't say the same for the other thirty-six.

"There you are."

She sucked in a breath and turned to see Ford striding toward her.

"You let my mother have a booth to find me a wife."

She started walking. "Get in line."

"What?"

"Everyone has something to complain about. I don't want to hear it."

Ford grabbed her arm. "Hey, my mother has a booth, and she says you gave her the permit."

She stopped and faced Ford. At least if she went after him, she wouldn't have to worry about hurting him or being sued. Of course, odds were he would kick her ass, but under the circumstances, that might make her feel better.

"She has a legal right to have a booth in the festival if that's what she wants. She isn't doing anything illegal and she paid her fees. It was my job to give her the permit."

He dropped his arm and stared at her. "But we're friends. You should have my back."

Those words cut her far deeper than any knife thrust. She clutched the tablet to her chest. "I'm sorry. I didn't think it was that big a deal."

"She wants me married off. She's taking applications."

He sounded really upset, she thought. "She's being proactive. It makes her feel better. You were gone for a long time, and she doesn't want to lose you again. Surely you can understand that. In a way, it's funny."

"It's not funny to me. You should have told me."

She tried to see the situation from his point of view. Just because she wanted to be paired up didn't mean everyone did. Look at Gideon, who avoided all emotional involvements.

"You're right," she said, nodding quickly. "I was wrong not to say something. I can see how you'd view my actions as a betrayal."

Ford shifted. "*Betrayal* is a little strong."

"No, it's not. I was a bad friend. I apologize."

"Jeez, Felicia, I was pissed, but it's not the end of the world."

"It was thoughtless of me." She felt her eyes burning, and it took her a second to realize she was starting to cry. "There's been so much going on. I'm trying to be understanding, because the changes are necessary, but everyone is resisting. There's more pushback than I anticipated and I haven't slept and now you're angry with me."

"I'm not angry," he muttered. "It's fine. Seriously. I'm okay. My mom's probably doing a good thing, right?"

"You're just saying that."

"I'll say anything if you promise not to cry."

She sniffed. "I'll do my best. However, once the sympathetic nervous system is engaged, it can be difficult to stop the process."

He swore.

She swallowed, still fighting tears. "You can go. I'll be fine. I feel better, knowing you're not angry with me."

"I'm not. Really. We're good. Okay?"

She nodded and he took off at a run.

Felicia walked through the crowds, trying to gather control. She generally didn't give in to tears, which just illustrated how much stress she was dealing with. Perhaps sugar would help.

In front of her, a boy of eight or nine stomped his foot. "This is stupid," he yelled at his mother. "I want an elephant ear. They're supposed to be right here. Why aren't they here?"

"I don't know. Everything's different this year." She looked at her husband. "It's just not as fun."

Felicia clutched her tablet tighter. "The elephant ears are over by the food court," she said, pointing. "Next to the lemonade stand. It's not very far."

"Thanks," the man said, putting his arm around his wife. "You know, a lemonade sounds good."

The family walked in the direction of the food court. Felicia stared after them, trying not to take the boy's comments personally, but it was difficult. She'd so wanted the festival to go well.

By eight that night, Felicia was ready to admit defeat. She'd been verbally chastised by both the honey vendor and a small boy looking for the lady who made the balloon animals. When Mayor Marsha walked up to her, she knew she had to come clean.

"It's a disaster," she said, facing her boss. "I'm sorry. I was so sure my way would be better. The flow is easier and I know there are more people listening to the music. But maybe I overestimated how much that would matter. Change can be difficult, I know. I took on too much."

The mayor waited a beat. "Is that what you really think?"

"No," Felicia told her. "I don't. Before, it was silly. With the corn dog vendor by the tarot card reader, people were eating when they came by. Even if they wanted a reading, they weren't always comfortable going into her booth while holding a corn dog. And the lines for the food spilled in front of other booths, blocking them. There wasn't enough seating for the various bands. This is better. Only no one believes me."

Mayor Marsha linked her arm through Felicia's. "In the words of Yogi Berra, *Imperfectum est dum conficiatur.*"

Felicia translated in her head. "It's not over until it's over?"

"Exactly. There are still two more days. Give people a chance to get used to things. I like what you've done, and I suspect they will, too."

"Is this before or after they lynch me?"

"Hopefully before."

Felicia stopped and faced the older woman. "Are you angry?"

"Not at all. You're doing your job."

"What if I ruined everyone's holiday? What if they don't have good memories of this Fourth of July?"

"You're assuming a lot more power than you really have. The memories are about them, not you. Searching for an elephant ear isn't going to ruin anyone's day."

"I hope you're right."

"I usually am."

Gideon went looking for Felicia around sunset. He found her by the park, on the edge of the crowd listening to the bluegrass band.

"What are the odds of them doing a cover of the Beatles' 'Hard Day's Night'?" he asked as he approached.

She surprised him by dropping her tablet on the ground and stepping into his embrace. She wrapped both her arms around his waist and hung on tight.

"Hey," he said, stroking her long red hair. "You okay?"

"No." Her voice was muffled against his chest. "I'm not. Everyone hates me."

"I don't hate you."

"Everyone but you. It's awful. I thought I was tough and brave, but I'm not. I'm weak. I'm a failure."

He touched her chin, nudging her until she looked up at him. Her green eyes were swimming with tears.

"You're also a little dramatic. Getting your time of the month?"

She managed a smile. "You're trying to distract me with sexist comments."

"Is it working?"

"A little." She drew in a breath. "The festival is a disaster, and it's all my fault."

He glanced around. "I don't know. People seem to be having a good time."

"They're not. No one can find anything. The vendors are furious. The band guy acted like I was stupid."

"That must have been refreshing."

She dropped her head to his chest. "You're not taking this seriously."

"It's a festival, kid. Not world peace. If you screw up, no one dies."

She raised her head and sniffed. "Perspective. You're right. I messed up, but I'll do better next time."

"There you go."

More tears shimmered in her eyes, and one trickled down her cheek. He felt like someone had kicked him in the gut.

"Why are you crying?"

"I feel awful. I'm not used to failure." She wiped away the tear, then leaned against him again. "When I was fourteen, there was this guy. Brent. He was one of the few students who would talk to me. Maybe because he was older. He'd been in the army, in Iraq. He'd lost both his legs and was in a wheelchair. He was like a dad to me."

She sniffed again, still hanging on to him. "He was in a lot of pain all the time, but he was so brave. I tutored him for a few math classes. He's the one who talked to me about becoming an emancipated minor. He helped me with the paperwork and went to court with me."

"He sounds like a nice guy," Gideon said, doing his best not to be jealous. She'd said *dad,* not *boyfriend.*

"Brent's the reason I joined the military. I wanted to honor him. Whenever I got scared, I thought about what he would do, what would make him proud." She stepped away and looked around. "If he were still alive, he wouldn't be very impressed with me today."

She drew in a breath. "Not by the mistake — everyone makes mistakes. But because I'm crying over it. Talk about stupid."

He realized several things at once. That from an early age, Felicia had managed to find what she needed emotionally. A mentor here, a father figure there. Justice was like a brother, as was Ford. She might have been abandoned by her parents, but she'd instinctively learned to take care of herself as best she could.

He also understood that she was harder on herself than any soldier he'd ever known.

"Are you right?" he asked.

She turned back to him. "About the festival?" She shrugged. "I know my theories are sound. So if I only consider the logistics, then, yes. But people are harder to quantify. Especially in a setting like this. I didn't take that into account."

"Standing up for what you know is right is the definition of bravery, Felicia. You have to believe in yourself."

She gave him a weak smile. "That's something Brent would have said. It's a soldier thing, right?"

"They beat it into us."

The smile strengthened before fading. "I

don't like that people are angry with me. I'm not used to being questioned. It makes me uncomfortable. Plus, what if I was wrong about the festival? What if I get fired?"

He put his arm around her shoulders. "I'll give you a part-time job at the station. You can work in the file room."

She gave a strangled laugh. "Do you have a file room?"

"No, but I also don't think you're going to be fired, so it's not a big deal."

She leaned against him. "Thank you."

"You're welcome."

She bent down and picked up her tablet.

"Come on," he said, heading toward the food court. "Let's go get an elephant ear. I hear they're tough to find, but worth the effort."

"Here." The tarot woman handed Felicia a pale green T-shirt. "To say thank you and I'm sorry."

Felicia wondered if there was a curse on the shirt. "Okay," she said slowly. "Um, you're welcome?"

The woman smiled. "I had a great festival. You were right about my booth. I got way more traffic. I hadn't realized how many people walked by without stopping because they were eating. This time, I had a line practically all four days. It was great. I'm sorry I was so difficult."

She turned to walk away, then looked back. "Whatever you want to do for next year? I'm up for it."

Felicia smiled at her. "I'm happy to hear that. Thank you."

The woman waved.

Felicia held out the shirt and grinned when she saw all the tarot cards displayed on the front of the shirt. A friendly gesture, she thought happily. Not the first of her Sunday evening, either.

Barely an hour before, two guys from different bands had stopped by to tell her that attendance had been up for their concerts, along with CD and T-shirt sales. Downloads of their music had gone through the roof. Three of the food vendors had wanted her to know they'd nearly doubled their sales from the previous years. There was still friction with the honey booth guy, but no situation was perfect and this was more of a win than Felicia had expected.

Patience and Lillie raced up to her. "Did you hear?" Patience asked. "It's Heidi. She had a girl. We're going to the hospital later to see her. It's the perfect end to a perfect weekend."

"I hadn't heard," Felicia said, thinking she'd only met Heidi a couple of times. The woman had seemed very nice. She had married the previous summer and was now a new mother. "Please tell her congratulations from me. I'm a tiny bit envious of her happiness."

Patience hugged her. "We'll find you someone. Did you go to Denise's booth? You could talk to her about Kent. Unless you're interested in Ford."

"I'm not, but thanks."

"Just as well. Despite her protests, I'm convinced Isabel still has a thing for him." Patience glanced at her engagement ring. "This town is just so magical."

Lillie tugged on her mother's hand. "Mom, we need to get to the hospital."

"You're right." Patience hugged Felicia again. "Come to Brew-haha soon. I want to hear all about your first festival."

"Sure."

They ran off.

Felicia circled the park and checked on the cleanup. The crowd had drifted away, and the booth vendors were busy breaking down their displays and packing them away. People called out to her as she moved by. She greeted them and wished them a safe journey.

She'd done it, she thought happily. Survived her first big event. It hadn't been easy, but she'd only had a mini breakdown and she had more information for next time. She would go a little slower with the changes and explain more. She would get input and then she would move forward.

She had a plan, she thought happily. Always a good thing.

She walked toward the front of the park. Gideon had said he would meet her there. She appreciated that he was checking up on her. She spotted him as she crossed the street, then realized he wasn't alone. There was a boy standing next to him.

The kid was maybe twelve or thirteen, with dark hair and eyes. Neither was unusual, so she shouldn't have found herself staring at the boy. Only there was something about him. Something almost familiar.

She wondered if she'd seen him that day. Or around town. There were so many children in Fool's Gold. He might be a friend of Lillie's or —

Gideon spotted her. His expression of both relief and panic had her walking faster. As she approached, the boy looked at her, too, and smiled.

The smile had her stumbling to a stop. She recognized it. Recognized the shape of his mouth, his eyes.

"You must be Felicia," the boy said. "Gideon was telling me about you. I'm Carter."

Felicia knew, even before he said the words, but still she had to hear them. "Carter?"

"Uh-huh. Gideon's my dad."

CHAPTER ELEVEN

"Your dad?"

Carter shrugged. "Yeah, I know. Weird, right?"

Felicia glanced at Gideon, but he wasn't talking. His gaze seemed locked on the boy, and if his trapped expression was any indication of what he was thinking, she would suspect he was seconds from bolting. A sniper rifle would make sense to him. An attacker would be quickly disabled. But a son?

Carter slipped his hands into his front jeans pockets. "My mom was Eleanor Gates. Ellie. They met when my d— Gideon was stationed in San Diego. He went overseas and then she found out she was pregnant. She always said he was a good soldier and she didn't want to get in the way of that."

Carter looked at Gideon. "Special Ops, right? That's what she said, but she wasn't sure. You didn't talk about it much."

"Need to know," Gideon said, then cleared his throat.

Carter flashed another smile. "And she didn't need to know. Kinda like in the movies. Anyway, she was pregnant and didn't want to get in the way. She said if you wanted to be with her, you'd come back."

The smile faded. "When you didn't, she decided not to put your name on the birth certificate. But she told me. You know, when I was older."

Felicia could hear the words and understand their meaning. But absorbing them was more difficult than she would have thought. Gideon had a son. Even without Carter's story, she could see the physical similarities.

"Where is she now?" she asked, afraid she already knew the answer.

"She died," Carter said simply. "A year ago. My best friend's parents said they'd be my foster parents, so that worked out. I lived with them. Only now they're getting a divorce and moving out of state. Neither of them wanted to take me, so it was find my dad or go into the foster system."

He sounded confident, Felicia thought. But she saw the telltale tremble in the corner of his mouth.

"How old are you?" she asked.

"Thirteen. But I know stuff. I'm not a kid."

"In many cultures you would be considered an adult male by now," she said. "Usually there are rituals to mark the passage from one stage of life to another. Here we consider adulthood to start at age eighteen, although it isn't difficult to become an emancipated minor."

Carter stared at her. "Okay," he said slowly. "You're agreeing I'm not a kid?"

"Not exactly. How did you find Gideon?"

"That was easy." He picked up the backpack at his feet and opened it. "I had his picture and his name. Once I knew about the divorce and having to find a new place to live, I went online and did some research. I'm good at computers and stuff."

"Obviously," Felicia said as she took the picture. It showed a younger version of Gideon with his arms around a pretty brunette. She was smiling with that "in love" glow Felicia had seen in other women but never in her own eyes. She passed the picture to him.

Gideon took it, then nodded slowly. "It's Ellie."

She knew there was no point in confirming the relationship. Carter was obviously related to Gideon. Not that he was prepared

230

to take on a child, she thought. There had to be a next step and she had no idea what it was.

It was nearly eight on a Sunday night. She'd planned to go home and sleep for at least twelve hours. Maybe longer. But what about Carter?

Mayor Marsha walked up and smiled at Carter. "Hello, young man. I'm Mayor Marsha and you're Gideon's son." She held out her hand.

"Carter," the teen said, shaking hands with her. "How did you know I was here?"

"I know everything, Carter. After you've been here a while, you'll accept that." She looked between him and Gideon. "I see the resemblance. Based on your wide-eyed expression, Gideon, I take it you didn't know about Carter."

"No," Gideon said. "I didn't."

"Then you have a lot to take in." The mayor turned to her. "You're exhausted, dear. This has been quite the weekend. But successful. Your first festival went extremely well." She turned back to Carter. "I admire your initiative. However, I'm sure you're aware there are consequences for your actions."

Carter sighed. "I didn't want to go into

the foster care system. You hear stories, you know?"

"I do know. But there are also laws, and you're still a minor. Plus, leaving a note for your guardians isn't going to reassure them."

"How did you know I left a note?"

She smiled. "Didn't you?"

Carter nodded. "I'm not a kid."

"You're a teenager, which is worse. Believe me, I know." She patted him on the arm. "You need a place to stay for the night."

"I have my dad."

"It's not that simple. Here's what I propose. You'll spend tonight with a foster family. I'll let your guardians know that you're safe. In the morning, we'll go see a judge I know. With no father's name on your birth certificate, we'll need to confirm the relationship with a DNA sample."

"Like in the movies?" Carter sounded impressed.

"Exactly like that. You'll get a cheek swab. It's all very high-tech. While the tests are being run, we'll get your father approved as a foster parent. We can figure out the rest as we go."

Carter slung his backpack over his shoulder. His expression turned wary. "I'd rather stay with him now."

Felicia understood that the thought of going to a strange place was frightening. Even if Carter had done it by choice, he didn't know anyone, nor could he believe everything was going to work out.

She thought about offering herself as a foster parent but knew she would have to go through the approval process, just like Gideon. And that couldn't happen on a Sunday night.

"You're not to worry," the mayor said gently. "I think you'll like these foster parents. Pia and Raoul Moreno have three children of their own. Peter, their oldest, was in foster care and they adopted him. Raoul used to be a football player. He was a quarterback for the Dallas Cowboys."

Carter brightened. "For real?"

Felicia nodded. "I know his wife. Pia's very nice. It's just for tonight, Carter." She thought about how to make him feel safer. "I have a prepaid cell phone at the CDS office." She had several, along with weapons and ammunition. Not that Carter would need any of that. "Why don't I activate one and drop it by Pia's house? I'll give you my number. That way if anything happens, you can call me and I'll come get you."

"You'd do that?"

"Of course." She moved close and lightly

touched his shoulder. "You traveled a long way by yourself to find your dad. Now you're here and everything is strange. It's going to take a while until you feel like this is home."

"Thanks," Carter said. He started toward her, then stopped himself. Instead he looked at the mayor. "I'm ready."

"I can see that. Let's go, then. We're going to walk. You'll find we can walk most places in Fool's Gold. Not that boys turning sixteen don't want a car. What is it with a young man's obsession about driving? Can you explain it?"

"Wheels are cool," Carter told her as they rounded the corner.

Felicia waited until their voices had faded, then looked at Gideon. "An unexpected development," she said.

He swore under his breath. "He just . . . showed up at the radio station. I didn't know what to do, so I came here. I can't have a kid. I can't. This is wrong. He can't live with me. What am I supposed to do with him? I'm not that guy. A father?"

He gave a laugh that was more bark than humor. "No," he said flatly. "It's not happening. He can go live with someone else."

Felicia placed her hand on his arm, just above the elbow. She pressed in hard, finding the nerve point that would trigger a more relaxed response in his sympathetic nervous system.

"Did Ellie have any family?"

"I don't remember." He drew in a breath. "I don't think so. She was an only child and her parents were dead. I remember thinking I wasn't the kind of guy she would want to take home, but that wasn't a problem."

He jerked free of her grip. "You can't calm me like some pet, Felicia."

"I wasn't trying to. I want to help, Gideon. You can do this."

"I can't. He needs to find somewhere else to live."

"You're going to put your son in foster care?"

"Better there than with me." He turned away, then faced her again. "I'm not shirking my responsibility. I'm telling you I'm incapable of being what he needs."

"You have plenty of spare bedrooms. That's a start." She thought about Carter and how he acted so brave and together, but inside he must have been terrified. With his mom gone, he was alone in the world. Gideon was his last chance.

"My parents handed me over to the university when I was four," she said quietly. "It took me a long time to understand what that meant. But by the time I was seven, I realized I was completely alone in the world. There was no one. Carter's older, but he's still very much by himself. He needs stability. He needs his father."

Gideon shoved his hand through his hair. "I get nightmares, Felicia. I wake up in a cold sweat, not sure if I'm going to kill someone or have a heart attack and die. A kid? No way. If you're so worried, you take him."

Her chest unexpectedly tightened. A child, she thought longingly. If Carter were hers, she would be delighted to welcome him into her life.

He swore again, then shook his head. He started to walk away, then turned back.

"You're right. I know he's my responsibility. I have to figure this out." He looked at her. "Can you help? Can you stay with me the first few days and get me through this?"

"Of course, but my understanding of parenting is less than yours. You grew up with a mother and father, in a home. You can draw on those memories. I have no working knowledge of that kind of relationship."

"You're a hell of a lot closer to normal than I am. You still have emotions. You feel things. Kids need that."

"You have emotions, too."

"Not the right kind," he said bitterly.

She stepped close and wrapped her arms around him. "I'll be there, for as long as you need me. I promise." She glanced up and smiled. "And when he's asleep, we can have sex."

Gideon gave a strangled laugh. "You're not boring, you know that?"

"I'm glad you think that."

"Wicked," Carter said, walking to the slider and opening it. Once he stepped on the deck, he could see even farther. His dad's house was on the side of a mountain.

He didn't know how high up they were, but all around were trees and mountain peaks and sky.

"Are there eagles?" he asked. "Does it snow up here in winter?"

"There are many different kinds of raptors," Felicia said. "As for snow, the elevation is such that there should be plenty." She looked amused. "Are you asking because you enjoy winter sports or because you're thinking it would mean missing school?"

"Both," he said with a grin. "I'd like to learn how to snowboard. I can surf. Not great, but I like it."

"Then you should have the balance necessary to snowboard. I have trouble with most sports." She leaned close. "I tend to fall a lot," she added in a whisper.

Carter laughed.

Felicia was strange. Totally hot, in a stepmother kind of way. He liked how she talked — all the big words challenged him. She was nice.

He was less sure about his father. Gideon stood across the room, watching, as if afraid to get too close. From what Carter'd been able to find out online, his dad had been through a lot of stuff in the military. Maybe he'd been hurt and wasn't right yet. That would be better than Gideon not wanting him around.

Most days Carter had been able to keep on doing what had to be done. He'd gone to class, done his homework, hung out with his friends. But at night, things were different. When it was dark and he was alone, he missed his mom. He cried, but no one had to know that. She'd been gone a year, and he still missed her. He wanted to feel safe again.

"Okay, your room," Felicia said. "It's back this way."

She walked through the large living room. There were sofas and stuff, but no TV.

"Is there cable?" he asked, wondering what he was supposed to do if there wasn't TV or internet.

"There's a media room downstairs," Gideon said stiffly. "Wi-Fi throughout."

Carter's mood brightened. "Good to know."

Felicia stopped and turned to face him. "Do we have to monitor your internet access?" she asked.

"I'm okay," he told her. "I don't go anywhere I shouldn't."

He did his best to look innocent and young.

Her green eyes gazed at him steadily. "You're thirteen. Biologically, you're dealing with a surge in hormones, stimulating sexual interest. Curiosity is natural. While I respect a quest for knowledge, you're still impressionable. Pornography will give you an unrealistic view of what it's like when a man and a woman —"

He winced. "Could we not talk about this? I know where babies come from."

"I'll need to do more research on the topic."

"Which topic?" He was sure hoping she wasn't thinking they needed to discuss sex.

"Rules and limitations for a boy your age."

"I'm a good kid. Everybody says so."

"I'm sure they do. Let's go see your room."

He followed her down a hallway. The first door on the left led to a large bathroom with a long counter and a big tub/shower combo. They went inside.

"This will be yours," she said, then frowned. "I think we'll have to get you new towels."

"They're fine," he said, pulling open drawers and opening the cupboard door below one of the sinks.

"They're beige." She glanced around. "Everything in this bathroom is beige."

He pointed to the toilet. "It's white."

"What colors do you like?"

"Blue and green. I like the color of your eyes. They're pretty."

He was tall and skinny, but she was taller by a couple of inches. She smelled nice. Like vanilla.

"You're really smart, right?" he asked.

"Yes."

"Supersmart? You went to college and stuff?"

"Yes. I have several advanced degrees."

"More than two?"

Her mouth twisted. "A few more than two."

"So you can help me if I have trouble with

my homework?"

"In every subject."

He grinned. "Except staying on a snow-board."

She laughed. "I don't think that's going to be an assignment."

She lightly touched his arm, then pointed out the door.

They went into the hallway and across to a guest room. It was big, with a large window facing the front of the house. There was a queen-size bed, a dresser and a door to the closet.

"Beige," she murmured.

Carter saw she was right. Beige carpet covered the floor, and a matching comforter draped over the bed. Felicia walked to the window, then back to the bed.

"You have room here for a desk. You'll need that for your homework. Are you too old for toys?"

"Have been for years."

She glanced at his backpack. "Do you have any other luggage?"

He shook his head, embarrassed, but determined not to show it. "I like to travel light."

Her green eyes settled on his face. "Your temporary guardians were too busy with the breakdown of their marriage to realize you needed new clothes and you were too proud to ask."

Heat burned on his face. "Look, I can take care of myself."

"You've done an impressive job, Carter. I grew up without my parents, but I had other adults who saw to all my physical needs. I was book-smart, but I doubt I could have been as innovative as you."

He felt his eyes burning and turned away. He was too old to cry in front of someone. "Yeah, I'm the man."

"It's good," Carter said, after he swallowed.

Felicia took a tentative bite, then nodded. "I agree. The lasagna turned out okay." She sighed in relief. "Recipes often seem designed to defy success. Although I understand directions and follow them, the result isn't always what I expect. Patience promised the recipe was foolproof, but sometimes people exaggerate about that. Or assume I have more ability than I do. People have been bringing casseroles to my office all day to help out while we all adjust to our new situation. So we won't have to completely rely on my cooking."

Gideon glanced down at his plate, wondering how he was supposed to fake eating. Or acting normal. Here he was, at his dining room table with Felicia and Carter. Felicia he could handle, but his kid? Jesus.

He was aware of the tightness in his body. Of the rapid pounding of his heart and the way it hurt to breathe. He needed to run until he couldn't go any farther or simply disappear into the night. Only he couldn't. Not now.

His gaze slid over Carter, then moved away. A son. He was unable to absorb the words or the meaning. If Ellie had told him about the baby before his time in the Taliban prison, maybe he would have felt different about being a father. Then again, maybe he would be dead now because of it. The other men there had crumbled under the torture because the longing for their loved ones had made them weak.

He remembered being held captive. The long nights, the longer days. How they'd beaten him, cut him, hooked him up to a battery until he'd screamed for mercy. One by one, the other men captured with him had given in to the darkness that claimed their souls. They'd died calling out for wives and children. Only Gideon had survived. He'd been able to go into himself, to think of nothing, miss nothing, be nothing. Loving had made the other men weak.

Carter glanced at him. "I saw the media

room. Sweet setup."

Felicia laughed. "I agree. You have an impressive man cave."

Gideon shrugged, unable to think of what he was supposed to say. "You, ah, know how to work everything?"

"Uh-huh." The teen nodded. "I looked over the movies. A lot of action flicks. Some are pretty old, but I'll try them." He looked at Felicia. "No *Sleepless in Seattle* for you."

"I haven't seen that movie," she admitted.

"You should. It was my mom's favorite. Kind of romantic. She always cried at the end."

"Happy crying?" she asked.

Carter stared at his plate and nodded.

Gideon sensed he was uncomfortable, no doubt missing his mother. The past year would have been tough for the kid. He was resourceful, which was good. Smart. Not Felicia smart, but she was in a class by herself.

He wondered what Ellie had told Carter about him. If she'd said much more beyond the fact that he wasn't father material. He wasn't angry with her decision — he agreed with it. Only now he was stuck and he didn't know what he was supposed to do.

He looked at the clock on the wall. It was barely seven, but he knew he couldn't stay much longer. The walls were closing in. He needed time by himself. A chance to disconnect. Only he hadn't eaten and there was Carter.

He reached for his glass of water, saw his hand was shaking, then dropped the arm to his side.

"Gideon, go." Felicia stared at him intently. "You have time before you have to be at the radio station. Go for a run. You can shower at the station afterward."

If he could run, he could breathe, he thought, not sure how she'd figured out what was wrong, but grateful she had. He nodded once and stood. Carter looked at him, but once again he had no idea what he was supposed to say.

Felicia followed him out of the kitchen. In the hallway, she spoke softly. "It will get easier."

He stared into her beautiful eyes. "Thank you," he said, meaning it more than nearly anything he'd ever said. "Thank you for helping. I couldn't do this without you. You're great with him."

She smiled. "I like him. Give it time. You'll like him, too."

"He's not happy to see me," Carter said when she returned to the table.

Felicia wondered if this was one of those moments where it was better to lie. She hadn't expected to have to make parenting decisions so unexpectedly. With a newborn, she would work her way to the more difficult conversations. Now she was thrust in the middle of a situation for which she had no training and minimal instincts.

"He's adjusting," she said. "Your father went through a lot. He was held prisoner for a couple of years."

Carter's dark eyes widened. "No way."

She thought about the scars on Gideon's honed body. "He's still adjusting. It's why he lives out here. So he can be alone."

Carter swallowed. "I shouldn't have come."

"He's your father. You need to be here. But it's going to take a while for the two of you to find your way."

"Are you dating?"

Felicia smiled. "Yes, we're dating." She wasn't going to explain that she'd made a deal with Gideon. "I'm going to stay here for a while. Until you and your father are settled with each other."

Carter stared at Gideon's untouched plate. "That could take a while."

"I have time." She took another bite and

chewed. "I've signed you up for a summer camp."

Carter groaned. "I'm too old for camp."

"It's called End Zone for Kids. Raoul owns it. You said you like him."

Carter smiled. "He was cool."

"Good. Then the camp should be, too. You'll be with teens your age. Making friends is the quickest way for you to feel safe and comfortable in Fool's Gold. You need a peer group."

"Another one of those rites of passage?" he asked, his voice teasing.

"Yes. Plus being in camp will fill your day. You'll have less time to brood."

"I'm a guy. I don't admit I have emotions."

"Already?"

Carter grinned. "Gotta start young if you want to get the cute chicks."

She tried to conceal her horror. "You're not dating yet, are you?"

"No. I'm thirteen."

"You seem mature. I'm going to have to find mothers in town and speak to them about this."

Carter looked panicked. "You're kidding, right?"

"No. I'm very serious. I have no experience with teenage boys. Gideon was one once, but I'm not sure he's comfortable with those memories."

"You're different from other adults I've talked to."

Felicia nodded, accepting that even children knew she was a freak. No wonder Denise Hendrix hadn't wanted her to apply to date her sons. "I've heard that before."

"It's okay. I like how you talk. You don't lie."

"How can you know that?"

He shrugged and collected another piece of lasagna. "I just know. Want to watch a movie after dinner?"

Felicia felt an unexpected warmth in her chest. Acceptance was always gratifying. "I'd like that very much."

Felicia was up before dawn. She hadn't slept much and by four had realized Gideon wasn't going to join her in the large bed in his room. She'd showered and dressed. After checking on Carter, she started coffee, then made her way downstairs to the media room.

Gideon sat on the black sofa, the news on. When she walked into the room, he acknowledged her with a nod.

"Did you sleep at all?" she asked.

"No."

"I'm going to take Carter to camp, then you and I need to go shopping."

"For what?"

"Everything Carter's going to need. A desk, clothes, toys." She drew in a breath. "He says he's too old for toys, but I looked online and there are several interesting options. There's a kit to build a solar power collector. I'd like that."

Gideon finally turned to her. "You want to build something with him?"

"Why not? It will be fun."

His dark eyes were unreadable. She sensed he was afraid but knew he wouldn't want to talk about that, wouldn't want to acknowledge his feelings. Having her around would be enough of an invasion, but a child was so much more. She knew there was damage from his imprisonment but had no way of knowing how much was permanent.

Carter was his son. Would Gideon be able to face that?

"We should drive to Sacramento," he said. "There'll be more selection."

"You'll go with me?"

"Sure. He's not your responsibility."

"I'll make a list," she told him and started to leave.

He called her back.

"Thanks for staying," he said, his gaze intense.

"I like Carter." She liked Gideon, as well, but knew he wouldn't accept the words as support or hear them as a good thing. Her feelings would be one more way he was trapped.

As she went upstairs, she wondered what he'd been like before he'd been captured. Given that he was a sniper and made his living killing people, she knew he would have been intense. But there must have been something lighter about him. Ellie had dated him, maybe loved him. In the picture, she'd been happy and affectionate.

Gideon might have laughed more quickly, gotten involved with the community. He might have trusted more easily. She knew there was no way she could begin to imagine all he'd been through. Torture was not an intellectual exercise. She'd been through mock imprisonments as part of her training. She'd been held in a windowless room, tied up and yelled at. But she'd known it wasn't real, and she'd been unable to summon any real fear.

No one had hurt her. No one had cut her or beat her. She hadn't thought she was going to die. Gideon had spent two years in hell, and that experience would have

250

changed him forever. The question that
remained was how much humanity remained and was it enough, now that he had
a son.

CHAPTER TWELVE

The next morning Felicia signed the paperwork to enroll Carter in the summer camp. Somehow Mayor Marsha had come through, and both Felicia and Gideon were cleared to be emergency foster parents. They'd been given joint custody of Carter until the DNA test confirmed what they all knew. But for the next few weeks, she was a mother, albeit a temporary one.

Dakota Andersson checked the form, then smiled. "Sorry this is going so slowly. Our normal clerk is out sick today, so I'm pulling front-desk duty. I'm not so good with the paperwork." She put the paper down and nodded at Carter.

"You're in. The way our camp works is we divide kids by age, interest and sometimes gender. You'll be with a group of guys who are your age. We have a buddy program. We assign you a fellow camper for the first week so you can meet people and fit in."

Carter leaned against the counter. "What happens on the first day of camp? Isn't everyone new then?"

"They are, which makes the buddy program pretty fun. No one knows where anything is and sometimes both buddies try to be in charge."

Felicia privately thought that was a flawed system, but she decided not to mention that. If Dakota wanted help, she would ask for it.

"Reese Hendrix is going to be your buddy," Dakota said. "He's my nephew, so he has to behave." She looked at Felicia. "He's Kent's son. Have you met Kent?"

"No, but I know who he is. I met your mother when she applied for the booth."

Dakota groaned. "That was not a fun weekend. Ford nearly went through the roof when he found out. Kent and Reese were out of town, so Kent missed the whole thing." She turned her attention back to Carter. "You ready?"

"Uh-huh. I left my lunch in the car. Let me go get it."

Felicia followed him back to her car. "You have the cell phone if you need to reach me. There's coverage up here, although I suspect the counselors frown on personal calls. An emergency is different."

Carter grinned. "I know the rules, Felicia. I've done this sort of thing before."

"That makes one of us."

She gazed at him, at his shaggy hair and disproportionate body. He'd reached the stage of growth where he was all arms and legs. Her chest felt tight again — a not unpleasant sensation.

"Don't worry," he told her. "I'll be fine."

"You're very brave." She paused, wrestling with the truth. "Is it all right if I give you a hug or would you consider it inappropriate?"

He surprised her by stepping close and wrapping his long arms around her. She hugged him back. He was so skinny, she thought. All bones, but strong. As they hung on to each other, she understood that she would do all she could to protect this boy, no matter what.

He stepped back. "Better?" he asked.

She nodded and collected his lunch.

"I'll be back at five," she told him.

He waved and walked toward Dakota. Felicia watched him go, her chest still tight, but this time with too much emotion rather than its usual emptiness.

She might not be very good at the traditional aspects of mothering, but she wanted to learn. And being around Carter made her believe she really had a shot at being like everyone else.

"I told you before," Gideon grumbled. "Beige is a color."

"Not for a thirteen-year-old boy."

Felicia looked at the striped comforter set. The shades of blue were trimmed with a masculine burgundy. The bed skirt was navy, as were the pillow shams. She'd already picked out sheets and a blanket. Next up were towels.

She put the comforter set into the large cart and followed the signs to the bath section of the huge store. She chose yellow towels with a blue trim, then spotted a bath accessory kit.

"I love it!"

Gideon followed her to the shelf. "Isn't he too old for dinosaurs?"

Felicia picked up the brightly colored toothbrush holder. There was a matching trash can and tissue box holder.

"Yes, by several years, but that's not the point. It will make him smile. In a few months we can replace it with something more age appropriate."

"If you say so."

She wasn't sure, but the decision seemed right. Carter would understand that she didn't see him as a little kid, but instead wanted him to feel comfortable. At least that was her hope.

After they paid for the purchases and loaded Gideon's already full SUV, they stopped for lunch before heading back to Fool's Gold.

They were seated in the outdoor patio of a small restaurant. Gideon leaned back in his chair, more relaxed than he had been in the past couple of days.

"You had a good time shopping," he said.

"It's fun. I hope Carter likes everything we got him."

They'd stopped by a toy store where she'd chosen a rocket that was supposed to go several hundred feet in the sky, a couple of science kits, including one that promised a working solar panel, and a book called *The Encyclopedia of Immaturity.* Gideon's picks had been more electronic in nature.

"You're handling this well," he told her.

"It's easier for me. He's not my child. You, on the other hand, just had this dropped in your lap." She paused to enjoy her use of clichés. "It's a lot."

Gideon sipped his iced tea. "I'm fine."

Exactly what Carter had said that morning. She wondered if either of them were telling the truth.

"He seems like a great kid. He's smart and mature. He has a good sense of humor."

Gideon smiled. "Which he got from his mother."

"Was she funny?"

"She was nice. It was a long time ago."

"Any regrets for what you missed?" Felicia asked.

"With Ellie or Carter?"

"Either. Both."

"No regrets. I wasn't cut out for what she wanted."

"Which was?"

"Same as you." His glanced at her. "She was all about getting married and having a family. I was still pretty young and looking to make my mark. A family was only going to slow me down."

"Did you tell her that?"

"Yeah. More than once. I'm not sure she listened."

"From what I've observed, many women don't listen when men tell them the truth. They hear what they want to hear. It's a failing I don't understand." She gave what she hoped was a genuine smile. "One of many. How did you meet Ellie?"

Gideon's mouth twisted. "Some jerkwad hit a dog with his car and kept on driving. I stopped. I could tell the back leg was

257

broken, maybe the hips, too. I picked him up and drove to the nearest vet's office. Ellie was fresh out of vet school. Smart, pretty. I paid for the surgery, but couldn't take the dog. She patched him up and found him a good home. Somewhere in there, I asked her out."

Gideon would have tempted any young woman, Felicia thought. He was strong and handsome, but more than that, he was capable. Back then he would have been more open, would have cared more easily. She wondered if their sexual chemistry had been as powerful, but found she didn't actually want to know the answer. If it was yes, she would be hurt. If it was no, she wouldn't believe him. How irrational. If she accepted the yes as truth, why not the no?

"Why are you smiling?" he asked.

"I'm having a female moment," she said happily. "My thoughts make no sense."

"Why is that a good thing?"

"It's progress. Before long I'll be snapping at you for no reason."

"Lucky me." As he spoke, he reached his hand across the table and took hers. "Thank you. For all you're doing."

"You're welcome. I like Carter. You don't have to be afraid of him."

He started to pull back, but she tightened

her grip.

"It's not him I'm afraid of," he admitted.

She understood that. He would be afraid of himself. Of what he was capable of. Or not capable of.

"You need to try," she told him.

This time he broke free and rested his hand on his lap. His face muscles tightened, and all emotion fled his eyes. She'd upset him, although being a man he would say that word wasn't correct. A human male could be pissed or angry but never upset.

"You're also avoiding me," she said, deciding he was unlikely to drive off without her, and she might as well say it all while he was already irritated. "If you want me out of your bed, simply say so. I can sleep in the guest room."

A muscle twitched in his jaw. "Stay in the damn bed. I'll join you."

She leaned toward him and lowered her voice. "If it makes you feel any better, I won't make any advances. I don't want you to be afraid of me sexually."

She hoped the outrageous statement would get some kind of response from him.

Gideon stared at her for a second, then closed his eyes. "Kill me now," he murmured.

She held in a smile. "I didn't mean to

intimidate you."

"You don't."

"Then why aren't you sleeping with me?"

He made a noise in his throat that sounded very much like a growl. "You want me there, I'll be there."

She did want him there. She wanted him naked and making love with her, but under the circumstances, that might be too much. At this point, she would take what he could offer and wait for the rest.

Their situation had shifted. They were no longer dating. She was fine with that, because what they were doing was even better. They were pretending to be a family.

"Felicia said I should come downstairs and —" Carter came to a stop in the center of the media room.

Gideon glanced up in time to see the teen grin as he picked up the cardboard carton.

"Xbox? You got an Xbox?"

Gideon pointed to the components. "It's the Kinect. We'll try it out after dinner."

"I played at my friend's house," Carter said, dropping to the floor. "It's fun. I can show you."

"Good, because I have no idea how this works." He motioned to a card on the coffee table. "That'll give you some time online. To play with your friends."

"Thanks." Carter picked up the card and studied it. When he put it down, he drew in a breath. "Do you remember my mom?"

Gideon turned so he was facing the cables, even though they were already hooked up. He'd known the question was coming. Even so, he didn't want to answer it. "Sure. I never forgot her. She was great."

"She told me how you met. She said you carried in that big dog even though it was in pain and could have bitten you."

Gideon chuckled. "Yeah, she yelled at me about that. Said I should have known better."

Without meaning to, he glanced at his son. Carter was staring at his hands. "Did you love her?"

Gideon instinctively wanted to surge to the door. He stopped himself in time and stayed where he was.

He knew the correct answer to the question, and he knew the truth. They weren't the same. Felicia would tell him this wasn't about him. That Carter was the one who mattered. For someone who'd never been around children, she seemed to have the instincts of a natural-born mother.

"I loved her," he lied.

Carter looked at him. "But you had to leave?"

He nodded. "I warned her from the beginning that I would be shipping out, and I didn't know how long I'd be gone. I never knew she'd gotten pregnant."

"She told me that. She said she thought about finding you, but by then 9-11 had happened and you would have been sent to war. After a while she stopped talking about you." Carter turned the card over in his hands. "When she got sick a few years ago, she told me your name. You know, in case she didn't make it."

"I'm sorry you had to go through that."

"Me, too. It was cancer. For a while we thought she was going to be fine, but then it came back and she died." He pressed his lips together. "She dated some, but she always said they didn't measure up." He raised his chin defiantly. "She wasn't waiting for you or anything."

Gideon hoped not. He wasn't worth waiting for. Worse, he'd never once thought of going back. Ellie had been in his past.

His son stared at him, as if waiting, as if needing something more. Gideon tried to figure out what he was supposed to say, but there was nothing. After a few minutes Carter got up and walked away, and Gideon was left sitting by himself.

Ford and Angel started up the ropes. Consuelo watched them intently. The two men kept pace with each other, then as they reached the end, Angel surged upward and hit the bell first.

Consuelo groaned. "How is that possible? Angel broke his shoulder years ago. That limits his range of motion. Ford should have won easily."

"Maybe he's distracted," Felicia said. "Or you're wrong about the shoulder."

Consuelo rolled her eyes. "Really? Wrong about it?"

"Sorry," Felicia said, grinning. "I forgot that you're never wrong."

"I can be wrong. Just not about stuff like that." She turned away from the ropes hanging in the outdoor workout center behind CDS. "At least this time the bet wasn't about cooking. I don't think I could stand another week of Ford's idea of gourmet cuisine."

"Pretty bad?"

"He's fine on the barbecue, but everything else is horrible." They headed for the offices. "This competition is getting out of hand. If they keep at it, one of them is going to kill the other. I told them one of them has to move out. They flipped for it. Ford's going to look for a place."

"Does that mean he won or lost?"

Consuelo considered the question, then laughed. "I don't know and I'm not sure if I care. Although Angel is the better cook. The things that man can do with pasta."

A plate of his seafood linguini meant doubling her workouts for a couple of days, but it was worth it.

They stepped inside. The temperature was immediately cooler, the light dimmer. She led the way to the break room and pulled two bottles of water out of the refrigerator.

Felicia studied her. "Don't you find it interesting that you live with two very attractive men and you've never dated either of them?"

"Neither have you."

"I don't know Angel very well, and Ford always thought of me as a sister."

Consuelo raised her eyebrows. "Meaning you would have said yes if he'd asked?"

Felicia tilted her head to the left, then the right. "Maybe when we first met but now I don't have any sexual interest in him."

"He's not my type, either." She wanted something else. Something impossible.

A normal man, she thought wistfully. One who didn't know a Glock from an M-16 and had never had to slit even a single throat in his life. A guy who watched sports on weekends and grumbled about taking out the trash. A man who called his mother every week and remembered birthdays and thought dinner and a movie was a pretty hot date.

Unlikely, she thought. She was sure such men existed, but they had no reason to be interested in her. Not if they knew the truth about her.

"How's it going with Carter?" she asked.

Felicia smiled. "Good. Even if I'm scared I'm doing everything wrong and Gideon spends his time with one foot out the door. This isn't anything he'd planned on."

"No one expects a kid to show up. Women have an advantage with that one. We always know if we have offspring."

"You have brothers," Felicia said. "What did they like to do?"

"Get in trouble. How old is Carter?"

"Thirteen."

Consuelo shrugged. "I'm not the person to ask about this. By the time they were thirteen, each of my brothers had already been arrested."

They'd taken the easy path — joining a gang. She wanted to blame them, but knew she hadn't had to make their choices. As a girl, she'd been able to avoid a lot of trouble. Her interest in getting out of their urban neighborhood had been concealed behind study and reading. Sure, the neighbor kids had thought she was weird, but because she was female, they'd left her alone. Her brothers had been forced to make a choice early. Join a gang or spend every day getting harassed. Sometimes worse. Sometimes kids who didn't fit in got dead.

"Has he made any friends?" she asked.

"He's been up at the summer camp for the past three days. They assigned him a buddy. Reese Hendrix. His grandmother was the one with the booth."

"I remember," Consuelo said. Reese's father had been the handsome man with the kind eyes.

Felicia sipped her water. "Are you still thinking about offering a self-defense class for people in town? What if you had a class for kids his age? I'm sure it would be popular, and then he could meet his fellow students before the school year begins. That would help a lot. I know how difficult it is not to fit in."

Consuelo groaned. "That's a lot of guilt in only a couple of sentences."

"Did I make you feel guilty?" Felicia

asked, sounding delighted. "I wasn't try-ing."

"That makes it worse. You were stating the truth as you know it. Come on. Let's go look."

They walked out of the break room and into the largest office. There were several desks pushed together, along with a big dry erase calendar on the wall.

"Yes," she said, crossing to it. "We're do-ing this the old-fashioned way."

Felicia winced as she stared at it. "Why isn't this on the computer? There are several excellent scheduling programs that could —"

"Spare me," Consuelo told her. "I don't do office and I don't want to hear about it. If you find this painful, talk to the boss."

She pointed to the column with her name. "I'm free on Tuesday evenings. Let's sched-ule it then. Get the word out and let me know when to be here. I'll teach them all how to kill each other."

Felicia wrinkled her nose. "That was humor, wasn't it? You wouldn't actually teach thirteen-year-olds how to kill each other."

"Only if they get on my nerves."

Carter sat at the picnic table, his lunch

unwrapped in front of him. Reese Hendrix was across from him. They'd already exchanged sandwiches and discussed getting ice cream when they were back in Fool's Gold.

"Have you always lived here?" Carter asked his new friend.

"Nah. We moved here a couple of years ago. After my mom split, my dad wanted to be closer to family. Mostly for me, I think. I have a bunch of aunts and an uncle." He grinned. "Two uncles, now that Ford's home."

"Your mom left?"

Reese nodded, then took a bite of his sandwich. "One day she was gone. My dad was pretty broken up about it. He didn't date or anything for a long time. He was waiting for her to come back."

Carter had also grown up without a parent, but he'd never expected his father to return.

"You don't see her on weekends and stuff?"

Reese put down his sandwich. "Never. She doesn't remember my birthday or anything. My dad tries to say she still loves me, but I know the truth. She bailed and it's done."

"I'm sorry."

Reese shrugged. "Whatever. I'm over it."

Carter thought his friend was probably lying, but wasn't going to call him on it.

"I didn't know who my dad was for a long time," he said. "When my mom got sick, she gave me his name so I could find him if something happened to her. She'd made arrangements for me to live with some friends, but they weren't adopting me." He thought about how they'd divorced and he'd been put into the foster system.

"You found him by yourself?" Reese asked. "Wicked."

"It wasn't that hard. With his name and knowing he was in the military, it was a pretty easy search." He gave a halfhearted grin. "It was harder to find Fool's Gold on a map."

"Yeah, the town is pretty small, but it's okay here. There's lots to do and we can go out by ourselves. I've only seen your dad a couple of times at festivals and stuff. He seems cool."

"He's okay," Carter said. "Felicia's nice. She likes to take care of me."

He was probably too old to allow much of that, but he liked her fussing. She worried he was eating enough and eating the right stuff. She'd done over his bedroom and the bathroom.

"She bought me this dinosaur trash can

and toothbrush holder for the bathroom," he said. "Little kid stuff. She said it was to make me laugh and we'd get something better later."

Reese grinned. "Is it funny?"

"Yeah, it is."

"You get along with your dad?"

"I don't know. He's busy a lot." Avoiding being at home, Carter thought. He wasn't sure what was Gideon's deal. If he didn't like all kids or just didn't like Carter. Either way, it was uncomfortable.

"You gonna stay around?" Reese asked.

Carter nodded. The truth was, he didn't have anywhere else to go. A thought that terrified him. But he was a guy, and he wasn't allowed to tell anyone that. He probably shouldn't even admit it to himself.

His friend handed him a chocolate chip cookie. "It could be worse," he said with a sigh. "Your dad could be a math teacher. Let me tell you, that does not make homework time fun."

CHAPTER THIRTEEN

Patience looked at the rack of white dresses. "This is silly. I shouldn't be here. I was married before."

"Very few women are virgins when they marry," Felicia said.

Patience stared at her. "Thank you for that interesting fact, but what does it have to do with anything?"

"I thought you were concerned about wearing white and how it represents innocence and virginity. Your previous marriage and, of course, your child would preclude anyone from assuming . . ."

Felicia stopped talking. Patience was staring at her as if she'd sprouted several heads like the mythical Hydra.

She mentally backtracked, searching for another reason why Patience would worry about buying a wedding gown. She was engaged, so it wasn't that she didn't expect to have a wedding in her future. She doubted there was a money issue. While Patience might not have a huge financial cushion, Justice had made large sums while working for his previous company. So it wasn't financial.

"You're thinking a second wedding should be smaller?" she guessed. "Not a big wedding gown event?"

Patience relaxed. "Exactly. I don't know if I'm being silly."

"It's Justice's first wedding," Felicia pointed out. "Won't the larger event make him feel special?"

She glanced around, hoping to be rescued by someone. Anyone. Reassurance wasn't her forte. But Isabel had run home to deal with a plumber, and there were no other staff on duty right now. Felicia had promised to explain that Isabel would be right back to any customers who might wander in.

Patience sighed. "You're right. He's talked about a big wedding, and I secretly want one. I guess I think I don't deserve it."

"Why not? You're getting married to a wonderful man who loves you. I would think a celebration is called for."

"Thank you. That was exactly what I needed to hear." She pulled a dress off the rack and studied the lace. "I like this one. Maybe I should try it on." She put the dress

272

back, then turned to Felicia. "But watching me look at dresses isn't why you wanted to talk to me, is it?"

Felicia shook her head. "I wanted to talk to you about Carter."

"Gideon's son? I haven't met him yet, but Lillie says he's really cute and all the girls have a crush on him. Lillie's only ten, so she still thinks boys are a little bit weird. For which I'm grateful, by the way. I know the teen years will be here soon enough." Patience motioned to the padded chairs by the mirror and took a seat. "What do you want to talk about?"

"I'm not sure," Felicia admitted. "I'm staying with Gideon for a few weeks, to help Carter settle in."

Staying in the master bedroom by herself, she thought. Despite her talk with Gideon, he had yet to join her in bed. When he got home from the radio station, he paced through the house. She'd see him walk through the bedroom a few times and knew he was barely sleeping at all.

"I want to make sure I'm doing everything right," she said.

Patience laughed. "With Carter? That's your question? How to do everything right?"

Felicia tried to ignore the laughter. "Yes."

"Oh, honey, that's not possible. No one

gets it right all the time."

"You do. Lillie is extremely well-adjusted. She's happy and bright, with excellent socialization."

"Thank you, but I can't take too much credit. She's a good kid and I've had my mother to help. Sometimes I get it right, and sometimes I screw up royally. We all do. In your case, you have a bigger challenge."

Felicia understood that. "He's not my child and neither of us know him. He's out of his element. From his perspective, he has no support structure, no one he can trust. Although his mother's been gone a year, I'm sure he's missing her a lot. He feels alone and unloved."

Patience blinked at her. "Okay, then. You're clear on his problems. What do you think of Carter personally?"

Felicia thought about the teen. "I like him. He's very resourceful and fun. From what I can tell, he has an excellent character and he's intelligent." She smiled. "He's much more socially normal than I am." She paused. "We hugged. I found the moment meaningful."

"I'm sure he did, too. However tall he is and socially capable, he's still a kid who's all alone. I would say, be on his side and let him know it. Be consistent. Knowing and understanding the rules will help him settle in. You want to have fun together, but also give him some space. This has to be overwhelming."

All things Felicia could do. It was the emotional connection that had her worried.

"How's Gideon holding up?" Patience asked quietly.

"This is hard for him. He's avoiding Carter." *And me,* she thought, but she wasn't going to say that. "He had no idea he had a child, and to have Carter show up with no warning . . . It's difficult. I worry that Carter will feel rejected."

"Sure. That makes sense. You don't want to push it, but try to get them to hang out together. Casual stuff where they're in the same room."

"Maybe a movie tonight." Felicia thought about the possibilities. "One they'll both like."

"Or one they won't," Patience said with a grin. "Give them something to bond over. A reason to roll their eyes together."

"Maybe an animated film," she said, pleased with the idea. "There are several I've wanted to see."

"That would work."

"Thank you. You're really good at this."

"I have a little more practice," Patience

said. "That's all."

"Are you and Justice going to have children together?"

Patience flushed. "Wow. Always with the direct questions."

"I'm sorry. Was that inappropriate?"

"No, just unexpected. To be honest, we haven't talked about it very much, but I would like to have children with him. I never meant to only have one. Lillie has made it clear she would like a brother or sister. Or both."

"Justice would worry that he has too much of his father in him to procreate. That he would pass along something bad. I believe in his case nurture is the more powerful influence. I could get you some articles, if you'd like them."

"Maybe they would help," Patience said, then smiled. "You're always so nice to me."

"I enjoy your company. You've been friendly and kind since I arrived, and Justice loves you."

"Because you and Justice are close. I should probably admit I didn't like you very much when you arrived in Fool's Gold."

Felicia felt her eyes widen. "Why?"

"You're so beautiful," Patience grumbled. "I mean, look at you. And then I found out you were really smart and you'd worked with Justice for years. I assumed you two had, well, you know."

"Been sexually intimate?"

Patience made a strangled sound in her throat. "Right. You're so good at reminding me to simply state the truth. Okay, yes. I was afraid you'd slept with him, and I could never measure up to all that perfection."

"The success of sexual relationships between people who care about each other is much more mental than physical. While technique can make things interesting, the emotional connection is far more important."

"I'm unmoved by your facts," Patience said, her tone teasing.

"Because your feelings are irrational. I go crazy when I see a spider, so I know what you mean." She leaned forward. "We never had sex. Justice and I are like family. We love each other — just not that way."

Felicia told herself not to mention that she'd begged Justice to sleep with her four years ago. Explaining she'd wanted the experience and not a relationship wouldn't make Patience feel any better. Besides which, Justice had refused and nothing had happened. She was learning some things were best left unsaid.

"Wow," Patience said happily. "If you're

like his sister, that makes you my sister-in-law. I'm getting a bigger family and you are, too."

Felicia stared at her as the truth of those words sank in. Belonging, she thought, stunned. It was really happening to her. Perhaps Patience would even ask her to be one of her bridesmaids. Felicia had never been in a wedding before.

"Are you okay?" Patience asked. "Was that the wrong thing to say?"

"No," Felicia said, smiling and feeling the need to cry all at the same time. "It was exactly the right thing to say."

"We're going to have movie night," Felicia said, holding up the Blu-ray feature she'd purchased that afternoon.

Gideon leaned against the kitchen counter. "Are you asking me or telling me?"

"Telling you."

He looked at the package. "It's a cartoon."

"It's animated. There's a difference."

"Not to me. If we have to watch a movie, can't we see one with a lot of car chases and shoot-outs?"

She would have assumed he'd seen enough violence for more than one lifetime, but he was a guy. Those kinds of movies generally had a specific outcome. Emotional

278

drama could be ambiguous, which most men found unsatisfying. It was why so few of them enjoyed foreplay without promise of orgasm. Not that Gideon had been seeking either from her.

"This will be fun," she told him. "And that was also an announcement."

"Can we negotiate?"

"No. I researched movies online. This one received excellent reviews and the themes are significant to our situation." She stepped closer and gazed into his eyes. "Please?"

He could have stepped to the side and escaped her. Instead he stayed where he was, his hands braced on the counter behind him. "Using your feminine wiles to convince me?"

"I'm trying," she admitted. "I don't think my wile skills are above average, but I'm hoping you'll overlook that."

She looked at his face, at the handsome lines. There were a few small scars, but they only added to his appeal. She could see part of a tattoo at the sleeve of his T-shirt. She knew about other marks and scars on his body and felt a flicker of desire. Heat and need burned through her, and she very much wanted to make love with him right that second.

But there was Carter to consider, not to

mention the fact that Gideon didn't seem overly interested in pursuing their chemistry right now. Probably because of everything going on, she thought. Having a son changed everything.

"You don't have to be afraid," she said, without thinking.

Gideon stiffened and slid away. "Let's go watch the movie."

She grabbed his arm, feeling hard muscles tighten under her grip. "I'm sorry. I shouldn't have said that. Challenging your masculinity is only going to make you more defensive and less trusting. You'll focus on what you have to prove rather than the situation at hand."

One dark eyebrow rose. "This is your way of making it better?"

"Too much analysis?"

"Oh, yeah."

"Are you angry?"

"I should be, but I'm cutting you a break. Mostly because I owe you."

She breathed a sigh of relief. Crisis averted. "So that's why you're not huffing and puffing about what I said?"

"Huffing and puffing?"

She smiled. "It's an accurate description."

"You're cute when you're intellectual."

She laughed. "I'm intellectual a lot."

"Yes, you are."

He rotated his arm, moving his hand up and around. Before she realized what he was doing, he'd pulled her against him, trapping the movie between them.

"You have too much free time," he murmured. "It's the smart thing. I read a short story years ago about a society where everyone was supposed to be equal. So the really strong guy had to walk around with a door strapped to his back."

"Carrying around a door wouldn't make me any less smart," she told him, aware of his body so close to her own. Of the heat of him and how she felt as if her insides were melting. They weren't, of course. But the sensation was pleasant.

"You'd figure out some kind of device to help carry the weight of the door," he murmured, lowering his head just a little.

"I would think my time would be better spent overthrowing such a ridiculous government."

"I'd help."

He kissed her. She'd hoped he would, and now she lost herself in the feel of his warm, strong mouth on hers.

His lips teased hers, almost nibbling her sensitive skin. She parted, wanting him to deepen the kiss. He obliged, slipping his tongue inside.

She wrapped her free arm around his neck and let her body sink into his. He moved his hands up and down her back, awakening need everywhere he touched.

She was aware of blood rushing to her breasts, of how they were suddenly more sensitive. Especially her nipples. She wanted him to touch her there, to tease her with his fingers, then use his mouth to suck and lick. The image made her insides clench. Sexual hunger made her uncomfortable with its intensity.

He lifted his hands to her shoulders and gently pushed her away. She opened her eyes.

"What?" she asked, when she really meant, "Why are you stopping?"

"The, ah, movie."

His low voice was thick and husky. She looked down and saw he was fully aroused. They could do it right here, she thought, thinking the counter height would be workable. He could —

She jumped back and sucked in a breath. The movie fell to the floor. "Carter."

"Right."

"I forgot." She'd been so lost in how Gideon made her feel, she'd forgotten there was a child in the house. "I'm a horrible person.

I need to be responsible and I forgot."

Gideon adjusted the front of his jeans, then looked at her. "You kissed me. It's not like you let him burn down the house."

"Carter's too responsible to burn down the house." She slapped her hand over her mouth.

"What?" he asked.

"I imagined us having sex on the counter."

Gideon stepped toward her. "You did?"

"We can't do that. Not with him here. He could have walked in on us. He's going through enough without having to deal with that visual." She closed her eyes. "I'm not ready to be a mother."

"Sure you are. You enjoyed kissing me. That's not a crime."

"I forgot."

"For ten seconds."

"That's all it takes for disaster to strike."

He lightly touched her cheek. "Don't you think you're being a little irrational?"

"Yes," she admitted. "I feel guilt. I'm overcompensating to distract myself from the guilt, which makes me uncomfortable. I do know that Carter is perfectly capable of taking care of himself for several hours at a time. While having a sexual encounter in the middle of the day in an open kitchen would be wrong, our kissing wouldn't be detrimental to him."

His gaze was steady. "But?"

"But I still feel guilty."

"Welcome to how the other half lives."

"You feel guilty?" she asked, surprised.

"Everyone does. We're not doing enough, we're doing too much. Hell, I feel guilty for not spending more time with Carter."

"So why don't you spend more time with him?"

When he just looked at her instead of answering, she understood. The fear. For what was taken and what had been left. For the kind of man he'd become. For all the things he thought he couldn't do and those he didn't want to do. Fear bred guilt which caused Gideon to withdraw.

"I feel guilty about you, too," he admitted.

That surprised her. "Why?"

"You're doing so much. I really appreciate how you've stepped in to handle a lot of this."

"I want to. I like him."

"He likes you, too."

Words that pleased her. "We should watch the movie," she said.

Gideon shook his head. "You go ahead. I'll catch up with you later."

Which meant he was leaving. "Why? You

284

were just laughing. We kissed. It was nice."

Something flashed through his dark eyes. Whatever he was experiencing emotionally, it wasn't pleasant.

"I'll be out on the deck," he told her, and then he was gone.

Felicia made her way down to the media room. Carter was reading one of Gideon's car magazines. He looked at the Blu-ray case in her hand.

"What are we watching?" he asked.

She showed him.

He groaned. "A cartoon."

"It's animated. There's a difference."

"Can we see something with car chases and bad guys and stuff?"

Which was almost exactly what Gideon had said. "This is better."

Carter grumbled something under his breath, but he turned on the TV and Blu-ray player and slipped the disc in place. Then he joined Felicia on the sofa as *Despicable Me* began.

She hadn't been sure she would enjoy the animated feature very much. Sometimes children's movies were too simplistic for her tastes. But the story of a man inadvertently discovering what it means to love and to create a family touched her more than she expected.

Partway through, she paused the movie to go get the brownies she'd baked earlier. Carter followed her up to the kitchen.

"Gideon left?" he asked.

"He's outside. He needs to be alone right now. He'll come back before his shift at the radio station." She paused, wanting to say Gideon wasn't avoiding him on purpose, only he was. She didn't like lying and felt it served no purpose. Carter would easily guess the truth.

She put brownies onto a plate. "Do you want a glass of milk?" she asked.

"I'll get it."

While he poured milk for himself, she put ice in a glass and then filled it with tea. They carried everything back down to the media room.

They sat next to each other on the sectional. Carter reached for the remote, but instead of resuming the movie, he turned to her.

"Why don't you have kids?" he asked.

The question surprised her. "I haven't been in a serious relationship," she admitted. "I understand that it's not technically necessary to be married to have a child, but I had hoped to follow that traditional path."

"Had hoped?"

"I still want to fall in love and get married." She nodded as an unexpected truth made itself known. "Either way, I want to have children. I want a family."

"You'll be a good mom," Carter told her.

She was less sure. "I don't know very much about raising a child. I don't have the advantage of having learned things from my own parents."

He reached for a brownie. "You have good instincts. You remind me of my mom, a little. She told me how things were. She didn't lie 'cause I was a kid. We were a team, you know? You'd be like that."

Felicia swallowed, her throat tight. "Thank you for the compliment. It's very meaningful."

He shrugged. "Having me show up like I did wasn't easy. But you've been right here the whole time. Not everyone would have done that." He picked up the remote. "The movie's pretty good. I like Gru, and the minions rock. I wish we could build some robots."

"They're not robots," she said. "They're life-forms. Ignoring the moral implications, ownership of life-forms destined to servitude fundamentally weakens a society."

Carter's eyes twinkled. "You're saying it's wrong."

"Extremely." She took in the twitch at the

corner of his mouth. "You're teasing me."

"You make it easy."

She sighed. "Just you wait. One day I'll be like everyone else."

He started the movie and flopped back against the sofa. "I hope not."

An hour later, Gru and his three new daughters had found happiness together. Carter put the disc back in the case, then turned off the TV and the player.

"That wasn't so bad," he admitted. "But next time, I get to pick."

"It's a deal." She stood. "You're going up to your room?"

He nodded, then stepped close to her. His long, skinny arms hugged her tight. She held on as well, feeling protective and caring at the same time. When he stepped back, she knew she was in danger of crying but couldn't for the life of her figure out why.

Gideon's feet hit the ground in a steady rhythm. The pace was challenging, and he knew he would be feeling the aftereffects in the morning. His regular workouts had been confined to a gym with a few miles on the treadmill and then weight lifting. Neither had prepared him for a run up the side of the mountain.

"Let's go, ladies," Angel yelled, and darted ahead.

"You live with that guy?" Gideon asked, then sucked in a breath.

"Not for much longer," Ford admitted, his breathing just as deep. "The competition's getting old. We work great together, but sharing a house is too much. Last week I beat him at arm wrestling, which he didn't like. Consuelo walked in on us trying to work out our differences, and I thought she was going to castrate both of us. I'm going to look for my own place."

"Angel and Consuelo will continue to share the house?"

"Sure. She does fine with either of us."

Gideon managed a grin. "If you can't be the solution, be the problem."

"You got that right."

The path shifted, heading nearly straight up. Gideon inhaled, then took the steep trail at a run. When he reached the top, he was gasping for breath, dripping sweat, but rewarded by a view of mountains that stretched on for what seemed like forever.

Except for his buddies' breathing, it was quiet. Even the hawk circling overhead moved silently as it searched for prey. Angel sprawled on the rocky ground. Due to a bet Gideon hadn't been part of, he was wearing a backpack. He opened it now and passed out bottles of cold water. Gideon drank nearly half of his in a single gulp, then sank down onto the flat top of the mountain.

The temperature was much cooler up here. It was hot down in Fool's Gold, but he was okay with that. Moving to the town had turned out to be a good decision. Without Felicia around to pick up the slack with Carter, he didn't know how he'd make it.

He finished the rest of his water, then stretched out on his back. No point in lying to himself, he thought. Felicia wasn't picking up the slack — she was doing all of it.

Angel sat up and stared at him. "What?" he demanded. "You look like you're about to take a bullet."

Gideon closed his eyes. "Shut up."

"I'm not the one making that face."

Gideon shook his head. "It's not a bullet. It's the kid."

Angel must have mouthed a question because Ford whispered, "His kid. The one who showed up."

"You really didn't know about him?" Angel asked. "I thought that was just some bullshit I was hearing."

"I really didn't know about him." Hadn't had a clue.

"If it had to happen anywhere, better here," Ford said. "The town is safe, he can't get lost. Carter's making friends."

"What? Is there a town gossip column?" Angel asked.

"My nephew told me. Reese. He met Carter up at camp and they're hanging out together. Reese is a good kid. His dad, Kent, is a math teacher."

Angel snickered. "Seriously? Your brother?"

There was a brief tussling sound, followed by a groan and silence. Gideon didn't bother opening his eyes.

"You handling it?" Ford asked.

As he was the one speaking, Gideon was going to guess he'd won the fight. "Not even a little."

"It's gotta be hard for both of you," Ford said. "I remember when my dad died. I was a year out of high school. My sisters were still in school and Kent was away at college. Ethan had to take care of everything. Mom fell apart. It was a tough time. Nothing made sense."

Gideon opened his eyes and glanced at his friend. "I'm sorry."

"It was a long time ago."

Angel sat up. "I was a kid when I lost my mom. Too young to remember much. My dad was a mess, though. I remember him being sad. I lived in a small town, a little like Fool's Gold. People stepped in to take care of things."

Gideon wasn't sure what he was supposed to do with the information. Everybody suffered. Life was hard. None of which helped him deal with Carter. His bottom line was he'd seen what caring did to people.

"What are you going to do about Carter?" Angel asked.

"Hell if I know. There's nothing *to* do. He's my kid. I'll deal."

One way or the other.

He wanted to tell himself it would get easier with time, but he wasn't sure he believed that.

CHAPTER FOURTEEN

Felicia woke to the absence of sound. She was alone in the big bed in Gideon's room. She rolled over and saw it was nearly three in the morning. Gideon should be back from the radio station by now, but once again he'd decided to sleep somewhere else. Assuming he slept at all.

He'd gone running with Angel and Ford the day before. She'd hoped hanging out with his friends would help, but he'd been distant afterward. She wanted things to be better between him and Carter, but didn't know how to facilitate any changes in their relationship.

She turned on a lamp and used the restroom, then decided she was going to find Gideon. If nothing else, he needed to sleep. She brushed her teeth and combed her hair, then pulled a short robe over her thigh-length summer nightgown. With Carter in the house, she didn't think it was a good idea to walk around partially undressed.

She passed through the living room and made her way out to the deck. Gideon was stretched out on one of the lounge chairs. She knew he was aware of her approaching, but he didn't bother to look at her. Instead, he stared up at the stars.

"Ever been to the Southern Hemisphere?" he asked, still studying the sky. "It's all different down there." He looked at her. "Feel free to give me a lecture on the placement of various star clusters. I'm also interested in your thoughts on the expansion of the universe."

She looked into his eyes. In the darkness of the night, she couldn't tell what he was thinking, but she felt his pain. It radiated out from him, warning her he was a wounded animal and she should do her best to keep herself safe. Only she wasn't interested in safe. Not with Gideon. She wanted to help, and barring that, she wanted to be near him. He was avoiding Carter, and by avoiding his son, he was avoiding her.

She grabbed his hand and tugged. He was big enough and strong enough that she wouldn't be able to get him to move without his cooperation. Not unless she used some warrior moves she'd been trained for. Luckily he cooperated and rose to his feet.

"What?" he asked, staring into her eyes.

There were dozens of things she could have said, but suddenly none of them mattered. She continued to hold on to his hand as she drew him inside, then led him to the master bedroom.

Once there, she closed the door and locked it, then dropped her robe on the floor. Her nightgown quickly followed. She slipped out of her panties, then waited.

One eyebrow rose. "Direct," he said, his voice low and velvety.

"I'm not very good at games," she told him, willing to wait him out.

"You're very good at games. You win all of them."

She smiled. "Regular games. Not the boy-girl kind."

He didn't smile back. He cupped the side of her face, then slid his fingers through her hair. From there he trailed his way down her back. When he reached the top of her hip, he slid down the curve, across her belly and up the center of her ribs.

Heat followed him, burning her skin and making her want to squirm. But she forced herself to stay completely still, letting him take charge. When his hand closed over her breast, he leaned in and kissed her.

The combination of his mouth on hers

and his fingers stroking her breast aroused her to the point where she couldn't think. An unusual but appealing circumstance. Sensation ruled. The insistent, erotic stroking of his tongue against hers, the light whisper of teasing as he gently squeezed her tight nipple before rubbing it. She went from aroused to desperate in the space of a second and wrapped her arms around his neck.

As she pressed against him, wanting to feel his body against hers, he began to explore her. He ran his hands up and down her back before squeezing her butt. She arched against him, bringing her belly in contact with his erection. Muscles clenched as she imagined how much she would enjoy having him push inside her.

He withdrew slightly and kissed his way along her jaw. When he reached the sensitive skin below her ear, he licked and she moaned. She reached for his shirt — one with buttons down the front — grabbed firmly and pulled. She applied just enough pressure to cause the fibers to rip and buttons to pop.

Gideon straightened and looked down at his now-destroyed shirt. "You could have asked," he said with a slow, sexy grin. "I would have taken it off."

"I'm asking now. And not just the shirt."

"Demanding."

"I think I'd be comfortable taking charge, if that arouses you."

"Maybe later."

He quickly stepped out of his jeans and boxers. The shirt fluttered to the floor, and he was naked.

She immediately reached for his penis, wanting to touch him. The tangible proof of his arousal excited her nearly as much as the physical contact. Although she would be hard-pressed to say that it was better than having him stroke her breasts. Or kiss them. Or lick her clitoris. If she had to put the three of them in order, she would have to admit that —

Gideon swore under his breath, then pushed her toward the bed.

"You can't do that," he growled.

"Do what?"

"Look at me like that."

"I was looking at your penis."

"Same thing."

He drew back the covers and urged her onto the mattress. After pulling open the nightstand drawer, he tossed a couple of condoms next to the lamp and joined her on the bed. As soon as he was horizontal, he drew her against him, holding her tight and kissing her deeply.

She savored the feel of his tongue circling hers as much as the pressure of his strong body next to hers.

Anatomy was so interesting, she thought. His chest was sculptured in a completely different way than hers. The basics were similar but the execution created so many erotic possibilities. She loved the feel of her breasts flattening against him. The light dusting of hair tickled. Their legs slid so easily together, his slipping between hers.

He gently eased his knee up until it rested against her vulva. Instinctively she tilted her hips, bringing her in more direct contact. She began to rock back and forth, but it wasn't enough.

She moved her hands up and down his muscled back. She felt frantic. Desperate. Hunger burned, and finally her mind began to shut down. There was only need and what he could do to her.

She drew back. "Gideon," she said, gazing into his eyes. "Would you please lick my clitoris?"

His mouth turned up in that slow, sexy grin of his. "With pleasure," he murmured, already shifting to his knees.

He nudged her onto her back and pressed his lips against her collarbone. From there he trailed his way down her chest. She closed her eyes. He licked between her breasts before pausing. She waited, not sure what was next but confident she would enjoy it. He didn't disappoint.

He touched his tongue to one breast, then the other. While the ripples of pleasure were still coursing through her, he settled his mouth over her left nipple and sucked. As he drew in the tight tip, he used his tongue to circle and tease.

She found herself clutching at the sheets with her fingers and breathing more quickly. She'd passed through the stages of arousal with great speed and now found herself hovering on the edge of an orgasm. Her muscles were tense, and she was swollen.

Before she could tell him, he abandoned her breasts and continued his journey down her belly. Lower and lower until he'd reached the very heart of her.

She parted herself for him and waited. A whisper of warm breath was her only warning before his tongue lightly stroked her clitoris.

She groaned. She parted her legs as wide as they would go, then bent her knees and dug her heels into the bed. Nerve endings fired in a sequence designed to fill her with pleasure, and it worked. She was helpless, close to begging.

He licked her again, then circled her swollen center. Slowly at first, slow enough that she could catch her breath with each cycle, then faster. Her body became a symphony, each muscle an instrument tuned for exquisite pleasure. He played her, making her gasp as she drew closer and closer to her climax.

Suddenly he stopped. She was so close, she thought.

"Gideon," she breathed.

His mouth returned, but this time he sucked, drawing in her clit, even as he thrust two fingers inside her.

She came with a scream, her body surrendering to him and the moment. Shudders took over, and she could only do as he bid, coming and coming until there was nothing left. Only then did he sit up.

"I always have these big plans," he said, reaching for the condom. His hands shook as he tore the wrapper and slid on the protection. "How I'm going to go slow and make it last. But how the hell is that supposed to happen when you come like that?"

She didn't think he expected an answer to his question, which was good, because before she could think of one, he'd already thrust inside her.

He filled her completely, only to withdraw and fill her again. His pace was nearly frantic, his breathing already fast. He gazed into her eyes, pumping harder, faster. Over and over until he came.

Later, when they were under the covers, he pulled her close. He wrapped his arms around her as he had before, holding on as if he would never let go. If only, she thought.

"Felicia?"

"Yes?"

"I probably shouldn't tell you this, but if it ever seems I'm not in the mood for sex, all you have to do is ask me to lick you and I'm done."

She raised herself on one shoulder. "I don't understand."

"It's the sexiest thing ever."

"But I'm just asking for what I want."

"Yeah, and it turns me on."

Men were strange, she thought, settling back into his arms. "What about if I asked you to rub my back?"

"Not as interesting." She felt as well as heard him chuckle. "Now if you asked for a spanking, that might work."

She smiled. "Especially if I told you I'd been very, very bad?"

"Oh, yeah."

■ ■ ■

The CDS logo, a target with the initials spelled out in bullet holes, was enough to make a guy think before entering the building. Carter had a feeling they didn't take any crap in this place. He wasn't nervous, exactly. Just . . . cautious.

Reese studied the closed door. "They're serious, huh?"

"Felicia knows the guy in charge. Justice. He's not running the class or anything but she likes him."

They glanced at each other. Carter shrugged and reached for the handle.

Inside, the ceilings were high, the floors concrete. A tall man with big shoulders, scary gray eyes and a scar across his throat was waiting in the foyer.

"Names," he barked.

Carter did his best not to jump.

"Reese Hendrix!"

"Carter, ah —" Carter hesitated, not sure what last name Felicia would have used.

The man glared at him. "You don't know your name? Then we can't help you."

Carter swallowed. "I just got to town. My dad is Gideon Boylan. I didn't know how Felicia registered me for the class."

The man smiled. "That Carter, huh? I've got you right here. Good to meet you." He held out his giant hand. "Nice to meet you both."

The transformation to nice guy was nearly as frightening as the scowl had been.

"Nice to meet you, too," Carter said in a small voice, shaking hands with the man. Reese did the same.

"I'm Angel. You got any questions, come see me. You're going to work out in the main fight room. It's this way."

He led them through several short hallways. They stepped out into a big open gym with punching bags along one wall, ropes dangling from the ceiling and a big area in the middle covered with thick, padded flooring.

Angel looked at his watch. "You've got about ten minutes, if you want to stretch."

Reese nodded and Angel left.

Carter leaned toward his friend. "You know how to stretch?"

"No, but I wasn't going to tell *him* that. Did you see his scar?"

"The one on his neck? Yeah. You think someone tried to kill him?"

"I don't know."

They sat on the edge of the mats.

"I wonder how many other kids'll come to

the class," Reese said.

Carter didn't know enough guys his age to guess. Although there could be girls in the class. He wasn't sure how he felt about that. He wouldn't be comfortable fighting a girl.

"Felicia's picking us up when we're done here," he said, to change the subject. "She's busy getting ready for the book fair this weekend, but said she had time to take us to lunch."

"You still doing okay with her?" Reese asked.

"Yeah, she's cool. It's harder with my dad. He mostly avoids me."

"They're not married?"

"No. They're . . ." Carter shrugged. "I don't know what they are. She likes my dad and I'm pretty sure he likes her. It's hard to tell. My mom didn't date much, so I haven't seen how people in love act with each other."

"Don't look at me," Reese told him. "My mom took off years ago. I could ask my dad, though, if you wanted me to. He might remember."

"No, I don't want him telling anyone. You know how grown-ups talk."

Reese sighed. "All the time. My grandma is great, but she goes on and on about stuff.

How my aunts are doing. Who's pregnant, which of my cousins is having a birthday. They're babies. It's not that fun hanging out with them."

Carter thought about the problem. "Maybe I could find some information online or something. There are a lot of weird articles and —"

His brain shut down. One second there were ideas and the next, nothing. He scrambled to his feet and stared at the most beautiful, sexy, incredible woman he'd ever seen.

She wasn't that tall — maybe three inches shorter than him. Her long, dark hair was wavy and curly in that sexy way girls had with their hair. Her face was all big eyes and lips, but what really got his attention was her body.

He didn't know where to look first. Her boobs or her butt. She had on a clingy workout tank, and pants that came to just below her knees. His body turned to fire and he was terrified he was going to be unable to control himself.

Reese mumbled something under his breath. Carter glanced at his friend and saw Reese looked as stunned as he felt.

The woman put her hands on her hips and shook her head. "I'm way too old," she told them flatly. "Don't even think about it."

"You could wait for me," Carter said before he could stop himself. "I'll be eighteen in two years."

Reese snorted. "You mean five years."

"Shut up."

"You're thirteen. She's not going to believe you're sixteen. She's hot, not stupid."

Carter jabbed Reese in the stomach and walked toward the goddess.

"Hi. I'm Carter." He hoped she would shake hands with him, like Angel did, but she only smiled.

"Consuelo. I'm going to be your teacher."

"Really?"

"Uh-huh." She put her hand on his shoulder. "Don't worry. By the end of the hour, you'll be hating me."

"Not possible."

He was having trouble breathing. Being this close to her was torture. He wanted her. He wasn't exactly sure what he wanted her for, but he needed to claim her, to tell the world that she belonged to him.

"Give me your hand," she told him.

He held it out and braced himself for the sweetness of her touch. She took his hand in hers. Her skin was cool, her fingers —

Everything spun as he found himself jerked up and over. The ground came up fast and hit him hard on the back.

"Wicked," Reese breathed. "Can you teach me how to do that?"

"You're both going to learn how to do that and other things, as well," Consuelo said, helping Carter to his feet.

"You flipped me," he said, unable to believe what she'd done, despite his battered body.

"Yup."

Her skills only made her more amazing, he thought.

Consuelo sighed. "You're going to be stubborn about this, aren't you?"

If that meant he would love her forever, then the answer was yes.

Gideon stood in the middle of the street, across from Brew-haha, and wondered how the hell he was going to get through the day. The annual book fair had turned much of the city into a giant bookstore with signings, readings and booths everywhere. Because Felicia was in charge of the festivals, she was working from dawn until eight or nine at night. Today was Saturday, which meant no camp, no classes, no way to keep Carter busy. Worse, tomorrow was Sunday. Gideon had two days with his kid and no idea what he was supposed to do to fill the time.

"You want to walk around?" Gideon asked.

"Sure."

"You read much?"

"Some."

Gideon wandered past a booth with a display of books on how to make furniture out of twigs. Next to that, a lady was demonstrating various quilting techniques. The day stretched out in endless minutes to be filled.

"There was a festival when I showed up, too," Carter said. "Does the town have them a lot?"

"Every couple of weeks in the summer. A little less the rest of the year, but at least once a month. Tourists are a big part of the economy. The festivals bring them in."

Carter looked around, then frowned. "I don't get it. Felicia runs this?"

"She organizes the events." He pointed to the list of signings and arrows pointing to the different venues. "She says where all the booths go and makes sure there are plenty of bathrooms. All the advertising runs through her, along with the permits. The Fourth of July Festival was her first one. She just started the job."

Carter's eyes widened. "She's good," he said. "I can't believe she's the boss of all these people."

"She's made some changes." Despite his apprehension at being with his son, he grinned. "There was some pushback last time, but she won everyone over to her way of thinking. Now they're all excited about the new setup. Want a lemonade?"

"Sure."

They walked over to the booth and Gideon ordered for them. People moved all around them. Families, couples. There were strollers and toddlers and teenagers. He'd never paid much attention to the ages of all the children before. Not that he spent a lot of time at the festivals. He preferred to stay in the background. Like narrating the Dance of the Winter King last Christmas. That was more his speed. But he'd always liked kids from a distance at least. Thought they deserved a fair shot — a chance to be special. But that was an idea born of generic concepts. He'd never thought he would be dealing with his own kid.

"How long have you lived in town?" Carter asked.

"About a year."

"Before that?"

"Here and there."

Carter sucked on his straw. "You don't want to talk about it."

No, he didn't. But what he wanted didn't seem to be an option. "When I got out of the military, I had some healing to do. That took a while."

He braced himself for more questions, but Carter only shrugged. "Makes sense. What about Felicia? How long has she lived in Fool's Gold?"

"A few months. She came in with CDS. Not to work for them. More to get the business up and running. But she was looking for a different kind of job, and when she was offered a chance to run the festivals, she was excited."

Which was almost true. She'd also been nervous about not getting it right. She had a strong sense of duty and wanted to fit in. A woman with principles.

"And before that?" Carter asked.

"She was in the military, too. She handled logistics for a Special Forces unit. She got them and their supplies where they needed to go and made sure they had a way out."

"They let girls do that?"

Gideon chuckled. "I suggest you avoid asking Felicia that question directly."

Carter grinned. "You're right. She's really smart, but nice, you know? She cares about people."

"She does have a big heart." And an amazing body, which wasn't anything he was going to discuss with a thirteen-year-old boy.

"She always has an answer," Carter said, then drank more of his lemonade. "I think my mom would have liked her."

"I'm sure she would have."

"Do you know Consuelo Ly?"

"I've met her a couple of times. Why?"

"She's teaching the class I go to at CDS." The teen grinned. "She's hot."

Crap, Gideon thought. Was he going to have to deal with hormones in addition to everything else?

"She's a little old for you, isn't she?"

Carter sighed. "Yeah. I asked her to wait, but I don't think she will. I wonder if she has a boyfriend."

"You know she could totally kick your ass, right?"

Carter grinned. "I know. She's already flipped me on my back. It hurt, but it was cool, too. You know? When I grow up, I'm going to get every girl I want, no matter what."

"It's not always that simple."

"Because they don't always like you back?"

"Sure. Or the timing's wrong. Or she's

with someone else."

The teen's grin turned cocky. "If a girl doesn't want me, then there's something wrong with her."

"You've got attitude," he said, chuckling. "I'll give you that." He looked around at the various booths. "You want any books?"

"No. I don't read books. Not paper ones. I read them on my laptop. Felicia bought me a couple the other night."

Great. So if books weren't interesting, what was he supposed to do with Carter? He glanced at his watch and held in a groan. It was barely noon. How was he supposed to fill a whole day?

"Any suggestions for the afternoon?" he asked.

Carter finished his lemonade, then nodded. "Sure. We can have lunch, then you can show me around the radio station."

"You're interested in the station?"

"I've never seen one before. I want to see where you work."

Something he'd never considered. "Okay," Gideon said. "Let's go get lunch."

After they'd grabbed pizza from a vendor, Gideon drove them out of town and to the radio station. As it was the weekend, the regular office staff were off.

"Not many people are in today," he said. "On weekends we run the station with a computer."

Carter followed him to the door. Gideon unlocked it and they stepped inside.

"You mean there's no people?"

"There's one guy to make sure the computer works. I usually hire college kids who can use the time to study. Watching a computer do its thing isn't that interesting."

Gideon led the way back to the engineering booth. A blond-haired guy looked up and grinned. He stood as Gideon and Carter stepped into the room.

"Jess, this is, ah, my son, Carter. Carter, this is Jess."

"Nice to meet you," Carter said politely.

"You, too."

"I'm showing him the station."

Jess nodded. "Not much to see these days. Most radio stations are run by a computer. No people required. Except for me. I make sure it all doesn't break down." His grin returned. "Like I'd know how to fix it. I'm really here to call in the tech experts if something goes wrong."

Carter glanced at all the equipment. "So the computer says what songs play?"

"More than songs. Commercials, too. Weather, even local news can be synced in.

I recorded a bunch of announcements about the festival yesterday, and they'll play all day." He cleared his throat and lowered his voice. "*New York Times* bestselling author Liz Sutton will be signing at three today, outside Morgan's Books." Jess shrugged. "Stuff like that."

Carter glanced at Gideon. "Do you ever do recordings?"

Jess chuckled. "He's the *man.* Nearly every local customer wants Gideon to do the commercials. Chicks dig his voice." He paused. "I probably shouldn't have said that, boss."

Gideon waved away the comment. "It doesn't matter because you're exaggerating. Half the people at the station work on commercials."

"But I thought everything was on the computer," Carter said.

"We buy blocks of on-air material," Gideon told him. He walked over to the computer and showed him the information on the monitor. It showed where they were in the program, what was playing now and what was in queue.

"We can insert our own commercials into what we've bought. We can do local news, too. The whole system uses the atomic clock so the timing is perfect. No one can tell

314

what's done by us and what's bought."

Carter frowned. "Is that good or not?"

"Some days I'm not sure. There's no way for a small station like this one to survive with live broadcasts. They're expensive to produce."

"At night, is it you or a recording?"

Jess grinned. "It's Gideon. The boss does his own shows the old-fashioned way. You should show Carter what's what."

"Sure."

They walked to the booth in the back, the one that no one else used because the equipment was so old. Carter slipped inside and sat at Gideon's chair. "Look at all this," he said.

The *this* was a stack of CDs. Some were compilations, others complete albums. Everything was numbered and neatly organized.

Gideon pulled a second chair. "I have a database I use to keep track of everything. I plan some playlists in advance, but not always. Sometimes it's a mood thing. People call in with requests."

Carter picked up the headphones, then put them down. "What's this?" he asked, pointing.

Gideon grinned. "A record player."

"You have records?"

"You don't have to sound so shocked. Yes, I have records." He pointed to the wall behind them.

Carter spun in the chair. "Whoa. Look at them."

Gideon followed his gaze. The record collection filled a specially built case that nearly covered the wall. He would guess he had close to a thousand records, some collected when he was a kid, some bought in the past couple of years at estate sales and auctions.

"I've never seen a record before," Carter said as he stood and crossed to the wall. "On TV and stuff, but never in person." He glanced back. "Can I touch one?"

"Sure. But hold it by the edges or the middle."

"Like a DVD." Carter pulled out a sleeve, then carefully slid out the record. He held it reverently. "So, these are like, what? A hundred years old?"

Gideon sighed. "It's from the '60s." At Carter's blank look, he added, "The 1960s. Barely fifty years ago."

"Fifty is pretty close to a hundred."

"I'm ignoring that." He held out his hand. "I'll play it for you."

Carter looked at the title. "*The Beatles Second Album?* That's the name?"

"It's actually the third album they released

in this country. They're a British band."

Carter handed him the record. He put it on the turntable and carefully placed the needle so they would hear his favorite track, the classic "She Loves You."

"Why do you like this music?" he asked as the first strains began to play.

"I can understand the words," Gideon said with a laugh. "I like the message of songs from the '60s. Life was simpler."

Carter shook his head. "Yeah, yeah, yeah? That's a message?"

"It was at the time."

Carter settled back in his chair and listened. When the song was over, he asked to have it played again.

Gideon studied the teenager who was his son. For the first time since Carter's arrival, he saw him as a person rather than a problem. A kid with hopes and dreams.

The song ended and he turned off the turntable. "You're going to have to tell me what I'm supposed to be doing," he said, putting the record back in the sleeve.

Carter's dark eyes flashed with emotion. "You mean about me?"

Gideon nodded. "I'm not exactly father material."

"You're doing good," the teen said quickly. "I'm not that much trouble."

"Nice to know. Should we talk about anything? You making friends okay? Anything with girls?"

Carter grinned. "I know about sex, if that's what you're asking. Besides, it's a little early for that. Get back to me in a couple of years."

Longer would be better, Gideon thought. "If you need anything or want to ask me any questions, you can. I won't lie to you."

"I'm glad. I'll try not to lie, either."

"I notice you didn't promise."

Carter smiled. "What can I say? I'm a kid. Things happen." His brows went up. "You know, we could talk about me driving."

"You're thirteen."

"It's never too early to start."

"It's highly illegal."

"Okay, but just so you know, you'll need to get me a car when I turn sixteen. So you might want to start saving now."

With any luck, he would start getting the hang of this "dad" thing before then, Gideon thought.

CHAPTER FIFTEEN

Felicia sat at the long table, feeling more than a little out of place. She was used to meetings that involved moving a six-man team into enemy territory with two tons of equipment and then extricating them with less than three hours' notice. That she could handle. A city council meeting was more than a little frightening.

She recognized the mayor, of course, and Charity Golden, the city planner. There were a few other people she'd seen at various functions. She was pretty sure the two old ladies sitting in chairs by the wall were Eddie Carberry and her friend Gladys.

"We have a revised agenda," Mayor Marsha said, standing with several sheets of paper in her hand. Slowly she put on her glasses and studied the sheet on top. When she raised her head, there was a slight tightness in her jaw. Almost as if she were grinding her teeth.

"Someone made changes," she said sternly. "Was that you, Gladys?"

One of the old ladies grinned. "Yup. We have a few things to discuss."

"We, in fact, do not," the mayor told her.

Eddie stood. She had on a bright fuchsia tracksuit that flattered her coloring. With her short, white hair, she looked like a cheerful, rowdy grandmother. Which she probably was, Felicia thought.

"The calendar last year made a lot of money," Eddie said. "We need to do something like that again. We could become known for our sexy calendar."

Felicia leaned toward Charity. "There was a sexy calendar?"

"Clay Stryker used to be a butt model. He brought in several model friends to pose for a calendar to raise money for the fire department. It was a big hit."

"This is a town," Mayor Marsha said slowly. "Not a club or a bar. We will not be known for anything but a civically focused calendar."

"I say we do butts," Gladys announced. "Naked male butts. You there. New girl."

Felicia realized they meant her. "Ma'am?"

"Those men you had moving the boxes. They're the bodyguards, right?"

"Yes."

"Use them. Don't they have nice butts? You've seen them, haven't you?"

"Don't answer that," the mayor instructed. "Either question."

"I'd like to know," Eddie said. "I'd like to judge for myself. Why should she get all the fun?"

"I'm so sorry," Charity whispered with a grin. "But now I have to know. Have you seen their butts?"

"Yes," Felicia said primly. "But only in a professional capacity."

Charity blinked at her. "That sounds interesting."

"I didn't mean it to. Sometimes they needed to get cleaned up, and we were still having a discussion. I went into the locker room. It wasn't romantic or sexual, if that's what you're curious about."

Charity fanned herself. "Oh, my. You had the most interesting job."

"They're whispering," Eddie complained. "She's sharing secrets, and I'm the one who deserves to know. This is my idea."

"Mine, too," Gladys said.

"Her, too."

Mayor Marsha groaned softly. "Stop, I beg you. There isn't going to be a calendar. Stop asking about it or talking about it."

Eddie and Gladys both sat down. They

weren't smiling now, and although Felicia couldn't explain it, she was sure they looked smaller somehow.

The mayor looked at them for several seconds, then sighed. "All right," she said. "I was going to save this information for later, but I'll share it now. We're going to have another new business coming to Fool's Gold."

Gladys and Eddie perked up. "Are there good-looking men?"

"Several. Three former football players have a PR firm called Score. Raoul Moreno knows them. They came to visit him and liked the town."

"Football players work," Eddie said. "Maybe we can see their butts."

"If we ask nicely," Gladys said.

"One of the principles is a woman," the mayor added. "Will you want to see her butt, as well?"

"Probably not," Eddie said.

Felicia turned to Charity. "Are they always like this?"

"Pretty much. You get used to it."

The mayor passed out the agenda. "We'll ignore the added items," she said.

There was a fifteen-minute discussion on a parking garage for the local community college, a report by Police Chief Alice Barns on how the usual summer tourist season was affecting crime, followed by an overview of the year-to-date budget.

Finally the council turned to the matter of the festivals.

"I see attendance was up," the mayor said, smiling at Felicia. "The lines were very long at the book festival."

Felicia stood and prepared to give her report. She mentioned the changes she'd made, along with some of the complaints she'd received. She talked briefly about the increased revenues and how next year they could support more vendors if that was what the city wanted.

"I heard most of those who complained at the Fourth of July festival were converts by the end of the long weekend," the mayor said.

"Ignore the whiners," Eddie called out. "You obviously know what you're doing. Stick to your guns."

Gladys nodded. "She's right."

"Thank you," Felicia said, gratified by their support.

"While I don't like to encourage them," the mayor said, "I have to agree. We're all very pleased with the changes you're making. Stay the course, dear. This town is lucky to have you."

Felicia nodded, her throat too tight for her to speak.

Gideon checked his watch again, then wondered if he'd made a mistake. He'd been in town earlier when he'd seen the display of mountain bikes outside the sporting goods store. He had the idea that it was something the three of them could do together. Not only would it help to fill the weekends, but the days were still long enough that they could go riding when Carter got back from camp.

But from the second he'd unloaded the bikes, he'd started to think he'd made a mistake. Carter might be too old, or think the idea was boring. What if Felicia didn't know how to ride a bike? He didn't like the worry, and he sure didn't like not knowing if he'd done the right thing.

Before he could pack everything up, Felicia and Carter drove up the mountain and pulled into the driveway. He was stuck standing by the garage, the bikes right in front of him.

Carter climbed out of the car and hurried over.

"You got these?"

Gideon nodded.

"Wicked. I've seen bikes like this in a

magazine, but I never thought I'd have one." He went over the bike, calling out details. "Can we try them out now?" he asked eagerly.

"Sure."

"Did you get helmets?" Felicia asked.

"Killjoy."

She walked over to him and put her hands on her hips. "If you like, I can provide you with the statistics on bike safety and brain damage that results from bike accidents."

"With a breakdown by age group?" he asked.

"If it's important to you."

If Gideon hadn't already been climbing on his bike, he would have pulled her close and kissed her.

"I got helmets," he said instead.

"Carter," she began.

"I know, I know," the teen grumbled, getting off his bike and walking over to her. "Helmet first." He took his and put it on, then waited while she adjusted everything.

"I can do that myself," he told her.

"I know, but I feel better doing it."

Carter glanced at Gideon and rolled his eyes. "Women."

Gideon chuckled.

Once they'd all put on their helmets the three of them set off up the mountain.

Carter led the way on the private road by the side of the house, pedaling fast. "We'll go really high," he called over his shoulder.

"There's a lookout about two miles up," Gideon told him.

"As long as we don't go onto the highway," Felicia said, keeping up easily. She was wearing khakis and a sleeveless white blouse, but her office clothes didn't slow her down.

"No highway," Gideon agreed.

"I heard that," Carter yelled. "I'm old enough to stay safe."

"No highway," Felicia repeated.

"Is there a back way to town?"

"We'll find one," Gideon said.

The sun was high overhead, but the tall trees provided shade. In Fool's Gold the temperature was probably close to ninety, but up here, it was a good ten or fifteen degrees cooler.

"When did you learn to ride a bike?" he asked.

"One of the lab assistants taught me." She pedaled steadily beside him, her face a little flushed. "He thought I should know how. Later he convinced the professor in charge of me to sign me up for swimming lessons."

"He sounds like a nice guy."

"He was. I think he felt bad I was alone in

the lab so much, but by then, it was all I knew."

By then. Meaning she'd known something else before. She was so intelligent, he hadn't given much thought to the connection between what had happened to her and how it must have felt for a four-year-old little girl to be abandoned by her parents.

"You must have had someone looking after you at first," he said.

"The university hired a nanny to stay with me. There were houses for professors on campus. I was given one of the smaller ones at first, and there was always someone to prepare my meals and stay with me at night. Later, when I was about twelve, I moved into one of the living units in the applied sciences building. There were a handful for the graduate assistants."

"You were on your own from the time you were twelve?"

"Mostly. By then I'd published several papers and cowritten a book, so I had income to buy food. I saved the rest of it. Having a way to support myself financially made it easier to show the judge I was ready to be an emancipated minor."

Despite his months of torture, Gideon knew that pain came in more than one form.

"You did a good job raising yourself."

"I dealt with what I had," she said with a smile. "I like to think my studies have helped other people, so when I have regrets about what happened, I remember that."

"Does it make a difference?"

"Sometimes."

Carter disappeared around a bend in the road. Felicia started to pedal faster.

"Don't worry. The road dead-ends at the lookout. He's got nowhere to go."

"Over the edge."

"You're a worrier," he told her. "I wouldn't have guessed."

"Just because I can calculate the odds of various outcomes doesn't mean I'm a worrier."

"Sure it does."

Felicia was concerned that Gideon was being critical, but from the way he was looking at her, she thought maybe not. If she had to guess, she would say his voice had a teasing quality to it.

They rode around the side of the mountain and found themselves on a large flat plateau. Trees and rocks provided a natural wall on three sides, while the fourth was a stunning view of the entire valley. She could see the town and the vineyards beyond. In the distance turbines spun in the afternoon breeze. Carter had leaned his bike against a rock. His helmet was on the ground, and he was standing with his back to them.

"What do you think?" Gideon asked, coming to a stop beside her.

Before she could say she was impressed, she noticed Carter's hunched shoulders were shaking.

"Leave me alone!" he yelled without turning around. "Just leave me alone."

His reaction was hostile, almost angry, she thought, taking in his body language. She saw the stiffness in his legs and the odd way he held his arms. For a second she thought he'd fallen and was hurt, but then she understood he was upset for reasons that had nothing to do with physical pain.

"What the hell?" Gideon muttered, starting toward him.

"Stop." She grabbed his arm. "He needs to be alone for a few minutes."

Gideon took off his helmet and glared at her. "Why?"

She drew him to the other side of the plateau. "He's crying."

"What? How do you know?"

"I'm not sure. I'm guessing."

He stared at her. "You're guessing? You don't guess."

"I think that's what's wrong."

"Why's he upset?" Gideon asked. "Why now? It's been a couple of weeks. Everything is going okay. I thought he and I had fun at the radio station. Was I wrong?"

"No. He liked spending time with you. Maybe that's the problem." She felt as if she was stepping through a minefield without a map.

"He's been through a lot," she continued. "Losing his mom, the foster care situation, finding you. He had no way of knowing if you'd want anything to do with him. He just showed up. That's very brave, but also terrifying. What if you'd rejected him? What if you still might?"

"I wouldn't have thrown him out or anything. His home is with me." Now he was the one to shift uncomfortably. "I know I'm not the best dad, but I'm working on getting more involved with him."

"I know, but he doesn't. Give him a moment. He'll be fine."

"I don't like it."

"Him crying? That's a response to socialization. If he were a thirteen-year-old girl, you'd be more understanding. As a society, we don't like our boys to cry, but they need the emotional release just as much. It's not unhealthy."

Gideon's mouth twisted. "I meant I don't

330

like you being insightful. You're already too smart. If you understand people as well as everything scientific or mathematical, how can we ever have a fair fight?"

She smiled, feeling a little proud of herself. "You'll always be able to best me physically."

"Like I'd hit a girl."

Felicia pulled the brownie pan from the oven. The smell of chocolate drifted throughout the house, which was enjoyable on its own, but what really pleased her was the satisfaction she received from baking. Logically, it made no sense. The creation of a brownie from disparate ingredients was the result of a chemical reaction when heat and time were applied. There was no magic. She'd performed much more complicated experiments in a lab. There, the results had had significance. Still, baking brownies was better, she thought happily, and she couldn't begin to say why.

She also found pleasure in knowing her way around the large, open kitchen. At first she'd been intimidated by the cupboards and drawers, not knowing what went where or what half the items were for. Gideon had admitted to hiring a decorator to furnish the house. He'd bought the bed in the master and the sofa in the media room and had left everything else to her, with instructions to keep things simple and masculine.

The woman had taken his instructions to heart everywhere except the kitchen. While the plates were simple white squares and the appliances were stainless, the decorator had bought every kitchen gadget ever made. Felicia was still figuring out what some of them were. She was intimidated by the food processor, although the thought of using the dough hooks that had come with the passive mixer was getting more interesting by the day. She could imagine the comforting smell of baking bread on a cold, snowy winter day.

As she put the brownie pan on the cooling rack, she wondered if she would still be living here when it was snowing. She and Gideon hadn't discussed their future. Per their agreement, they were supposed to date and nothing more. He was teaching her how to be with a man so she could find someone normal to fall in love with. Carter had shown up and challenged all that. Now she wasn't actually dating, but she was living with a man. She thought maybe that was instruction enough.

But she was less sure about leaving. She liked the big house and the views of the mountains. More, she liked being around Gideon. Even when he was emotionally distant, walking the floors in the hours of darkness, she felt closer to him than she ever had to anyone else. She liked knowing he was nearby.

Since they'd made love again, he slept with her — those few hours when he slept. Knowing he was going to be in the bed with her made her feel safe. Odd, considering she rarely felt *unsafe.* She supposed it was because he understood her better than most and still seemed to like her. She could be herself and know she wouldn't be judged. She trusted him.

She heard footsteps and turned to see Carter walking into the great room toward the kitchen. The teen had been quiet all through dinner. Her instinct had been to let him be. He would talk when he was ready. She hoped she was doing the right thing by letting him decide when or even if he wanted to talk.

When it came to him, she was never sure she was doing the right thing. She found herself worrying about him at odd moments, which made no sense. He was obviously capable. But she couldn't shake the feeling.

He leaned against the counter. His face

was pale and his eyes slightly red. She wondered if he'd been crying again. The thought of his emotional pain made her own heart ache.

He pointed at the pan. "The brownies smell good."

"The scent of chocolate baking diffuses very nicely."

He flashed her a smile. "There you go again, with the funny talk."

She sighed. "I'm too literal, but I'm working on it."

"You shouldn't change. You're honest. You've been there for me."

Felicia wasn't sure where "there" was, but she decided it didn't matter. "You've been through a lot. I respect how you've handled a difficult situation. I was on my own when I was your age, and I know it's tough. You're here now, and I hope that makes you happy. I want us to be friends."

He nodded and glanced away. "I'm sorry about what happened before. On the mountain."

"You don't have to apologize."

"I yelled at you and Gideon, and you hadn't done anything wrong."

"Was it because you were having . . . a moment?" she asked, hoping she wasn't saying the wrong thing.

He shrugged. "I guess. I miss my mom."

Her mind searched for linkage and possible solutions. She ignored everything that was logical and went with what made emotional sense.

"Are you worried that liking your dad and living here is being disloyal to her memory?"

"And you." He swallowed. "My dad is kind of distant. He was better over the weekend. We talked and stuff and I liked that. But you're the glue."

"Oh, Carter."

She crossed to him and wrapped her arms around him. He hung on, holding her so tight it hurt. But she didn't complain, didn't ask him to let go. And when his body shook and she heard the cries he tried to silence, she promised herself she would never let go. Figuratively, of course.

After a few minutes, he straightened and drew back. He wiped his face with the back of his hand.

"I miss her," he admitted, his voice thick with emotion. "Every day."

"Nothing is going to change that. Your feelings for your mother have a special place in your heart. She will always be your mother. Given the choice, I know you'd rather be home with her than adjusting to life here." She paused, wanting to get it right. "But whatever happens, Carter, you can always come to me."

"Are you and Gideon going to get married?"

An unexpected question. "No. He doesn't want that kind of involvement."

"Don't you love him?"

Another unexpected question.

"I'm not sure. I've never been in love before. We're dating. I like him very much."

Carter surprised her by flashing a smile. "Like I said. Honest. So what's his problem? You're beautiful, smart, funny and caring."

"Thank you. Those are lovely compliments. As for your father, he had a difficult time a few years back. I told you he was held prisoner, but it was more than that. He was also tortured."

Carter's smile faded. "I didn't know that part."

"The conditions were horrible. When he was finally rescued, he needed time to heal. It's not the sort of experience a man walks away from easily. He'll always have some part of that inside him."

And she'd assumed the greatest challenge of her evening was going to be making brownies, she thought, putting her hand on Carter's shoulder.

"Your father wants you to be happy. He's

still getting used to you, but he bought those cool bikes. That's progress. You need to give yourself time to adjust, and I think he deserves leeway, as well."

Carter studied her for a second. "Okay. I get what you're saying. But for the record? If my dad doesn't marry you, he's an idiot."

"What do you think?" Noelle asked.

"You've done a very thorough job," Felicia said, able to appreciate good planning when she saw it.

Noelle had figured out several layouts for her store. She'd made cardboard "footprints" of various shelving units and cabinets, each marked with what it was supposed to represent. Round disks represented Christmas trees that would be set up. By setting them on the floor and moving them around, she was able to play with the different configurations.

Isabel walked around, and shook her head. "You're good. Seriously. This is impressive. You have several plans to choose from and time to make a decision. Look at you, all savvy with the retail."

"Thanks," Noelle said with a laugh. "I'm down to three main concepts for the floor plan. I was hoping you'd help me pick the right one. The remodel starts on Monday, and I'm going to have to tell the contractor where the built-in units are going."

The future location of The Christmas Attic was nearly square. Big front windows let in light and offered plenty of room for displays. The ceiling was unusually high. Maybe eighteen or twenty feet, Felicia thought. She'd never had an innate ability to estimate distances by sight.

"Which configuration is your favorite?" Felicia asked. "Let's set up that one, then we'll start at the entrance and walk our way through the store."

"Good idea. I've done that, but I'm to the point where I can't see anything new. Bookcases over there, cabinet on the wall opposite the windows, cash register stations are here."

It took them a couple of minutes to get everything in place. They walked to the open door and stopped.

"You'll have a stack of baskets for shopping?" Felicia asked, remembering her experience at similar stores. She'd never been in a place that solely celebrated Christmas, but she'd been in craft stores and one shop in Santa Barbara that specialized in tiny figurines.

"Right here." Noelle pointed.

The other woman had pulled her hair

back in a ponytail. She wore a pink T-shirt and white capris. She was thinner than average and there was something about the way she moved that made Felicia think Noelle had suffered some kind of physical trauma in the past year or so. Not a car accident, she thought. That left a person bruised and battered in a different way.

She knew that from personal experience. She'd been hit by a car when she was eighteen and on leave. She'd ended up with several broken bones and a mashed face. The plastic surgeon had worked miracles, correcting all her facial imperfections. She'd been young and healthy and had healed quickly. It seemed like a lifetime ago.

"Here you go," Isabel said, pretending to hand her something. "Your basket."

Felicia bent her elbow, as if she were placing a handle over her forearm. "What's first?"

"The trees are toward the back, drawing you there. Most of the ornaments will be on them, although I'll have boxes of some sets on shelves. I want customers to step into the store and not clog up the entrance." She smiled. "I'm assuming I'll have more than one shopper at a time."

"You will," Felicia assured her. "Your local clientele might wait until closer to the holidays to buy but tourists will know they aren't coming back and want to take advantage of your inventory while they're here."

She and Isabel did pretend shopping. They went through the store's layout. Felicia did her best to imagine what it would look like.

"Your idea of having the children's books and the teddy bear collections together is very smart," she said. "How are parents supposed to resist either?"

"And it keeps kids away from the breakables." Isabel looked around. "For what it's worth, I like that layout best."

"Me, too." Noelle grinned. "Let's take a break for a second and clear our heads. I have soda. You two want one?"

"Sure."

Noelle disappeared into the storeroom, then reappeared with three cans of diet in her hands. She, Isabel and Felicia sank onto the floor and popped the tops.

"I'm a little more encouraged than I was," Noelle admitted when she'd taken a sip. "I was thinking my Christmas store idea was just plain idiotic. Then I started getting things ready. I swear, every day I leave that front door open, someone wanders in to see what I'm up to."

"This town takes an interest in its citizens," Felicia reminded her.

Noelle flashed a grin. "Not always a good thing. It would be a lousy place to try to sneak around." She looked at Isabel. "Although you're doing a good job."

"I'm not sneaking. I'm stealthy."

"Oh, like there's a difference," Noelle said, her voice teasing.

Felicia started to point out there was, but then stopped. This was not the time to be defining words.

"I've never been especially stealthy or sneaky," she said instead. "I like the warmth and sense of community here."

"Me, too. It's way different than Los Angeles." Noelle glanced at Isabel. "And New York."

"You don't regret your move?" Felicia asked.

"No. It was impulsive, but I'm happy here. Making friends helps." Noelle poked Isabel in the arm. "You're going to find it hard to leave."

"I hope not." She wrinkled her nose. "I have appreciated the chance to get away from my trouble, though. The reminders."

"Not missing men yet?" Noelle asked.

"No. Not yet."

Felicia smiled at Noelle. "Are you seeing anyone?"

Noelle sighed. "Dating? No. I had a really bad breakup not long before I moved here. We were together three years. I kept putting off the wedding because of work and stuff, which turned out to be a good thing." She paused as if she was going to say something else but had changed her mind.

More secrets, Felicia thought, knowing there was no point in speculation.

"You're still living with Gideon," Noelle said.

"I am. Carter is wonderful. He's a lot of fun to be with. The adjustment is difficult, but he's working his way through it."

"You sound like a mom."

Felicia flushed with pleasure at the compliment. "I'm trying to be supportive and take care of him. I know that being around him has confirmed that I want to have a family of my own."

"With Gideon?" Isabel asked.

"He's made it clear he's not interested in anything long-term." Something she'd always known, but saying the words just now made her oddly sad. "I know Gideon's been through a lot, but he's less damaged than he thinks. We all have problems and flaws. I believe he feels he's less human than the rest of us, but that's not true. Only I don't think he can be convinced. He has to learn to believe in himself, and I'm not sure he's willing to take the risk."

Noelle stared at her. "That was an impressive assessment of him. If I'd been that clearheaded about my fiancé, I wouldn't have stayed with him for so long."

"I could be wrong," Felicia said.

"It doesn't sound like you are," Isabel told her. "I'm impressed, too."

Noelle smiled. "When I first met you, I thought you were some brainiac who wouldn't know an emotion if it bit you on the butt. I was wrong, and I'm sorry for judging you that way. You're very warm and caring, and you really get people." She groaned. "Oh, God. You're perfect. Now I have to hate you."

Felicia laughed. "I'm not perfect and I don't really get people. I wish I did. I'm better than I was, but I still feel awkward in unfamiliar situations and I'm not sure what to say."

Noelle raised her can of soda. "We can be imperfect together."

Just then, a tall, dark-haired woman with blue eyes walked into the store. She had on a black suit and elegant pumps with four-inch heels that were so beautiful Felicia wondered if she could ever learn to walk in such ridiculous footwear.

"Hello," the woman said. "I'm . . ." She paused and looked around. "I'm apparently lost and in the wrong place." She frowned. "That's repetitious, isn't it? If I'm lost I can't be in the right place. I need coffee and sleep and very possibly a way to kill my business partners."

She gave them a weary smile. "Sorry. I'm exhausted and rambling. I'm Taryn Crawford with *Score.*"

"What's Score?" Isabel asked.

"A new business in town. Or it's going to be. Assuming there's no partner death in the near future." Taryn gave a little shrug. "For the record, I'm kidding about killing him. Sort of. I wouldn't know how to go about it. Jack is friends with Raoul Moreno who, apparently, lives here. Jack came to visit, loved the town, talked to the other partners, convinced them we had to relocate, and here the hell I am."

Felicia put the pieces together and remembered her recent city council meeting. "You're with the football players."

"Don't remind me," Taryn grumbled. "What's that expression? It's like trying to herd cats. I was supposed to meet a real estate agent about some property. I don't have time to be looking, but I can't trust one of the guys with it. We'd end up with a

344

corner in a sports bar. There are days . . ." She drew in a deep breath. "You know the kicker in all this? They're great with the clients."

"Which is why you haven't killed them yet?" Noelle offered helpfully.

"Pretty much. That and prison. I wouldn't enjoy prison." She glanced around. "Great space. Like the light. What's it going to be?"

"A Christmas store," Noelle told her. "The Christmas Attic."

"Nice." Taryn looked up. "You should put in some framing to make it look like a real attic. The ceilings are high enough. It wouldn't be expensive, just a few beams to give the look. Then you could add shelving at the base of the framing for displays. A Christmas store." She paused for a second. "What about a train set? It could circle the store, do that toot-toot thing they do. Kids would love it. The noise might make you want to run screaming into the night, but retail comes at a price. So, where did I go wrong? I was looking for Frank Lane and Fifth."

Isabel pointed to the door. "That's Frank. Take a left and go a block and a half. You'll be there."

"Thanks. I'm sure I'll see you around."

Taryn waved and left.

"I love her," Noelle said reverently. "She's brilliant. I can make my store look like an attic. I can't believe I never thought of that myself. It makes sense. Did you see her shoes?"

"Beautiful," Isabel said, watching her walk away. "I'm so with you on the shoes."

"That's because you have a shoe thing, too. I'd fall and break an ankle if I tried to wear them," Noelle said. "But it might be worth it."

"I liked her, too," Felicia admitted. Taryn had been extremely straightforward in her speech. And she had attitude.

"She's very beautiful," Noelle added. "I wonder if Denise Hendrix would like her for Kent."

"Or Ford," Felicia added, then laughed. "The danger with that match is Ford really would know how to kill her business partners."

"Hey," Isabel said. "Not Ford. We're not finding a woman for Ford."

Noelle raised her eyebrows. "You said you weren't interested in him."

"I'm not. I'm sure of it." She clutched her can of soda. "At least I'm pretty sure."

CHAPTER SIXTEEN

Reese held out the bowl of popcorn to Carter. It was raining, and they were at Reese's place, watching movies. In the past couple of days, Carter had started to feel a little better. Maybe it was okay for him to be happy here, in Fool's Gold. He knew his mom wouldn't have wanted him to forget her, but she also wouldn't expect him to be unhappy all the time. And she would have liked Felicia a lot.

"You think about your mom?" he asked.

Reese paused the movie. "Not so much anymore. I did when she left. More than I wanted my dad to know. For a while I was afraid he'd take off, too. But he kept telling me he would always be there for me. Moving here helped. Being close to family." He shrugged. "I know that's kind of lame, but it makes a difference."

"I know what you mean. Without Felicia around, things with my dad would suck. I think he likes me, and we have fun and stuff, but it's not the same. We don't talk the way Felicia and I talk." He didn't mention the hugs because that would make him sound like a baby. But having her hug him was important. He just felt better when she did.

She made it clear she was interested in him and listened to what he was trying to say. She was logical in a way his mom hadn't been. He didn't think he could freak her out about anything.

"She's learning to bake," he said. "It's pretty funny. Everything is so precise with her. She measures exactly. My mom just threw stuff in a bowl and it always came out great. With Felicia, we follow the recipe." He reached for another handful of popcorn.

"My grandma is determined to get my dad and Uncle Ford married," Reese said. "Last month she had a booth at a festival. She's got all these applications and wants my dad to start calling the women she's picked."

Carter stared at him. "No way. Is your dad pissed?"

"Kinda, but he doesn't want to say anything. I told her I'd check out the ladies ahead of time, but she didn't like that idea."

"You think your dad will start dating?"

Carter asked.

"He said he would. It's time. Mom's not coming back, and I like the idea of a step-mom."

Carter grinned. "You like the idea of someone cooking and doing your laundry."

Reese chuckled. "Sure. Why not? Plus, she'll want to show I'm important, so she'll buy me presents."

Carter laughed with his friend, but knew his needs were different. He wanted Gideon and Felicia to stay together permanently, so they could be a family. Right now, they could walk away from each other at any second.

"I need a plan to get Gideon to marry Felicia," he announced.

Reese shook his head. "You're not going to make that happen, bro. They're adults. We're thirteen. What do we know about getting people together? Your mom was single your whole life, and my mom walked out on my dad. It's not like we've seen it happen and can follow the steps." He held out a hand. "Don't say you're going to find something on the internet. It's not that simple."

"So how does it happen? People meet, they start dating, they fall in love."

"Gideon and Felicia are already living

together. They don't have to date."

Carter saw his point. But he was pretty sure most couples lived together because they were in love, or something close. Felicia had moved in because of him. He was in the middle of what they were doing.

"They should have a date night," he said, wondering how he was going to make that happen. "I could tell Gideon that Felicia deserves a night out after everything she's been doing."

"You think he'll fall for that?"

"Maybe. If I mention the baking. I can stay here that night and then they'll be alone and it can be romantic."

"You think they're doing it?" Reese asked.

Carter punched him in the arm. "We can't talk about that. It would be like your dad and some girl."

Reese shuddered. "Okay, you're right. I don't want to go there. Old people shouldn't do that sort of thing."

Carter understood his friend being grossed out, but as far as he was concerned, Gideon and Felicia *should* be getting it on. They should be together in other ways, too. From what he could tell, marriage was like a team. He needed to get them on the same side. It would move them closer to falling in love with each other and getting married.

Once that happened, he would have a permanent home and not have to worry anymore.

"This is nice," Felicia said as she and Gideon walked into Angelo's. The Italian restaurant was crowded on a Friday night, but the hostess smiled at them and said she had their reservation.

"Inside or out?" Gideon asked, putting his hand on the small of Felicia's back.

"Out," she told him.

They were shown to a table on the patio. Although there were plenty of other people around, the strategic placement of plants provided the illusion of privacy.

She and Gideon sat across from each other. The hostess put menus in front of them, then left.

Gideon leaned toward her. "You look great. Did I mention that?"

"No, but thank you for the compliment. You look great, as well."

He chuckled. "Thanks. Carter helped me pick out my clothes."

Which explained the black shirt and black jeans, Felicia thought. Gideon wasn't usually that formal or into dark clothing.

"He made me try on a bunch of shirts," Gideon told her. "He's a stern taskmaster."

He sounded relaxed as he spoke, as if the idea of a son was no longer so startling. They were all settling in, she thought happily. Finding their way.

"How was your bike-riding this afternoon?" she asked.

Gideon and Carter had started riding bikes together, after camp. They were generally gone about a half hour while she started dinner. Then Carter set the table while Gideon pretended to help in the kitchen. Their own ritual, she thought fondly.

"Good. He's enjoying camp and has made a lot of friends. He and Reese Hendrix seem to be getting close."

"I'm glad. Ford is sometimes frustrated by his family, but from all he's said, they're loving and supportive. They'll draw Carter in and give him a sense of belonging."

Gideon's expression tightened, then he relaxed.

"What?" she asked.

"I was thinking of my brother," he admitted.

Felicia didn't know much about Gideon's family. "Your twin."

"That's him. He's a doctor. Good guy. Plays by the rules."

"Which you don't approve of?" she asked.

"I like rules just fine."

"So long as you can ignore them."

"I did kind of get over them in the army." One corner of his mouth turned up, which she found disproportionately sexy.

"What kind of twins?" she asked.

"Fraternal."

"So there's no connection beyond being the same age and your time in the womb?"

He grimaced. "Don't talk about me and my brother being in the womb, okay? It's creepy."

She laughed. "You were once little more than a zygote, my friend."

"Fortunately, I can't remember back that far."

"Too bad. It would be fascinating. I enjoy speaking with identical twins. There have been studies that suggest an almost psychic connection. If it exists, I believe it comes from sharing DNA." She paused. "We were talking about your relationship with your family."

"The DNA stuff is much more interesting."

"Liar. You're trying to distract me."

"And it nearly worked." He shrugged. "I do okay with my family."

"By what scale? You never see them or call them."

"How do you know I don't call them?"

"I haven't heard you on the phone with anyone since I moved in."

"Maybe I call from work."

"It's the middle of the night anywhere in the continental United States."

His eyebrows drew together. "Sometimes you being smart is a real pain in the ass."

She smiled. "I've heard that before."

Their server, a college-age guy in black pants and a white shirt, stopped by their table. He explained about the specials, then offered to get them drinks. Gideon named a bottle of wine.

When the server had left, Felicia rested her elbows on the table and her chin in her hands. "We were talking about your family," she said, her voice teasing.

"Figures you wouldn't forget. Fine. I don't see them very much."

"Or talk to them."

"Yeah, yeah. I don't talk to them."

"They don't know about Carter, then?"

He drew in a breath. "I don't know what to say. My mom will want to meet him. It complicates things."

"They must be very proud of you, of your service."

"They're grateful I'm not dead," he admitted, then sighed. "Okay, sure, they're proud. They're good people. My dad was career army. We moved around a lot. I knew I wanted to be just like him. Gabriel wanted to be a doctor. He got the army to send him to medical school. Slick trick, if you ask me."

"He's still in the service?"

"Last I heard."

Their server brought them bread. Gideon offered her a slice. She took it and set it on her side plate.

"I think you're right to wait on letting your parents know about Carter," she said.

"Really?"

"Carter's still adjusting, as are you. If you were close to your parents, their presence would be welcome. But you're not, so they would be one more stressor. In a couple of months, when you and Carter have a closer relationship, it will be easier."

She wondered if she would still be living in Gideon's house when his parents arrived. She wanted to be. She liked her new life. Was this what it was like to be married? Sharing chores, doing things together. She cooked, but Carter and Gideon cleaned up after. They watched movies, rode bikes, worried about Carter's adjustment. It all felt so normal.

Was it love? she wondered. She had strong feelings for Gideon. Not just sexually, but in other ways. She liked him and respected him. She missed him when she wasn't around him. She could imagine herself staying with him indefinitely. But was that love? She had no way of knowing what love felt like.

"Have you been in love?" she asked.

He froze in the act of buttering his bread. "Excuse me?"

"Were you in love with Ellie?"

"No. She was a sweet girl, but I was pretty young. I didn't love her." He shook his head. "Carter asked me the same thing, and I lied."

"Lies aren't always destructive. Sometimes they're told out of kindness. Him believing you loved his mother will make him feel safer. There's no reason for him to know otherwise."

She wanted to ask again if he'd ever been in love, but sensed it wasn't a topic designed to get Gideon to relax. Maybe she should speak with one of her friends about love. Isabel had been married before. She would know what love felt like.

"Do you know about the new PR firm moving to town?" she asked. "It's owned by several football players."

"I've heard something," he said. "Raoul Moreno brought them here."

"One of the owners is a woman. Taryn

Crawford. I met her the other day. She was very direct. I liked her a lot. A lone woman among alpha guys. I can relate."

"The old ladies are going to want some kind of strip show for sure," Gideon said with a grin. "Eddie and Gladys do like their beefcake."

"Have they asked to see your butt?"

"No, and I'm not offering. They're pretty wild women."

"Imagine what they were like forty years ago."

The server returned with the wine. They placed their orders, and the server left. As he did, a dark-haired woman in her forties walked over to their table and smiled at Gideon.

"I'm Bella Gionni," she said. "I own House of Bella. You've been in to have your hair cut."

"Nice to see you again," he told her.

"I hate to pry, but I heard about your son. If you need anything from the community, we're here for you. You just have to ask."

Gideon looked like a deer in the headlights. Felicia wasn't sure how to help.

"The town is so welcoming," she said, and held out her hand. "Hi. I'm Felicia Swift."

"Nice to meet you." Bella's gaze settled on her hair. "Your hair is a lovely color. Is it natural?"

"Yes. I'm lucky."

Bella returned her attention to Gideon. "You're dealing with so much. You might want to talk to Ethan Hendrix. Do you know him?"

"He owns the turbine company outside town." He looked at Felicia. "Wind turbines. They're used for electricity."

"I'm aware of that," she began, only to realize saying that was *his* way of creating a distraction. "Um, yes. Windmills. What do you know about them?"

Bella shot her a look that clearly stated she thought Felicia was the village idiot. "As I was saying, Ethan went through a little of what you're dealing with now. It's a complicated story, but by the time he found out he had a son, Tyler was eleven or twelve. It nearly broke his heart."

"That he had a son?" Felicia asked.

"No, dear. All that he missed." She put her hand on his shoulder. "I know you're working through that, too. Those early years. Him being born, the first step, first word." Her eyes filled with tears. "That first day of school. All gone. And you can't get them back."

Gideon looked as if he was going to bolt.

"Carter's mother seems to have done an

excellent job with her son," Felicia said.

"A boy needs his father," Bella said, glaring at her, before turning back to Gideon. "I'm just saying, Ethan has been there and he can help you through the adjustment period."

She smiled once more, then left.

Felicia picked up her wineglass, then put it down. "I have a strong urge to apologize, but I'm not sure for what."

"I missed stuff," he said, sounding dazed. "Years when Carter was younger."

Thirteen years, she thought, but decided that information wasn't helpful to the discussion at hand.

"Does that give you a sense of loss? Are you angry with Ellie?"

"No." He stared at her. "I never thought about it before. About him being younger and growing up. I don't need to know about that. I don't want to know."

"Somehow thinking Carter appeared fully formed made him less scary?"

He swore under his breath. "I thought you were supposed to be socially awkward."

"I'm less so now," she said proudly. "But you're avoiding the question."

"I don't have an answer for you. Maybe that's part of it. He's not so bad. We're starting to figure out what to talk about." He glanced around. "Damn this town. Why can't they leave me alone?"

Bella's words might have triggered his feelings, but Felicia suspected Gideon had been fighting the walls closing in for a while. He was a man who sought out solitude. He lived away from other people. He meditated, practiced Tai Chi and ran miles at a time. All alone. He specifically worked at night when most of the world was asleep. He didn't seek involvement, yet it had been thrust upon him.

"We can go," she told him. "We don't have to stay and eat dinner."

"This is your date night."

Your, she thought sadly. Not *our.*

"Another time," she said, waving to their server. "Let's just go home. You can drop me off, then head into the station. Get set up for your show."

She wanted him to say no. She wanted him to say that being with her was relaxing. That while he was interested in getting out of the restaurant, being with her wasn't like being with other people.

"Thanks," he said, pulling a credit card out of his wallet. "I promise to come to a full stop at the house and not ask you to jump out while the car's still moving."

"I could do a tuck and roll."

"Not in those shoes." He reached across the table and squeezed her hand. "Thanks."

She nodded because she was afraid if she spoke, she would betray her disappointment. As they left the restaurant and she faced a long evening of missing Gideon and wishing they were together, she realized that caring for someone came at a price. To open one's heart meant letting in all emotions, not just the good ones.

"If you don't focus, I'm going to hit you," Consuelo said, glaring at Ford.

"Sorry."

He gripped the punching bag more securely. Just as she shifted into position, he stepped back.

"It's my mother," he admitted.

"Do I look as if I care?"

"You heard about the booth?"

"Everyone heard about the booth, and we're all laughing at you. Now, can we get back to the workout?"

They were supposed to be sparring together. When he'd been too distracted for a decent round or two, she'd suggested they move to the punching bags.

"Consuelo, you don't understand. She's taken applications from different women and sorted through them by likable attributes. She's been emailing me the information and then following up to see if I've called them yet."

Ford was about thirty-three, over six feet tall and all muscle. Although she would never admit it to anyone, she was pretty sure he could take her. So it was unexpected, to say the least, to watch him practically tremble at the thought of his mother sending women his way.

"Tell her no," she said.

"My mother?"

"Isn't that who we're talking about?"

"I can't. She won't understand. She went to a lot of trouble."

"It was a booth for two days. She had fun. It's not like she was in an Iranian prison on a hunger strike."

"She's my mother."

Now he was giving her a headache. "We've established that. If you say she's your mother again, I'm going to hit you in the balls. Is that clear?"

Ford stepped closer to the bag, as if that would offer protection. Idiotic man.

"What do you want?" she asked, digging deep for patience she didn't naturally possess.

"Her to leave me alone. I made the mistake of mentioning I was moving out, and she wants me to move back home. I already spent a few days there. It's not going to work."

"And you can't tell her?"

"I don't want to hurt her feelings." He narrowed his gaze. "Before you get on me about that, you wouldn't hurt your mother's feelings, either."

"No, I wouldn't." Assuming she were still alive, Consuelo would want to do everything in her power to make her mother happy and proud of her.

"So you have two problems," she said. "Living quarters and the women. Let's take them one at a time. Where are you going to live? You can't stay in the house."

Ford and Angel were going to kill each other, which she could live with, but then she would have to clean up the mess, which annoyed her.

"I've got a lead on an apartment. I'll know if I got it in a couple of days. It's above a garage, very private."

"Sounds nice. So don't tell your mother where you're going to be."

His expression turned pitying. "This is Fool's Gold. There are no secrets. Even if I don't tell her, someone else will."

Consuelo began unfastening her gloves. Obviously there wasn't going to be a workout with Ford this morning. When he was done whining about his problem, she was going for a run. A long one. Then she was going to soak in the big tub in her bathroom. Later, there would be wine. She was sure of it.

"There's a difference between lying and withholding information."

"Not a big one," Ford said.

"Then you're going to have to deal with her knowing your whereabouts. It's a small town. It's not like you'll have distance on your side."

"I never should have moved back."

She glared at him. "No, what you never should have done was promise me a workout and then gotten all girly about your problems."

"I'm sharing something personal here."

"Cry me a river."

"You're not very feminine."

"That makes one of us." She drew in a breath. "Okay, this isn't working. You're getting an apartment and you're going to have to deal with your mother dropping by. Do you see another solution?"

"No."

"Great. Problem solved. Or if not solved, then something we don't have to talk about anymore. Next, the women applying to marry you. You know, if we'd recorded this conversation, all you'd have to do is post it on YouTube and they'd run in the opposite direction."

"Why do I remember you being more helpful?" he asked.

"Hell if I know." She dropped her gloves to the mat and flexed and opened her hands. "Have you talked to any of them?"

"The applicants? No. Why would I?"

"I don't know. Because you need to get laid and they're offering. They can't all be bad."

"I don't want to get married." His voice was two parts stubborn, one part whine.

"All right. I'll bite. Why not?"

"I just don't."

"Okay. As long as it's a *good* reason." She decided if she moved just a little closer, she could nail his groin with a quick kick. Then the issue of having children would be off the table. But despite his annoying honesty and soft spot for his mother, she sort of liked Ford. If she couldn't enjoy hurting him, there was no point in causing the pain.

"Go out with them," she said.

"What?"

"Go out with them. How bad could it be?"

"Bad."

"You don't know that. Your mom knows

you pretty well. She put up with you for years."

"I was a kid. I've changed."

She was about to make a smart-ass remark when she realized he was telling the truth. Ford had become a SEAL. He'd been around the world, seeing and doing things that very few people could understand. That had a way of changing a man . . . or a woman.

"So, distract her," she said. "She's also looking for a wife for Kent. Tell her you need more time to settle into civilian life, that you'll be difficult to date. She should understand that. Say she can practice on Kent."

Ford's worried expression relaxed. He circled around the punching bag, heading toward her. Consuelo started backing away.

As she'd feared, he was both stronger and faster, and apparently more determined, she thought grimly as he grabbed her in his arms and swung her around.

"That's perfect!" he crowed, squeezing tight. "I'll get my mom to focus on Kent." He put her down and released her. "He can be her practice case."

She took a deep breath, just to make sure there weren't any bruised ribs, and told herself she didn't care if Ford's brother started dating other women. It's not like she knew the man. "So much for brotherly love."

"Lorraine left Kent years ago. He's got a kid. He needs to get married."

"I'm sure he'll appreciate your professional assessment." She cleared her throat, then did her best to sound casual. "Do you know why she left?"

He shrugged. "She was a bitch." He held up both hands. "My mom's exact words. I'm not being critical of a woman. Don't hurt me."

"I won't."

Ford dropped his arms to his sides. "Kent was crazy about her for years, and they had Reese together. He's a stable kind of guy. A math teacher. As far as I know, he never cheated. When we spoke right after the divorce, he was pretty broken up about it. I felt kind of bad."

"Do you think he's looking to get involved again?"

A stupid question, she thought angrily. It wasn't as if she was right for him. Even if he found her attractive, he would only want her for sex. Normal men wanted normal women to marry. He was an intelligent single father with kind eyes. Whether he wanted to or not, he wouldn't stay single for long.

"He told Mom he was. At least he's not disinterested, which is pretty much the same thing." He started toward her, but she shook her head.

"No more hugging?" he asked.

"No. But I understand you're grateful. You've bought yourself some time. But once Kent is happily involved, your mother is going to go looking for a woman for you."

"I'll figure out something," he said.

"Great. Problem solved." She started out of the gym.

"Wait." He walked alongside her. "Where are you going?"

"For a run."

"Want some company?"

She rolled her eyes. For all their toughness and attitude, she would swear the guys she worked with were like puppies. Annoying and underfoot, but ultimately kind of adorable.

"Fine, but you have to keep up."

He winked. "I'll leave you in the dust."

"In your dreams."

CHAPTER SEVENTEEN

Mornings were Gideon's favorite time of the day. He liked the quiet when he was alone in the house, the coolness before the sun had completely cleared the mountain. He stood on the widest part of the deck, his elbows bent, his arms moving as he completed the movements. He focused on his breath and flow, feeling the energy in his body.

The slow-paced exercise, a kind of moving meditation, kept him grounded. When he was faithful in his adherence, the nights were less long, the dreams less violent. He'd been distracted, with Carter's arrival and having Felicia around, and he'd paid the price. Now he inhaled to a slow count of ten and reminded himself he would never be able to forgo the simple practices. They kept him able to function.

He pivoted on his back foot and tightened his muscles as he shifted his weight. Carefully he —

"Yoo-hoo, Gideon? Are you home?"

He brought down his right foot and turned, able to see through the house to the two women peering through the big front window. The old ladies, he thought grimly. Eddie and Gladys. They'd followed him home.

He shook his head and went in through the sliding door on the deck. He was halfway across the living room when he remembered he was wearing nothing more than sweatpants. Sweatpants that sat very low on his hips.

"Goddamn sonofabitch," he grumbled, detouring into the kitchen where he'd left his T-shirt. He jerked it over his head and pulled it down as he continued walking toward the front door.

"What?" he barked as he jerked it open.

Eddie and Gladys both stared at him. Eddie's mouth curved up in a smile.

"Were you in the shower?" she asked hopefully.

"No. I was exercising."

"Naked?"

"Not naked."

The first shiver of fear replaced annoyance. He shook off the sensation. They were old ladies. They weren't going to hurt him . . . were they?

Gladys pushed her friend aside. "We want to talk to you. It won't take long."

Good manners overcame common sense. Gideon stepped back and let them in.

"How can I help you?" he asked as they prowled the living room.

Gladys turned to him first. "What? Oh, why we're here." She smiled. "We want you to sponsor our bowling team. We have the shirts all picked out. We've chosen the colors and everything. Show him."

Eddie plopped down on the sofa and pulled a picture out of her large handbag. He inched forward and took it, then stepped back out of range.

"Okay," he said slowly, studying the fuchsia-colored bowling shirts. They were a new level of ugly.

"You can see why we want them," Gladys said.

"Not really."

Eddie ignored him. "Our names get embroidered on the front and the radio station logo goes on the back. That's advertising for you, which is why you'll want to pay for the shirts. Lots of people come to the bowling alley. They'll see the call letters and want to listen." She paused as if she thought he needed time for the concept to sink in.

He'd been in more dire situations before and understood the need to have a plan of action. However, none of his military training had prepared him to face two old ladies on a mission.

"I get a pretty decent audience share right now," he said.

Gladys put her hand on her chest and actually seemed to go pale. "You're telling us no?"

Eddie's mouth quivered. "I have to sit down," she said, then shook her head. "Oh, I am sitting. It's just the trembling gets so bad." She looked at Gideon, then lowered her voice. "It's my condition."

Gladys sat next to her and squeezed her hand. "Honey, you know it upsets you when you talk about it."

Eddie nodded. "I know. It's just I really thought with the new shirts and all we had a chance at winning. Just one last time before . . ." She swallowed. "You know."

Death, he thought grimly. She meant death. He couldn't shake the feeling he was being played, but he also wasn't willing to take the chance.

"Fine," he snapped. "I'll buy the damn shirts. Order them and send me the bill."

Eddie beamed. "Do you want to approve the design?"

"No," he told her, then remembered who he was dealing with. "Yes. I want to see what you're putting on the shirts before I pay for them."

"No problem."

Eddie stood with amazing agility for one so close to her final chapter. Gladys bounced up next to her.

"Thanks so much," Gladys said, leading the way to the front door. "We appreciate it."

They walked to the front door and let themselves out. Halfway down the driveway, they turned to each other and did a high five. Octogenarian hands slapped loudly in the quiet of the morning.

He'd been had. Suckered by two old ladies, and there wasn't a damn thing he could do about it. As they drove away, he figured he'd gotten off easy. No doubt they would go perform their show in front of someone else to get another sucker to spring for new bowling balls.

He started to go inside, then saw a mail truck pulling into the driveway. A young woman with a ponytail got out.

"Mr. Boylan?"

"Yes."

"I have a certified letter I need you to sign for."

"Sure."

He scrawled his name, then took the slim letter.

"Have a nice day," she called as she got into her small truck.

He nodded.

The return address was from a medical lab outside Sacramento. There was only one reason he would be getting correspondence from a lab this way. Inside was the information on Carter.

He went into the house and stood by the front door. For a second he thought about not opening the envelope. He could cheerfully go a long time without knowing. Except he already knew. In his gut and maybe even his heart. There were plenty of clues and lots of physical evidence. The report would only confirm the information he already had.

Still, he tore off the end and pulled out the single sheet of paper. When he read the report, he went to the study and put it in a drawer. Then he walked away.

Saturday afternoon Felicia walked into the kitchen, not sure what she wanted to do for dinner. She had lots of ingredients but no real sense of how to put them together. Maybe she could go look on the internet.

But her search for inspiration stalled when she saw several dirty dishes sitting on the counter, along with an open package of bread and a jar of peanut butter. The knife was still sticking out of the jar and half the bread was spread over the counter. Two slices had fallen into the sink.

Gideon was out running errands, so she knew he hadn't done this, which left only Carter. While he wasn't perfect — most mornings he tossed his dirty clothes on the bed rather than putting them in the basket she'd provided — he was generally neat and considerate. He'd made his own lunch and snacks before, and he'd never left such a big mess.

A sense of unease washed over her. Something was going on, and she didn't know what. Even more troubling, if someone had stopped and asked her how she knew there was a problem, she couldn't begin to tell him or her.

She walked down the hall to Carter's room. The door was half-open. She knocked as she entered.

Carter was sitting in front of his laptop, slouched in his chair. His feet were up on the desk, and he was playing a computer game with lots of shooting and what looked like purple-skinned space aliens.

"Carter," she began.

"Give me a sec."

He twisted in his seat as he fired several more times. His shooting style was inefficient, she noted. He wasted a lot of energy and had less than fifty percent accuracy. Not that she was going to give him tips right now.

"Carter," she repeated. "I need to speak with you."

He sighed heavily, paused the game and turned to face her. His feet hit the floor with a thunk.

"What?"

She hadn't realized so much information could be contained in a single word. Not that any of it was good.

For a second she felt as if she'd intruded, that she should apologize and leave him alone. The sense of being uncomfortable, of not fitting in, nearly had her backing away. Then she remembered the kitchen.

"You made a peanut butter sandwich a little while ago."

"So? I was hungry. Are you saying I shouldn't eat? Do you want to starve me?"

Felicia processed the words twice and still found no linkage between her comments and his. "I'm saying you left a mess in the kitchen."

"Oh. That."

He turned back to his computer screen and picked up the controller.

"Carter."

"What?"

He didn't bother turning around.

Frustration joined confusion. "Carter, I'm speaking to you."

"We're the only two people in the room. I get that. Unless you want to have a meaningful conversation with the bed." He chuckled.

"I have no reason to speak to the bed," she began, only to realize he'd distracted her again. An excellent ploy, she thought with some respect. So this was what it meant to deal with a teenager. Carter had been so easygoing and polite that she'd assumed he wasn't going to ever be difficult. A mistake on her part. Perhaps he'd just been settling in. Now he was more comfortable and could act like a regular thirteen-year-old.

"Please put down the controller and face me."

There was another very heavy sigh, but he did as she requested. He raised both eyebrows. "What?"

"You left a mess in the kitchen."

"Didn't we already have this conversation?"

"We didn't finish it. You need to go clean up everything."

"Sure." He turned back to the game.

"Now. You need to do it now."

He spun back to her so quickly, she half expected to see him go flying off the chair.

"You don't tell me what to do," he yelled. "You're not my mother."

He stood and moved toward her. Nothing about the move was threatening, yet she sensed he meant it to be.

"I don't have to do what you say," he said, his voice still loud, his posture aggressive. "You're not my *mother*!"

Felicia took a step back. Not because she was afraid, but because she felt as if he'd slapped her. She and Carter had gotten along from the first day. They hugged before he went to bed. They hung out together. She cared about him.

Had it all been an act? A way to gain her trust? If so, what was there to achieve from a pretense of affection?

"Repeating a fact we both already know won't increase its significance," she said quietly. "Our relationship has little bearing on how you conduct yourself in this house. We are a family unit, however loosely formed. Each of us has responsibilities for the greater good. There are rules and considerations. One of them is that you don't leave a mess in the kitchen. You will clean it up now."

He glared at her, his dark eyes bright with emotion. She wasn't sure what he was going to do, but after a few seconds, he stalked past her. She heard his heavy footsteps in the kitchen, then the slam of cupboards and the refrigerator door.

She had no explanation for his harsh words, his attitude. Her chest was tight, and she suddenly knew she was only a few seconds from crying. Something she instinctively guessed she couldn't let him see or know about.

She hurried down the hall. The master was on the other side of the house. She sank onto the bed and tried to steady her breathing. But it was too late to stop the tears. They filled her eyes and spilled down her cheeks. The pain in her heart overwhelmed her. She felt betrayed and hurt and so very small. As if she could no longer protect herself.

Even though she couldn't say from what, she knew that Carter was somehow at the root of it all.

■ ■ ■ ■

Gideon knew something was wrong the second he stepped into the house. There was a change in the energy. If he were on the other side of the world, he would be pulling his gun and bracing for an ambush. As it was, he could only move quietly and be prepared for whatever happened next.

He walked through the kitchen, but all seemed well there. A few crumbs on the counters, but nothing out of place. He paused, not sure which way to go next. He started toward Carter's room, then changed his mind and went into the master.

Felicia sat on the bed. At first he didn't understand her posture. The slumped shoulders were at odds with her usual upright, take-charge self. Then she looked up, and he saw tears in her eyes.

He found himself pulling her to her feet and holding her tight. She clung to him, her pain as raw and open as a wound.

He stroked her hair and her back. "What happened?" he asked. "Are you hurt?"

"No," she managed, her voice a choked sob. "I'm fine. Or I should be." She sniffed and stepped back. "It's Carter. We had a fight."

She moved away. "That's what it was. A fight. I've never had a fight with anyone before. It's awful. How do people do it all the time? Why aren't they crushed? He made a snack and left everything out. The bread, the peanut butter. He doesn't do that, so I was confused. I went to see him to ask him to clean up what he'd done and he —"

She paused, her mouth trembling.

So far he didn't see the issue, but she was upset and that made this his problem. "And?"

"He yelled at me. He said I wasn't his mother and I couldn't tell him what to do. The way he looked at me . . ." More tears fell. "I thought we were getting close. I thought he liked me."

Gideon pulled her close again. "He *does* like you."

"You didn't see him. I'm trying to tell myself that he's thirteen and there are hormones, or maybe he's testing me to see if I'll stand by him, no matter what. I hope it's one of those, but I never thought it would hurt so much."

He held her, knowing there was nothing he could say to make the situation easier. But he could try to understand it better.

"I'm going to talk to him."

Felicia nodded. "I guess one of us should, and I don't think I can right now."

He was halfway down the hall when he saw the front door just out of the corner of his eye. It would be so easy to head out. Take off. Run up the mountain or get in his car and disappear. Leave all this emotional crap behind. Simple solution that wouldn't solve the real problem. Because the letter he'd gotten two days ago said no matter how long he was gone or how much he avoided his responsibility, Carter was still his son.

He walked into his office and pulled the envelope out of his desk, then went down the hall. When he reached Carter's room, he found the teen lying on his bed, staring at the ceiling.

"Go away," he said as Gideon entered.

"No such luck, kid."

Gideon pulled the desk chair next to the bed and sat down.

He'd been a teenager once, although trying to summon the memories was useless. During his captivity, he'd done his best to forget everyone and everything he'd ever known.

But now, as he stared at the boy who was his son, he had no way to connect. No funny stories about his past to share. He'd done a good job of forgetting, never thinking that if he survived, there might be a price to pay.

"You gonna be a shit much longer, or is this about over?" he asked, his voice conversational.

Carter sat up and stared at him. "What are you talking about?"

"Don't pretend you don't know. Felicia's the smartest one in the house, but neither of us is stupid. What's your endgame? Does hurting someone who cares about you make you feel like a man?"

Carter flinched. "She's upset?"

"She's crying."

The last vestige of defiance faded, leaving behind a frightened and ashamed boy. "I'm sorry."

"Don't apologize to me."

Carter hung his head. "I was mean to her." He cleared his throat. "I don't know why I did it. I really like Felicia. She's cool, you know? Always nice and interesting."

Gideon searched for the right words, for some parable to explain what was going on. The problem was, he didn't understand Carter any more than he understood the two old ladies who had invaded his space a few days ago. The only thing he knew for sure was Felicia was hurting, and he wanted her to feel better. And his son was confused, and he needed to help him.

Carter nodded. "I get it. I'm testing her, right? To make sure she's going to be there. She's so patient and understanding. I want this to work. I want the two of you to get married and stuff, but what if you don't? What if she leaves?"

Gideon was on his feet and nearly out the door before he caught himself and turned around. Fortunately, Carter was busy trying not to cry and hadn't noticed.

"Married?" The sound was more croak than word.

He couldn't get married. He couldn't. That part of him had been beaten, electrocuted or just plain starved out of him. No way.

Carter looked up at him. "Sure. You like her, and she gets this funny look when you're around. It makes a stable home for me. But if you don't, she'll leave eventually. I mean come on, she's hot. Some other guy is going to snatch her up if you don't make your play."

"You fought with Felicia because you think she's going to start dating another guy?"

Carter gave him a half smile. "No. I don't want her to leave."

"I don't want her to leave, either."

The smile broadened. "Cool."

"No, not cool. Not anything. What happens or doesn't happen with Felicia doesn't change what you did to her. And it doesn't change this."

He pulled the envelope out of his back pocket and dropped it on the bed. "The DNA results are back. You're stuck with me, kid."

Carter stared at the paper but didn't touch it. "You're my dad?"

"Uh-huh. Not a surprise for either of us. I'll talk to a lawyer and find out what the next step is to make it official. There will be a few legal things. You can keep your last name. It's what you know and a connection with your mom."

Carter drew his knee to his chest and poked at the envelope. "Felicia told you that last part, didn't she?"

"Yes. She said it was important for you to maintain your identity. Or at the very least, that it should be your decision."

He had more to say, but Carter was already running down the hall.

Gideon followed more slowly. He found them in the center of the master, Carter nearly wringing his hands as he apologized.

Felicia let him finish, then shrugged. "We need to establish some rules and consequences."

"I can help with that," he told her earnestly. "I'm sorry I hurt you." He brushed away tears. "I mean it."

"I know."

Carter sniffed. "He's my dad."

"Are you surprised?" she asked.

"No, but it's nice to know for sure."

"Confirmation can be soothing."

Carter started to laugh. Gideon expected him to hug her now, but the kid turned and reached for him. The teen pulled her along and it was the three of them, holding on for a very long time.

Gideon suddenly understood what Dickens had meant. The best of times and the worst of times. Unexpectedly, he started to laugh.

"What's so funny?" Carter asked.

"Felicia." He looked at the woman in question. "You're a dangerous influence."

She smiled. "I try to only use my powers for good."

CHAPTER EIGHTEEN

"You're not going to believe it," Isabel said, reaching for a chip.

Felicia dipped into the guacamole and waited for the news.

Lunch with her friends was always fun and interesting, she thought. There were plenty of jokes and a real sense of caring and connection. Just a few months ago she'd been a stranger in a new town, but now she belonged. She had a job she loved, girlfriends to hang out with, a gorgeous man in her bed and a growing bond with a teenager. The best part was she honestly couldn't say which element was the most surprising. She never would have expected to be so happy, but here she was.

Patience smiled at Isabel. "We're not, so tell us."

Isabel waved her chip. "I got an email from my parents, who are very close to Hong Kong, by the way, and they've rented out the apartment over the garage. Just like that. A note telling me the tenant will be moving in at the end of the week, and could I please get the cleaning service in and air out the place."

"Who's the tenant?" Noelle asked.

"I have no idea."

"Could be a serial killer," Charlie said cheerfully. She was looking tanned and relaxed after her exotic honeymoon.

"Thanks for that," Isabel said with a grimace. "I can't believe they didn't ask me to interview whoever it is. Or at least meet them."

"If he kills you in your sleep, they'll feel guilty," Noelle said. "I mean that in a helpful way and it didn't come out exactly as I planned."

"Oddly, I know what you mean," Isabel said and bit down on her chip.

"I understand your point," Patience told her. "The apartment is close enough that you'll be seeing a lot of your new tenant."

"Not if he only goes out at night," Charlie pointed out.

"Somebody kick her," Isabel said.

"While I'm closest and capable," Felicia said with a smile. "I don't want to take Charlie on."

"Thanks." Charlie grinned. "Because, of

everyone here, I think you're the only one who could take me." She looked at Consuelo. "Okay, you, too. Even though you're small."

Consuelo winked. "People underestimate me all the time. It takes away the challenge, but I always enjoy having the advantage."

Jo appeared with a big tray. "It's food time, people. Move your stuff."

Salads, burgers and tacos were passed out. Felicia accepted her BBQ chicken salad and wondered what Carter would make of the place. While he was too young to come into the bar at night, during the day, children were welcome. There was even a play area in the corner for the toddler set.

She thought he might get the joke of reality TV playing and the female-skin-tone-flattering paint colors. He'd been home the past couple of days with a cold. She'd stayed with him, and they'd enjoyed hanging out together.

Since the big fight a few days before, life had been a lot calmer. She and Carter had written up house rules and consequences. He'd been extremely fair when suggesting punishments, offering up items he valued most. He'd admitted to testing boundaries and apologized for hurting her.

For reasons she couldn't explain, the

incident had brought them closer. Logically she should have been worried he would hurt her again, but she wasn't. Gideon, on the other hand, seemed to be more wary around them. She suspected having the DNA test confirm his relationship with Carter was something he had to deal with. Connections were difficult for him, and there was no way to un-make Carter his son.

"If you're really worried about your new tenant," Charlie said, picking up her burger, "ask the police to run a check on the guy. Assuming it's a guy."

"Women can be killers," Consuelo pointed out.

Noelle smiled at her. "You say that so cheerfully."

"I don't like discrimination." She grabbed a French fry and turned to Felicia. "Carter's doing really well in class. He's got some talent."

"He probably gets that from his dad. He's loving the class. And he has a big crush on you."

"He'll get over it."

"Are you going to offer self-defense classes?" Patience asked. "I'd love to take one."

"I could," Consuelo said. "If you think people would be interested."

"It's Fool's Gold." Isabel rolled her eyes. "Nothing scary ever happens here."

"That's not true." Patience waved her fork. "Lillie was kidnapped."

They all nodded. "That was awful," Charlie said.

"And remember after Brew-haha opened and there was that guy?" Patience asked.

Consuelo looked confused. "What guy?"

"It was great," Patience told her. "This guy came in with his wife. He was awful. Abusive and mean. Felicia walked over to him and took him down."

Felicia shook her head. "I immobilized him until the police could come. Nothing more."

"Impressive," Isabel said. She turned to Consuelo. "If you're teaching that, sign me up."

"I can show you how to kick a little butt."

Felicia felt both pleased and uncomfortable with the praise.

"I remember her," Charlie said. "Helen. She left him. Relocated and is starting over. Good for her."

Maybe it was the town, Felicia thought, glancing out the window. It empowered people to change. There were —

Her brain came to a complete stop. There was a woman outside walking her dog. Not an unusual occurrence. People walked dogs all the time. Except . . . Except . . .

She pushed back her chair and sprang to her feet. "I forgot!"

Everyone stared at her.

"What's wrong?" Consuelo asked. "Are you okay?"

"No. I can't believe it. I forgot. It's Tuesday."

"Did she hit her head?" Isabel asked.

Horror had a metallic taste, Felicia thought, barely breathing as the truth rushed into her brain like the tide. How could she have forgotten?

"I was working on it all last week. I knew. And then I had the fight with Carter and I just forgot." She stared at them. "It's the Dog Days of Summer festival on Friday."

"Oh, that," Charlie said and picked up her burger. "Sure. Same weekend every year."

"But I'm not ready," Felicia shrieked. "Do you see any decorations? Signs for parking? Have there been any announcements on the radio? I forgot. It's my job and I forgot."

She reached into her pocket and pulled out a twenty, then ran out of the bar. Once on the sidewalk, she came to a stop, not sure what to do next.

There should be decorations, she thought

frantically. Due to a scheduling mix-up, the city crew wasn't available to put up the signs, but she'd been given a budget to hire high school and college kids to hook the banners to the light poles. She had a three-page, single-spaced list of all she was supposed to accomplish. Instead of checking that in her office, she'd been home with Carter. She'd been so focused on him, she'd forgotten about the festival.

Indecision clutched her like big hairy monster hands. She couldn't move, couldn't think. Help. She needed help.

She pulled her phone out of her purse and pushed in Gideon's number.

"Hey," he said when he answered.

"I forgot the festival," she said, her voice breathless. "I forgot. I don't know how it happened. I've never forgotten anything. It's in three days and I'm not ready."

"Festival?"

"The Dog Days of Summer. There are no decorations, no pooper-scooper stations. I stayed home with Carter instead of going to work. I was out to lunch with my friends. I forgot! I never forget. I have a perfect memory."

She clutched the phone with both hands as panic made it impossible to breathe.

"Slow down," Gideon said. "What do you need?"

"I don't know. Everything. The festival is ruined."

"Can't ruin what hasn't started. Figure out what you need and call me. I'll head to the station and put the word out. We have three days. In Fool's Gold time, that's a month. We'll get it done."

"I hope you're right," she whispered and disconnected the call.

Her office, she thought. She had to get to her office.

She turned to head that way and found all her friends standing on the sidewalk.

"You were eating lunch," she said, confused to see them there.

Charlie waved her burger. "You can get food to go. Jo grumbles, but she'll do it."

Patience touched Felicia's arm. "You're in trouble. We want to help."

Isabel smiled. "We heard what you said on the phone. We're going with you to your office, and we'll split the to-do list. Gideon can put out a request for help on the radio and you'll have plenty of volunteers."

"That's what he said," Felicia murmured, still unable to grasp what would happen. "You can't help me. You're all busy."

Noelle shook her head. "Nothing that

394

can't wait. You need us. Later, you'll return the favor. No big deal."

"Let's call Dellina," Isabel said. "We all saw what she did with Charlie's wedding. The girl has mad skills."

"Thank you," Felicia said fervently. "I'm so confused, I don't know where to begin."

"Admitting there's a problem is always the first step," Patience said, putting an arm around her. "Now, let's go to your office and get this festival going."

At six, Felicia made her way through the corridors of city hall. She'd phoned ahead and had an appointment with the mayor. She'd already printed out and signed her letter of resignation, which she couldn't bring herself to think about. Every time she did, her stomach hurt and she thought she might throw up.

She loved Fool's Gold more than any place she'd ever lived, and she'd let down the town. She'd messed up her job, and she was only in month two. She honestly wasn't sure which was more surprising — her shock at forgetting or how devastated she felt for having forgotten. She hadn't known she was capable of feeling so much guilt and remorse.

The mayor's door stood open. There was

no one sitting out front, so Felicia knocked on the door frame and stepped inside.

Mayor Marsha sat at a large desk. Behind her were a U.S.A. flag, a state flag and a city flag. Big windows framed a view of the town. Mayor Marsha looked up and smiled.

"There you are, Felicia. Have a seat."

Felicia moved to the offered chair and sat down. She put the folder on the desk and pushed it toward the other woman.

"What is this?" the mayor asked, reaching for the folder.

"My letter of resignation. I'm sorry I didn't get it to you sooner."

Mayor Marsha picked up the folder, turned in her chair, bent over and started a machine. Felicia heard a whirring sound, followed by the grind of shredding paper.

"I don't think so," the mayor said as she straightened. "You're not getting away from us so easily."

Felicia shook her head. "You don't have to be nice to me. I messed up. I forgot the festival. I got caught up in my personal life and I forgot. I have no excuse other than carelessness. I deserve to be fired."

"I doubt that. Besides, the more important question is what the town deserves. I believe we should have the very best, and that, my dear, is you."

For the second time in less than a week Felicia was fighting tears. "You don't understand," she said, blinking rapidly. "I was wrong."

"You were human."

"I wasn't thinking about work."

"Bravo."

"Wh-what?"

"There has been too much work in your life. You copublished your first scientific article when you were eleven. Growing up in that university, you worked in the lab seven days a week. Did you ever take off even a day? Go on vacation?"

Felicia considered the question. "A professor and her family took me to see Mount Rushmore once."

"How lovely. But a child needs more. We need you, Felicia. We need your intelligence and organizational skills, but we also need your heart. I've seen you with Carter. I've heard how much he cares about you. You're building a family, and that's something to be very proud of."

Felicia twisted her hands together. "Please don't be nice to me. I did a terrible thing."

The mayor smiled. "I'm sorry, but I'm not going to punish you. I learned many, many years ago that harsh words can never be unspoken, and they have consequences.

Since then I have vowed to weigh what I say first. You need to learn to accept your flaws and forgive yourself. A wise man I know has told me the same thing, and I suspect he's right." She smiled. "Sensible words from a handsome man. What is the world coming to?"

Felicia had no idea what she was talking about. "The festival," she began.

The mayor cut her off with a shake of her head. "Come here."

Felicia rose and followed her to the window. They could see down Fourth Street to Frank Lane. Everywhere she looked people were hanging banners and putting out pots of flowers. As she watched, a truck pulled up. Two men started unloading dog water stations.

"In two days, the booths will be put up and the vendors will start to arrive. The dog costume parade will begin on time, as will all the demonstrations and lectures. Most of the festival was already put in place. You forgot a few window dressings."

"But it's my *job* and I screwed up."

"I see. What have you learned from this experience?"

"That I'm not infallible. That I can be distracted, which I never knew. I learned I need to check my calendar before I take a day off and . . ." She paused, aware the mayor was staring at her expectantly. As if none of these answers had been correct.

She thought about how she'd felt when she'd realized what she'd done. Sick to her stomach. But Gideon had been there for her, as had her friends.

"I learned it's okay to ask for help," she murmured.

The mayor put her hand on Felicia's shoulder. "Exactly. You're one of us now, child. And we take care of our own." She glanced at her watch. "It's late. You should get home to your family."

Thursday afternoon Felicia checked her diagram against the construction being done in the park. Part of the Dog Days festival included a show ring. The local "best dog" contests would be judged here, and there would be demonstrations by different canine groups. A rancher from Stockton was bringing his herding dogs, and a local agility club would show off their dogs. Montana Hendrix-Bradley would give a lecture on service dogs.

"There you are!"

Felicia turned and saw Pia walking toward her. The other woman, finally showing her pregnancy, grinned as she approached.

399

"You screwed up," Pia said, hugging her. "I'm so happy."

Felicia stood still, not sure what to say.

Pia continued to smile. "Thank God. All I've been hearing is how amazing you are, how much better the festivals have been since you took over. I was getting a complex. Now I discover you're really human, so I can like you again." She linked arms with Felicia. "Okay, show me what you're doing so I can coo over it."

It was a quick emotional roller coaster, but still impressive for all its brevity. Felicia pressed her free hand to her chest. "You're going to need to give me a minute to catch up."

"Pshaw. You're doing great." They started toward the park. "I have to say this is one of my favorite festivals. You know it's not just dogs, right?"

"What do you mean?"

"People bring all kinds of pets. They dress them up, too. You haven't truly lived until you've seen a pair of tuxedo cats dressed like a bride and groom."

"Why would someone do that to pets they supposedly love?" She shook her head. "Never mind. As a culture we want to anthropomorphize everything from cars to animals. I've never been able to figure out if it's because we think we're the best species or if we enjoy communication so much, we want to pretend everything around us can talk. I wonder if anyone has done a study on that. It would make a very interesting dissertation for a variety of fields of study."

She realized they'd come to a stop and Pia was staring at her.

"You are so weird," the other woman said. "But I still like you. I'll admit, I was reluctant to hand over my festivals to anyone, but you're the perfect fit."

"You're only saying that because I messed up."

Pia laughed. "In part. When I realized I couldn't do the job anymore, I went to Mayor Marsha. We each made a list of the five people we thought would do the job best. You were number one on both our lists."

"But you didn't know me."

"I'd heard about you. I asked around." She started walking again. "Okay, show me where the iguana display is going to be."

Felicia blinked. "There's supposed to be an iguana display?"

Pia grinned. "Kidding. You're so easy. But I happen to know the funnel cake guy is all set up. Let's go there and I'll buy you a funnel cake."

■ ■ ■ ■

Gideon and Carter strolled through the center of town. The sidewalks were crowded as people waited for the costume parade.

Carter looked around at all the people with their pets. "I thought it was the 'Dog Days' of summer," he said quietly, pointing. "That lady's holding a rabbit."

"It's kind of a town thing." Gideon figured in Fool's Gold people wouldn't want to restrict themselves to simply celebrating dogs.

"I've never been anywhere like this before," Carter told him. "It's strange, but still nice. Felicia was saying that in the next festival some guy gets his heart cut out."

"I'm pretty sure that's symbolic and not genuine."

"You mean there won't be any blood?"

"Sorry. They don't even use a real knife."

"Bummer." Carter grinned at him. "It would be a great threat to use all year."

"Take out the garbage or I'll sign you up to get your heart cut out?"

"Sure."

"I didn't know you were so bloodthirsty."

They were still snickering when Eddie joined them. Today her tracksuit was apple-green. She hurried over, her expression determined.

"We're getting our bowling shirts next week," she announced. "I saw a sample, and they're going to look wonderful. They're fuchsia."

Gideon stared at her. "Wasn't I supposed to approve the sample?"

She waved her hand in a gesture of dismissal. "They're fine. You'll love them." Her smile turned sly. "I took the liberty of ordering a couple of extras. One for you and one for Carter."

"Cool," Carter told her. "Thank you."

"You're welcome." She looked at Gideon. "He's a very nice young man. You should get him a dog."

With that, she left.

Carter stared up at him. "A dog?"

"No."

"But a boy needs a dog."

"Did you two plan this?"

"No. I've never met that lady before in my life."

"You'll have to make do with a bowling shirt. By the way, they're pink."

"She said they're fuchsia."

"Do you know what color fuchsia is?" Gideon asked.

"No."

"It's pink."

"About that dog," Carter began.

Fortunately, they turned the corner and Gideon saw Ford up ahead. He waved to his friend, who headed toward them.

"Have you seen my mother?" Ford asked, looking over his shoulder.

"No. Carter, this is Ford Hendrix. Ford, my son, Carter."

"Hey," Ford said, holding out his hand. "Nice to meet you." He looked around. "She's here."

"Who?"

"My mother. She wants to find me a wife."

Gideon remembered talk of the booth at the Fourth of July festival. "That's right. She's taking applications. How's that working out for you?"

Ford glared at him. "If there wasn't a young man standing here, I would tell you exactly how it's working out for me."

"I don't mind if you swear," Carter told him. "I've heard it all. Why don't you want to get married?"

"It's a long story."

"Are you in love with someone else? Because if you're not, Felicia's awesome. She's totally hot and she can cook and she's very organized."

Now it was Gideon's turn to glare, but at

his son rather than his friend. "What are you doing?"

Carter shrugged. "Felicia wants a family. She told me. If you haven't made your move yet, Dad, you need to step out of the way and let some other guy have a shot at her. She's a babe. Not to me, because she's like a stepmom, but Reese thinks she's all that."

Ford patted Gideon on the shoulder. "All right, bro. You have bigger problems than me. I find that comforting. Good luck." He started to walk away, then turned back. "You should get that kid a dog."

Carter beamed.

Gideon found himself wanting to pummel his friend and ground Carter for the next year. "Felicia can get her own guy."

"She won't go out with anyone else while she's still with you. Unless you're in love with her. You don't have to tell me, of course," he added. "I'm just a kid."

He started to say he wasn't in love with Felicia, that he was never going to love anyone. He couldn't. To love was to be weak. But Carter wouldn't understand that.

"You guys are great together," Carter added. "If you're worried I'll be upset because you didn't marry my mom, I won't be. I promise."

"Good to know."

■ ■ ■ ■

Sunday afternoon Carter and Reese lay on the grass in Reese's front yard.

"I'm not getting anywhere," Carter admitted, staring up at the blue sky. "Gideon won't make his move." Reese already knew about the fight the previous week. Although it hadn't been part of his plan, afterward he'd realized they'd had to pull together to deal with him. He'd waited for days, hoping for a sign that things had progressed.

"You're sure he didn't say he loved her?" Reese asked.

"I'm sure. I practically asked and he didn't answer."

"Maybe he doesn't want to talk about his feelings. My dad never does."

"I don't think it's that simple. He wasn't happy when I suggested Ford go out with her, but he also didn't say no." Carter needed Gideon and Felicia to get together. He needed them to be a family, and he was running out of ways to make that happen.

Reese sat up. "Okay, I have one more idea, but it's risky. And we could both get in a lot of trouble."

"Trouble isn't always bad if it brings Felicia and Gideon together. Tell me what you're thinking."

Felicia couldn't remember being this tired before, except maybe after the last festival. She had spent the past three days running from around six in the morning until midnight. Now it was close to ten Sunday evening and she could barely keep her eyes open.

"Thanks for picking me up," she said, trying not to yawn.

"I know how long the days are," Gideon told her as he drove up the mountain. "We'll get your car in the morning."

She leaned against the door and closed her eyes. "I'm not worried. No one is going to steal it."

"Succumbing to small-town charm?"

"Uh-huh."

She could feel herself starting to drift off. The sound of the car was soothing, and being around Gideon always made her feel safe. Sleep, she thought drowsily. She needed sleep.

"You know Ford Hendrix, right?"

"What?" She opened her eyes. "Sure. For a long time. He's friends with Justice. A SEAL, but we don't hold that against him."

"You ever date him?"

"No. Ford falls into the brother category.

Not as much as Justice, but close. His mother's trying to find him a wife. I don't think he's excited about the prospect."

"So if he wanted to go out with you, you wouldn't be interested?"

Surprise added to alertness. "No. What a strange question. Ford and I are friends." The only man she could imagine herself being with was Gideon. The thought of trying to be intimate with someone else made her uncomfortable.

Pair bonding, she thought. She'd bonded. She wasn't sure that was the same as love, but it was a step on the road. Another sign of normal, she thought happily. If only she could figure out his feelings for her.

"Do you think we should get Carter a dog? A couple of people mentioned it today."

"There are many reasons to have a dog in the family. They teach responsibility and demonstrate loyalty. Does Carter want a dog?"

"He said he did."

"Do you?"

"I'm not sure."

They arrived at the house. He parked in front. She climbed out of her side and started toward the house.

The night was dark and still. In the distance, she heard the soft hoot of an owl.

"There aren't any lights on in the house," she said as Gideon unlocked the door. "What time was Kent dropping off Carter?"

"Around nine. That's what Carter said. Maybe he went to bed already."

"He never has before. He always waits up."

But he wasn't in the living room. Felicia found herself coming completely awake as irrational panic swept through her.

"Carter?" she called as she hurried to his bedroom.

"He's not in the media room," Gideon yelled from downstairs.

He wasn't in his bedroom, either, but he'd left a note on his desk.

Gideon and Felicia — I've run away. I'm out alone in the world. It's a dangerous place. Who knows what could happen to a kid my age. You should probably come find me.

CHAPTER NINETEEN

It took the Fool's Gold police department less than an hour to set up a command station. While Gideon waited for Ford, Angel and Justice to arrive, Felicia moved her computer into the dining room. The police might technically be in charge, but she was going to be running the show.

She had trouble with her computer. Something was wrong with the keys. They weren't responding. It took her a second to realize she was shaking so hard, she wasn't pressing them right. Then she sank down in a chair and covered her face with her hands.

She couldn't do this, she thought as panic and helplessness wrestled for control. Couldn't not know, couldn't feel these feelings. All around her police officers spoke on cell phones and called out instructions, and all she could think was that Carter had run away.

Had she done something wrong? The

question repeated itself over and over in her brain. She waited for some logical response or a pithy phrase in Latin. Instead there was only fear and the knowledge that if it would bring him home, she would gladly cut out her own heart and offer it to whomever was interested.

Someone pulled her hands away from her face.

"They're ten minutes out," Gideon said, his expression tense and determined as he crouched in front of her.

"Justice and the guys?"

"Yeah. They're who I'd want on my team."

He was trying to make her feel better. She wished it could work. "We need to find him."

He straightened. "We will. I'm going to call in a heat-seeking helicopter."

Not the technical term for the cameras that were sensitive enough to differentiate various temperatures from hundreds of feet in the air, but she got the point.

"Maybe later. First, we should start by searching the old-fashioned way." Mayor Marsha walked over to them. She took Felicia's hand and squeezed her fingers. "I know this is hard for both of you."

"He ran away," Felicia said, still trying to believe the words. "He ran away because I

411

did something wrong."

"While it would be easy for you to blame yourself, I doubt either of you are at fault," the mayor told her. "Let's think about this from Carter's point of view. He's a thirteen-year-old boy who's had his life turned upside down. A year ago he lost his mother. Three months ago, his living situation dissolved and he knew he was going to be thrust into the foster care system. He had to find his father, make his way to Fool's Gold, all on his own, and start over. A lot for anyone, but for a young man of his age?"

Felicia nodded. "You're right. But he did it. All of it." She looked at Gideon. "He's so strong. I think he gets that from you."

Gideon raised his hands and took a step back. "Do we have to talk about that now?"

"No. You're right. We have to find Carter."

"Did he take his bike?" Mayor Marsha asked.

Gideon shook his head. "It's still in the garage with the other two."

"Well, then, he's traveling on foot." The older woman smiled and released Felicia's hand. "He can't have gotten far."

"Unless he got in a car with someone." Felicia pressed her hand to her mouth. "What if he's been abducted?"

"He left a note saying he ran away," Gideon reminded her. "He wasn't abducted."

"I agree." The older woman drew in a breath. "Boys do love to explore. There are so many trails in the mountains. Caves and old shacks. We have a lot of ground to cover. I've already put a call in to Max Thurman. Two of his older service dogs used to work for the DEA. They're trained to find items based on scent. I wonder if they could help locate Carter." She sighed. "We really need an organized Search and Rescue operation in this town. I'll have to put that on the budget agenda for next year. But first things first. Let's find your boy."

The front door opened and Justice, Angel and Ford walked in. They were dressed in black and carrying backpacks. Felicia raced to Justice, who pulled her close.

"We'll find him," he said. "I promise."

"I want to believe you," she admitted. "I've never looked for a child. I'm not sure where to start first."

Patience stepped into the house and hurried to Felicia. "We start by calling his friends and talking to their parents."

"I've done that," Felicia said, relieved she hadn't wasted time with a useless task. "I spoke to all of them except for Kent. He didn't answer his cell. I left a message for him, and none of the other parents have seen Carter." She bit her lower lip. "Why would he do this?"

"That's for later," Patience said firmly, leading her back to the dining room. "First we have to find him."

Felicia nodded, even as she fought tears.

More police officers arrived, along with a few state troopers. They started to divide everyone up into teams. Police Chief Barns pointed at Felicia. "You'll be staying here."

"No way," Gideon said, before Felicia could say anything. "She's coming with me. She's as capable as anyone here, and she knows Carter the best."

"Thank you," she told him.

He put his arm around her shoulders. "I know you're scared. I'm scared, too. When we find him, I'm locking him in a shed until he's eighteen."

She managed a slight smile. "I wish we could."

Gideon's jaw clenched. "Damn kid. Fine. I'll admit the shed is a little extreme, but he's going to be grounded or something. This is irresponsible."

"I know. That's what confuses me. He's mature most of the time. I wish I understood what was going on."

The front door flew open, and Kent Hendrix stormed in. "Where is he? Where's my son?"

Felicia's stomach churned harder and faster. "He's not at home?"

"He left me a note that he was staying here tonight. Reese's been over here a couple of times, so I didn't think anything of it. Until I got your message."

Ford crossed to his brother. "Reese is missing, too?"

Police Chief Barns groaned. "All right, people," she said to her team. "We're looking for two boys and they could be anywhere."

"They're on the move," Carter said, watching the screen on his laptop. It had taken him some doing, but he'd managed to tap into the GPS on Felicia's cell phone a few days before and could now track her.

They were stretched out in sleeping bags in the caves on the Castle Ranch. They had lanterns, a cooler, an extra battery for the laptop and a portable Wi-Fi hot spot. The challenge was staying close enough to the front of the caves to get a signal, but far enough back so they weren't detected.

Fortunately, the only person who came into the caves was Heidi Stryker. She used the caves to age her goat cheese. But according to Reese, she only checked every couple of days, and the space she used was on the other side of the opening. To avoid her, they'd gone north instead of south at the fork.

Reese rolled onto his back and grabbed a fruit snack. He opened the package and tore off a strip. "How much trouble are we going to be in, you think?"

"Tons," Carter said, watching the small red dot moving on the screen. "You heard the police scanner. Half the town has turned out to look for us."

"Wicked!"

"You didn't have to do this," Carter reminded his friend. "You could have stayed home."

"And let you have all the fun? No way. Plus, once you get Gideon and Felicia married, I'll know you're staying around permanently. High school in two years, my friend. Then we get all the girls."

They bumped fists, then wiggled their fingers.

The search parties all started from Pyrite Park. A member of CDS was part of every team. Consuelo had joined them, giving them one more professional to help the townspeople. Gideon didn't know what to think about the sheer number of people who had turned out to aid in the search. Even Eddie and Gladys had come along to find the boys.

People he didn't know kept coming up to him and patting him on the back as they promised they would find the missing kids. He felt numb — almost disconnected. The attention was uncomfortable but necessary, he reminded himself. They had to get Carter back.

He couldn't figure out why the kid had done it. Sure, there'd been some adjustments, but he would have sworn things had been going okay. Carter knew Gideon was his father and that he wasn't going anywhere. Felicia made everything feel like a family event. What more did Carter want?

"We're going to walk a grid," Police Chief Barns said through a megaphone. "There are a few outlying areas we want to check, as well. Up the road by Gideon's house. Justice, you take your team there. Also, the summer camp. Consuelo, can you go there? Make sure a parent with a kid in the camp is on the team."

Gideon paced, waiting for them to be assigned. He kept having the nagging sense of missing something. That the *why* of it all was right in front of him, if only he could see it.

"You should go check out the caves by the Castle Ranch," Mayor Marsha told Felicia. "If I were a boy, that's where I'd go."

"Caves?" Felicia's voice rose in pitch. "That sounds dangerous."

"These are shallow. Heidi uses them to age her cheese, but only a few. They're safe enough — we had lots of people in them last year for . . ." She pressed her lips together. "That's not important. You two go ahead. I'll tell Alice."

"I'll come, too," Kent said grimly.

Gideon grabbed Felicia's hand and pulled her to his truck. "That's as good a place to start as any." He needed to be moving, doing. Standing around accomplished nothing.

"I don't want a random search," Felicia said. "It's late and I want to find him."

While it wasn't exactly cold in late August, there was still a slight chill in the air. What if Carter was scared? What if something had happened to him? What if he was hurt?

Gideon shook off the questions. He hadn't been in the field in years, but he knew the drill. Stay focused. Felicia might have the brains in the operation but he had the experience.

"How can anyone survive this?" she asked, sliding into the passenger side and closing the door. "The not knowing. It's horrible."

"I'm telling you, a shed is the answer."

Kent slammed the rear door. "I can tell you Reese isn't going to see the light of day until he's thirty-five."

They drove out to the ranch.

When they got there, several people were waiting for them. Rafe Stryker had already collected flashlights. Heidi, his wife, showed them some rudimentary maps of the caves, done years ago.

"This is where I store my cheese," she said, pointing. "I was just there this morning."

"Carter hadn't run away then," Gideon told her. "He was at the festival."

"See how the path splits," Rafe told them. He traced the line on the map. "Heidi only goes south. There's a whole maze of trails heading north. If the boys are in the caves, that's where we'll find them."

Shane, Rafe's brother, joined them. They walked past a barn and what Heidi identified as the goat house, then headed toward the opening to the caves. Everyone turned on their lights. Three minutes later, they reached the divide in the path. Heidi and Rafe went first.

"This way," Heidi said. "I spent some time in these caves last summer. There were cave paintings." She paused. "That doesn't matter. This way."

Felicia moved next to Gideon. He took her hand. She squeezed his fingers, and they walked forward.

After a few hundred feet, he heard something.

"Quiet," he instructed.

"I heard it, too," Felicia murmured.

Their group went silent. In the distance was faint music.

"That way," he said, pointing to a path that veered to the left.

"Carter!" Felicia called as she started to run.

Gideon kept up with her easily. His right hand kept reaching for a nonexistent weapon. The result of training, he thought grimly. No guns today, and no enemies.

"Carter!" Felicia screamed, running ahead.

Gideon kept pace with her. They rounded a bend and stumbled into a large open cave with high ceilings. Carter and Reese were sitting on sleeping bags, playing a game on a laptop, music blasting from speakers. There were lanterns and a cooler.

The teens scrambled to their feet as the

adults rushed in. Felicia pulled Carter hard against her.

"What were you thinking?" she demanded as she touched his face, then his shoulders. "Running away? It was horrible. When I read that note —"

Kent muttered something under his breath as he reached for Reese. Father and son embraced.

The rest of the team gathered around. Felicia kept touching Carter, as if reassuring herself. Then she started to cry.

Carter immediately stepped back and looked horrified. "I'm sorry," he said. "Don't cry."

"I was so scared," she admitted, her voice shaking.

"I didn't mean to frighten you."

"Too bad, because you would have achieved your goal. Oh, Carter." She hugged him again. "You know you have to be punished, right?"

He nodded.

"Okay, and you have to swear you'll never do this again." She cupped his face in her hands. "I love you. You need to get that."

Tears filled his eyes. "I love you, too, and I'm sorry."

"Me, too, Dad," Reese told his father. "It was a stupid trick."

"More than a trick. You're grounded, for starters. We'll take it from there."

Rafe headed toward the path. "I'll alert the others that the boys are found."

Gideon watched it all, physically there, but separate from what was happening. He could see Felicia's emotion but wasn't a part of it. Sure, he was glad the boys were fine, but he didn't have the same connection as the others. It was like being underwater and hearing sound. He knew it was there but couldn't recognize it.

And then he knew. Whatever had been done to him, whatever had been beaten from him, whatever had allowed him to survive when the others didn't, wasn't because he was stronger than them. It was because there was something wrong with him. He wasn't like other people. They had loved once, and losing all they loved had destroyed them. He'd thought them weak, but he was wrong. They were completely human.

And he wasn't.

He didn't have the same emotions, the same needs. Perhaps the flaw had always been there, and the torture had brought it to the surface. Maybe he'd been more whole before, but what had happened to him had caused breaks. He didn't know, and it didn't matter. Except he had a child now.

What was he supposed to do about Carter?

It didn't take them long to get back to the park. Nearly everyone who had turned out to help them with the search wanted to see the boys, as if to be reassured that they really were okay. Carter stayed close to Felicia, and she did the same, as if they both needed reassurance.

Finally the mayor started telling people to head home.

"It's late," she reminded them. "Tomorrow's a workday, everyone." Then she looked at Carter. "Did you get what you wanted?"

Gideon frowned and Felicia looked confused, but Carter flushed.

"I don't know what you're talking about," he began, then shrugged. "I don't know." He smiled. "Felicia loves me."

"Was there any doubt?" the mayor asked.

"Not for a while now." Unexpectedly, he turned to Gideon. "Dad, were you scared about me being gone?"

Gideon sensed the trap and didn't know how to avoid it.

"I don't understand," Felicia said. "What are you talking about? Of course he was terrified. We all were."

"That's not what he means," Gideon said stiffly, as all the puzzle pieces came together. It shouldn't have taken him this long, he told himself. It's not as if the kid was subtle.

"He wants us to get together," he told Felicia. "He wants us married so he can have a family. That's what tonight was about. Scaring us into realizing our feelings."

Felicia wouldn't have thought she had any emotions left. The ups and downs of the past few hours, not to mention the long weekend of the festival, had drained her. But apparently there was also room for surprise.

"He's right," Mayor Marsha said quietly. "That's exactly what Carter wants. We've been talking about it a little. The one thing every child needs is stability." She smiled. "All right. Two things, because love matters, too. What's happening now is confusing. Carter needs to know where things stand."

Get married or split up, Felicia thought, barely able to process the information.

"We'll talk about it," she said.

Gideon didn't say anything.

They walked to the truck. Carter slid into the rear seat. Felicia climbed into the passenger seat as Gideon took the wheel. None of them spoke.

The drive up the mountain passed in a blur, but as they pulled into the driveway, she realized that she didn't need to go looking for an answer, that it had been there all along.

Telling Carter she loved him had been a spontaneous moment. A burst of emotion, followed by a complete sense of rightness. She might not be the best mother around, but she was willing to do all she could, to learn, to be supportive and to establish boundaries. She would give her life for him if necessary and pray it was all enough.

Now, as she searched her heart, she discovered she'd also fallen for another person, but in a completely different way.

Gideon. Always Gideon.

From the first moment she'd spoken to him in that bar in Thailand, he'd been a part of her life. He'd made her feel good about herself, had laughed with her, cared for her, taught her and made her feel safe. When she wasn't sure if she could fit in or where she belonged, she was comfortable with him. Loving him was so easy, she hadn't recognized the symptoms.

He pulled to a stop in front of the house. She turned to tell him, only to remember they weren't alone. A quick glance over her shoulder showed her a very sleepy teen who could barely crawl out of the truck.

"Can you punish me in the morning?" Carter asked with a big yawn.

"Sure."

"Thanks."

He hugged her, handed over his cell phone and walked inside. She and Gideon followed.

"What's the cell phone for?" Gideon asked.

"I'm not sure. I guess he's assuming he's going to lose it while he's grounded." She frowned. "I don't know what it means to be grounded. I'll have to do some research."

Gideon closed the front door behind them. They stood in the living room, not looking at each other. Tension filled the space, making her feel awkward and unsure.

"About what the mayor said," she began.

"I know what Carter thinks," he started.

"You go first," she murmured.

He walked toward the kitchen, then turned back to face her. "The mayor's right. Carter needs stability."

Felicia felt herself starting to bubble up with happiness. She was truly going to have it all. A man she loved, a child and a place to belong. Because the town had come through, not just for her, but for all of them. First, with the festival and then, tonight. As long as they lived in Fool's Gold, they would always have a community that cared.

"This relationship is confusing him," Gideon continued. "In the morning I'll explain it was never going to happen. Us getting married. I asked for your help and you were there for me, Felicia. I appreciate that. I don't want to stand in your way. I know you want to find the right guy and settle down, and that's not going to happen with me."

The pain was so sharp it almost didn't hurt. It was more concept than sensation. But the promise of agony whispered at the very edges of her consciousness, and she knew she didn't have long until she would be nothing more than an open wound.

"You want me to leave."

She wasn't asking a question, and a part of her was surprised she could still speak.

"I don't want to take advantage of you."

He was trying to make this about her, to be the nice guy. But it wasn't and he wasn't. He wanted her gone because he didn't believe he could be like everyone else. She'd always known that. Why had she allowed herself to forget?

She remembered telling Consuelo she wouldn't mind a broken heart. That she would appreciate having been in love and would accept the consequences. Her friend had warned her, but she hadn't listened. She'd been so sure she would be fine. She hadn't known what this could feel like.

"We'll talk in the morning," Gideon said. "You need to get some sleep. You're exhausted."

Sleep? She would never sleep.

"No," she told him. "I'm leaving now."

"Felicia, no. It's late."

He moved toward her, but she stepped away. She couldn't stand to have him touch her. No, she thought, shuddering. She desperately *wanted* him to touch her, and when he did, she would lose the little strength she had left. She would want to beg and plead, to prepare diagrams and flow charts explaining why he was wrong. Why this was so right for all of them.

Carter. She squeezed her eyes shut. She was going to have to tell him goodbye.

She would pack first, she thought. Complete the task and then tell him. She would make it clear he would always be welcome in her life and her home. That he could come stay with her, that they would talk every day.

Tears burned, but she refused to give in. That was for later. For now, she had to keep moving.

■ ■ ■ ■

Carter sagged against the hallway wall. Disappointment made it hard to swallow. He was out of ideas, he thought sadly. Out of ways to make Gideon see what was important.

He turned and walked to his bedroom, where he quickly collected his computer and a few clothes. The rest could wait. He didn't think Gideon would care if he came back and got it later. After zipping up his backpack, he walked down the hallway to the master suite.

Gideon stood outside the door. "You don't have to do this," he said.

Carter didn't hear Felicia answer, but he guessed it was something along the lines of not having a choice.

Carter moved past him and walked into the bedroom. Felicia looked up.

"Carter, what are you . . ." Her gaze settled on the backpack. "You heard."

He nodded.

"You don't have to leave, Carter. This is your home. Gideon is your father. He wants you with him."

"If he can't love you, he can't love me, either. I'm a kid, Felicia. I need to be where the love is." His heart stopped as he realized she might have just been saying the words rather than meaning them. "If you want me."

"Oh, Carter. I love you. Of course you can come live with me."

He didn't remember moving, but suddenly she was holding him and he was hanging on and neither of them was going to let go. He'd wanted it all — a set of parents and a home, but two out of three wasn't bad.

CHAPTER TWENTY

Gideon waited until dawn to go running. He'd wanted to leave earlier but knew the stupidity of heading up the mountain while it was still dark. He would take responsibility for breaking his neck but didn't see the point in needing a second rescue party in less than twenty-four hours.

As soon as the sun cleared the top of the mountain, he was out and moving. He drove himself hard, quickly breaking out in a sweat and breathing hard.

The uneven terrain challenged his body but left his mind free to wander. Free to think and speculate. What were they doing now?

He'd spent the night wandering the house. He'd tried to sleep a few times but hadn't been successful. The place he'd once seen as his haven was too large, too empty. The quiet had pressed in on him until he'd wanted to be anywhere else.

He tripped over uneven ground and went down on one knee. The sharp pain sent him back to his feet and he kept running. Blood trickled down his leg but he ignored it, ignored all of it. He could outrun anything. That was what he had to believe.

They were gone because he'd asked them to go. It was the right decision. He couldn't be what either Carter or Felicia needed. There wasn't enough left. He should be happy, or at least relieved.

But he wasn't. He was empty and hollow. He was as broken as he had ever been, and he was a man who had been to the edge of hell. He'd been dragged out of a prison cell maybe days or even hours before he would have died. He had bled into the ground of his captors' prison, and he would never be able to forget that. No matter what he thought or how he felt, he couldn't allow that to touch anyone else. Especially not Felicia or Carter.

Sometime later, exhausted and dripping sweat, he made his way back to his house. As he stepped out of the trees, he saw his truck parked in the driveway.

For a second he allowed himself to hope she'd returned. She'd taken his truck last night because they'd left her car in town. But as he approached the vehicle, he knew she hadn't been there at all. She would have sent Justice with either Ford or Angel to return it. She would take care of business. Take care of her responsibilities. But she wouldn't be back.

Felicia reacquainted herself with her kitchen. She'd been at Gideon's so long her rental had ceased to be her home. As she opened cupboards and checked the pantry, she realized she was missing most of the cooking gadgets she'd grown to love. And the space itself was way too small.

She'd rented the small townhouse back before she'd known if she could make a home in Fool's Gold. It was a simple, furnished two-bedroom unit with a small living room/dining room combination. The furniture was modern and masculine. The owner, a lawyer-type businessman named Dante Jefferson, had recently moved into a house with his new wife.

She heard footsteps on the stairs. Carter walked into the kitchen, still rubbing his eyes. He wore a baggy T-shirt and PJ bottoms. His hair was a mess, and his eyes were puffy.

"Get any sleep?" she asked.

"Some."

He'd obviously been crying, but she

wasn't going to mention that.

"Are you hungry?" She walked to the refrigerator and pulled it open. "There's nothing here, so I thought we'd go out for breakfast, then stop by the grocery store. Also, I want to talk to you about us moving. I rented this place when it was just me. I think we need a larger space. More living area and a bigger bedroom for you. Maybe a yard for a dog."

He stared at her. "You're really keeping me." He sounded surprised.

"Carter, I told you last night that you can stay with me. I'm all in."

"I'm all in, too." He glanced around. "This place is nice, but the kitchen is too small. Where will you put all your cooking stuff?"

"I know."

He shifted on his feet. "Can you afford something bigger? Because this place is fine if you can't."

She squeezed his shoulder. "Don't worry about money. I've been earning my way since I was only a little older than you. I developed a few patents years ago. In addition to my salary, I get very nice licensing checks every quarter and semiannual royalty checks from technical books I've written."

His eyes brightened. "Are you rich?"

"No, but we can afford a larger house."

"Cool!" He raced to the stairs. "Give me ten minutes and I'll be ready."

She leaned against the counter and told herself that everything would be fine. She was strong and capable, and she had a support system. As soon as her friends found out what had happened, they would surround her with love and encouragement. And, most likely, casseroles.

She had no empirical evidence for her supposition, but she believed it down to her bones. Until then, until she was brave enough to let them know she'd been desperately wrong about Gideon and her ability to handle a broken heart, she would focus on Carter. On getting him settled with her and figuring out how to keep breathing through the pain of missing the only man she'd ever loved.

On the third day, Gideon went into town. Without Felicia and Carter with him, he felt exposed, but that was the point. He was ready to take what was coming. To have the stones thrown at him. He knew he'd been a bastard and he deserved the punishment.

He'd hurt Felicia. He'd thought only of himself, of what he wanted, and never considered her feelings. He wasn't sure exactly *what* she'd wanted or expected, but it hadn't been to be dumped with no warning. He owed her an apology. Barring that, he should stay the hell out of her life. In the meantime, he fully expected the town to take her side.

He walked by the park and thought about stopping in Brew-haha. Patience was Felicia's friend. She would sure have something to say to him. But before he got there, he spotted Eddie and Gladys, who waved cheerfully and kept on walking. A few other citizens nodded as he passed, some called out greetings.

No one was pissed. No one yelled. He couldn't think of why, except that maybe Felicia hadn't said anything yet.

His chest ached at the thought of her going through this alone. While he wasn't sure if she'd fallen in love with him, he knew she cared. Felicia didn't hold back anything. So she had to be hurting. She needed someone to talk to. He had to speak to Patience and make sure she knew.

He turned and walked toward the coffeehouse. When he was across the street, Justice stepped out and moved toward him.

The other man's stride was purposeful, and Gideon knew this meeting wasn't accidental. Justice had been waiting. Justice, who considered Felicia a sister.

There was going to be hell to pay, Gideon thought, more than ready to take whatever the other man offered. He wouldn't defend himself. He would accept it, and maybe when it was over, he would feel better.

Justice stopped in front of him. "Come on," he said, pointing down the street. "We need to talk."

Gideon nodded and fell into step with him. He didn't know where they were headed, and he didn't care. Maybe back to CDS where Justice could work him over in the quiet of the gym. Or somewhere in the woods. He wasn't concerned. There was nothing Justice could do that hadn't been done to him already times a thousand, and in this case, he deserved it.

But instead of a dark alley — something tough to find in Fool's Gold on a Wednesday afternoon — Justice stepped into Jo's Bar and led the way into the back room.

Gideon avoided Jo's. Too many people, too many lights, and during the day, a play area for small children. Justice walked past all that. When he stopped, they were in a much smaller space. One with only a couple of windows up high on the wall. Flat-screen TVs were tuned to ESPN and a car auction. A couple of old guys sat at the bar, nursing beers.

"What can I get you?" the man behind the bar asked.

He looked familiar, but it took him a second to place the old guy. "Morgan? Shouldn't you be at your bookstore?"

"I will be," the white-haired man said with a smile. "I have some work to do here, first."

Justice took a seat on one of the stools. "What they're having."

Morgan poured two beers and pushed the glasses across the bar. Justice took one. Gideon ignored the other.

"You brought me here for a reason," he said.

Morgan nodded. "Good. You're not stupid. I'd hate to think of Felicia with an idiot."

Gideon felt his mouth drop open. "You know Felicia?"

"Sure. She comes to my store all the time. She likes to read paper books rather than electronic books. I like that in a woman." Morgan's smile returned. "She has eclectic tastes."

"That's one way of putting it," Justice murmured.

Morgan rolled up his sleeve, exposing a tattoo of a girl in a bikini. "Got that in the Philippines. They do good work. That was

438

after my time in Vietnam. Tough place to be for a farm kid from Georgia. Hell, before Uncle Sam drafted me, I'd never been past the county line."

"My brother went over there, too," one of the old guys said. "My number never got called." He gave a grin and picked up his beer.

Whatever was going on, Gideon wasn't interested. He started to get up. Justice clamped his hand around Gideon's forearm, holding him in place.

Breaking free would have been easy enough. Gideon knew all the moves. He could have had them all gasping for breath in ten seconds. He eyed Justice. Okay, maybe that would be a more difficult fight, but he figured he had a fifty-fifty chance. But was that what he wanted?

Gideon relaxed on the stool, and Justice released his arm.

"Civilian life was tough," Morgan continued. "My old girlfriend had married someone else. I hated the farm. I didn't know what to do with myself, so I took off. Hitchhiked around the country, did drugs, became a drunk. Somebody pulled me out of the gutter, and I started to get better. Then I met Audrey."

Morgan smiled, his gaze looking past them

to something only he could see. "Beautiful girl. Too good for me, which is who every man should marry. She was patient with my failings and loved me more than I deserved. But I couldn't love her back. I couldn't go there. The scars went too deep."

He looked at Gideon. "I was a fool, and I nearly lost her. Came to my senses facedown in a gutter, barely remembering my name. I nearly died from alcohol poisoning." He smiled. "That was thirty-five years ago. I have loved her every day since. We only had seventeen years together, then cancer took her. On her deathbed she made me promise I wouldn't give in to my demons again. I've kept that promise."

"I know what love does," Gideon said, figuring the truth was all he had left.

"No, you don't," Morgan told him. "If you did, you'd be with that pretty girl of yours and not here drinking with us. Love makes you strong. If you're brave enough to hand over everything you have and take that leap of faith. For me it was either love Audrey or stay in the gutter and die. You're in the gutter, my friend. The difference is, you can't see it."

He could see it all right, Gideon thought. What they didn't get was he didn't care. He belonged here.

Justice tossed a couple of bills on the bar and stood.

"Patience told you?" Gideon asked as the other man turned to leave.

Justice nodded. "Felicia told her yesterday. The women had one of their get-togethers last night. From what I heard, it was lots of margaritas and ice cream and calling you a bastard. They're all hungover this morning, so I'd stay clear if I were you." He started to leave.

"Wait." Gideon rose. "Aren't you going to hit me or something?"

"No need to hit a man when he's already down."

Gideon pushed the button and started the CD track. The Beach Boys' "God Only Knows" played in the studio. The same song went out on the airwaves, but he cared less about that. Tonight was about searching and hopefully finding.

He'd spent the day walking around town and his evening working out. He was exhausted but not tired, spent but not at peace. The ache inside him refused to go away, and sleep was impossible. He needed the one thing he could never have. Morgan had been right — he was in a gutter and he had no way to crawl out.

Without any conscious plan, he flipped the switch that activated his microphone. "Today, I want to talk a little bit about the past, about *my* past."

He paused, not sure what to say next. "Some of you know that I served in our armed forces. There are things that happened, things I saw, that challenged everything I believed in. I was taken prisoner with other men. Good men who served with honor. They loved their country and their families. For a long time, I knew the reason I'd made it and they hadn't was that they couldn't forget those they'd left behind. They missed them, longed for them, called out to them. Racked with fever from open wounds and burns, they thought they were back home and reading stories to their children. But they weren't. They were in a cell, and I watched each of them die until I was the last man standing. Because I was alone and I thought that made me strong."

He didn't have to close his eyes to see the other men. They were with him, always. "I don't know why I made it and they didn't. I only know that when my friends dragged me out of there, I knew I was never going back. I was never going to risk their pain. I had learned my lesson."

What if he'd known about Carter, he

thought grimly. How much worse things would have been. How —

Or was that true? He'd had nothing to miss, which he'd always seen as a strength, but he'd also had nothing to live for. Once he'd been rescued, he'd had nothing to keep him moving forward except the knowledge that he was alive.

Morgan had talked about being unable to fit in and how his Audrey had saved him. Would Carter have made a difference? Would Felicia?

The phone lines lit up. Gideon figured he was going to get an earful and pushed the first one.

"Don't you think you've been punished enough?" a woman asked. "Gideon, there's no reason to blame yourself for surviving when those other men didn't. Only God knows the answer, and if you spend too much time asking, you'll waste what you've been given. A chance with your son and Felicia. That's the real crime. Not that you lived, but that you're not living now."

He didn't recognize the voice, and he had no idea who she was. "All right," he said slowly. "Uh, thanks for calling."

The second caller was a man. "War is hell. Thanks for serving, son. Thanks to all who serve. Now, walk away from what you did and walk toward what matters. When you're old and ready to meet your maker you're not going to be thinking about what you did or what you owned. You're going to be thinking about the people you love. So get to it."

There were several more calls just like that, followed by what sounded like a teenage girl requesting less "really old songs and more Justin Bieber."

"I'll see what I can do," Gideon said with a chuckle and hung up.

He leaned back in his chair. This was what Felicia wanted, he thought, getting it for the first time. A community to care. People who would tell her when she was being an idiot and when she was on track. A safety net and all the other clichés about being surrounded by people who loved you and whom you loved back.

He stood, prepared to claim, to be a part of this. Then the memories were back, the screams, the pain. The knowledge that even though his body was alive, he'd already given up. And by giving up, he was dead.

The red button flashed. Someone was at the back door. He tore off his headphones and raced to the rear of the building. When he jerked open the door, he grimaced.

"You," he grumbled.

444

Angel raised his eyebrows. "I was expecting more of a greeting."

"You're not who I was expecting."

His friend studied him. "No. I'm not who you wanted. No offense, but you're not my type, either. I came to finish your shift."

"What do you mean?"

"You can't leave dead air out there. I've watched you put the CDs in and push the button. I can do it."

"I'm not leaving."

Angel shook his head. "You're as stupid as you look. You're leaving because a woman like Felicia comes along once in a lifetime. Because if you don't go after her, someone else will. You've been given a second chance. Didn't that guru guy in Bali teach you anything? The only way to heal what's wrong with you inside is to love her and trust her."

"Like you know anything about being in love?" Gideon paused, belatedly remembering that Angel's wife and son had been killed. "I'm sorry," he said quickly. "I'm sorry."

Something flashed in Angel's eyes. A sharp pain that cut to the soul. Gideon recognized it because he'd felt it himself.

"Apology accepted," Angel said. "Having gone through what I did, I know you'll

445

regret losing Felicia until your last breath. I know that you've finally found where you belong, and there's no way you can stay here without her. What's that line from that stupid movie? She completes you, bro. Only it's more than that. You have a woman who understands you and a kid like Carter and you're confused?"

Gideon felt as if someone had hit him on the side of the head with a two-by-four. For a second, the world went dark and quiet, and then it all cleared again. He had been looking for answers about why he had survived and there were none. Or maybe the answer was twofold: Carter and Felicia.

He looked at his friend, the one who had risked his own life to pull him from that Taliban prison.

"I owe you," he said quietly.

"Yeah, I know. Now get out of here."

Gideon pulled his truck keys from his pocket and headed for the parking lot. He turned back and yelled, "Keep it clean. We have kids listening."

Angel laughed.

Felicia drove quickly but carefully. She was willing to go five miles over the speed limit but not much more. Not while still in town.

"This is taking forever," Carter grumbled.

"I don't want to get in an accident."

"I know. Sorry. I'm nervous."

That was one word, Felicia thought. Terrified was another. Because while listening to Gideon, she'd realized she'd done exactly the wrong thing when she'd walked away. She'd taken the easy way out. Sure, she'd been hurt, but she'd also been scared. She hadn't stood up for herself. She hadn't told him what she wanted. She hadn't made it clear she loved him.

Gideon was dealing with a past that would have killed most men and had caused the death of nearly a half-dozen excellent soldiers. He would never be like everyone else, but that was why she loved him. Because of who he was now.

She turned left to head out to the radio station and saw a truck driving into town. She slammed on the brakes. The truck driver did the same.

She was out of her car in a second and running across the street. The truck door opened, and Gideon got out. They stared at each other. Behind her she heard a car door slam and assumed Carter was joining them.

Gideon looked wonderful, she thought, her heart aching. Tall and strong. Loyal. There were ghosts, but she was comfortable with his past. He would always have issues,

447

but no one was better at logistical planning than she was. They could figure it out together.

"I heard your show," she began. "We both did. That was brave."

"No. Brave isn't telling the truth."

"Sometimes it is. Sometimes it's easier to keep the secret. What if they'd confirmed your darkest fears? That you didn't deserve to be the one who survived?"

He flinched. "How did you know?"

"You weren't grateful to be alive. You were trying to figure out how to be strong, but you also suffered from survivor's guilt. A natural result of what you went through."

"Got a flowchart for that?"

"I could make one." She paused and held out her arm. Carter joined them.

Gideon looked at his son. There were explanations, he thought. For later.

He reached for the boy and held him tight. "I'm never letting go," he promised. "No matter what. I'm so grateful to have you in my life. I have a lot of work to do to show you how important you are to me. I've been . . . scared. Scared to let you in. Scared to disappoint you."

"Dad." Carter's voice was muffled. "We're going to be okay."

"Yes, we are, son. We are."

Felicia fought her own tears, watching the two men she cared about most finally connect. It was so perfect.

She drew in a breath, knowing it was her turn to be brave. "I've been keeping secrets, too. I didn't tell you I love you, Gideon, and I do. I want you and me and Carter to be a family. I want us to get married and have more children."

One corner of Gideon's mouth turned up. "That sounded a whole lot like a proposal."

"Oh. I hadn't considered that. I meant it to be informational. I would never propose. Socially, that's the man's purview, even if the truth is women hold families together much more than men. Women are also happier when they live alone, whereas men do better when they have a partner."

"Felicia," Carter hissed.

She turned to him. "What?"

"You're getting off the point."

"Oh, you're right." She looked back at Gideon. "I wasn't proposing."

"As long as that's clear. But you're saying I can't be happy without you."

"I didn't mean that, exactly." Why was this so hard? She loved him and wanted them to be together. She wanted to stop hurting inside and know that she could give her heart to him.

"Gideon, I —"

He moved closer and touched his fingers to her mouth. "You need to be quiet now."

His hand settled on her waist, and he pulled her against him. She went willingly, needing to feel the heat of him. In his arms, she'd found her home. Without him, she was broken. She would stay strong, for Carter's sake, but she wasn't looking forward to the struggle.

"I'm sorry for all I put you through." He looked past her. "You, too, son."

"That's okay, Dad."

Gideon smiled. "Okay." He returned his attention to her. "You never waver, Felicia, never take the easy way out. I admire you and I respect you. I want us to be together. You, me and Carter. Carter and I need you." He looked at Carter, who nodded. "We love you, Felicia."

She flung her arms around him and hung on, knowing she would never let go.

"All right!" Carter cheered. "I'm heading back to the car now, and I'm going to turn up the radio, if you guys want to kiss awhile."

"I kind of do," Gideon admitted, settling his mouth onto hers.

Felicia sank into him. In the distance, she heard Angel's voice coming from the speakers in Gideon's truck. "This one is for a very special couple. Unless my friend is an idiot, which is a real possibility."

Gideon chuckled. "I wonder what song he —"

Sonny and Cher's "I've Got You, Babe" began to play. Gideon raised his head and groaned. "No way. I hate that song." He touched her cheek. "Please don't make me dance to it at our wedding."

"Was that a proposal?"

"No. It was the promise of one. I thought I'd do it more privately when we're alone." He took her hands in his. "Please come home, Felicia. I miss you, and I miss my son."

"Can I drive?" Carter asked.

"I thought you weren't listening," Gideon said, his voice amused.

"Sorry."

Felicia smiled up at him. "I'll follow you," she promised as she reluctantly stepped back.

"No way," he told her. "You're going to lead. You've always known the right way home."

ABOUT THE AUTHOR

Susan Mallery is the *New York Times* bestselling author of over one hundred romances and women's fiction novels. Her funny and sexy family stories consistently appear on the *USA Today* and the *New York Times* bestsellers lists. She has won many awards, including the prestigious National Reader's Choice Award. Because her degree in Accounting wasn't very helpful in the writing department, Susan earned a Masters in Writing Popular Fiction. Susan makes her home in the Pacific Northwest, where she lives with her husband and toy poodle.

The employees of Thorndike Press hope you have enjoyed this Large Print book. All our Thorndike, Wheeler, and Kennebec Large Print titles are designed for easy reading, and all our books are made to last. Other Thorndike Press Large Print books are available at your library, through selected bookstores, or directly from us.

For information about titles, please call:
   (800) 223-1244

or visit our Web site at:
   http://gale.cengage.com/thorndike

To share your comments, please write:
   Publisher
   Thorndike Press
   10 Water St., Suite 310
   Waterville, ME 04901